Seven Archangels:

Shattered Walls

Jane Lebak

Seven Archangels:

Shattered Walls

Jane Lebak

Philangelus Press
Boston, MA USA

Other titles by Jane Lebak:

Honest And For True
Half Missing
Seven Archangels: An Arrow In Flight
Seven Archangels: Sacred Cups
The Wrong Enemy
Seven Archangels: Annihilation
The Seven Angels Short Story Bundle
Bulletproof Vestments
The Boys Upstairs
Pickup Notes

Sign up for Jane's mailing list:
http://eepurl.com/bcnCNX

Kindle ASIN: B01E7BUTEE
Print ISBN: 978-1-942133-20-9

Cover: C.K. Volnek

Dedication

After I published *Annihilation*, I set up email addresses for some of my characters, and one day, the archangel Remiel got a letter from a fan. So "Remiel" wrote back, and that began a correspondence spanning the next five years. The fan and I (and "Remiel" and "Gabriel") would send letters, packages, signed books, ecards, and handknits. She loved my angels, and my angels loved her. She called them her sweet friends, and I'm told their letters were the high point of her day. The angels would sign off with curious endings like, "Live in God's light" or "Be God's own," and she adopted those closings as well.

Last summer, I learned she died after a long illness. As I wrote Shattered Walls, I knew how much she'd have loved reading about Remiel again, and I'm sad that the world has lost such a bright light.

So Chantelle, I'm dedicating this book to you and to your memory, and to your mother, Sarah. Be God's own. Be God's, always.

ONE

Remiel drew all four of her wings tighter against her body, the inner set flush against her sides while the outer one iced over with Hell's lashing sleet. Squinting against the wind, she muttered, "They picked the right place to hide their project, whatever it is."

Ahead of her, Zadkiel shook her head, scattering ice crystals from her curly black hair. Why were they even here? Demons didn't use the ice fields for research and development. Hell's elite typically cordoned off the dark caves known as the lab area for their personal office space, and the rank-and-file spent most of their time in the hot interior or on the shores of the Lake of Fire itself.

But the ice fields? Demons hated them. For research and development, or even for just talking, this part of Hell had too much weather and were too tumultuous. The rumors Michael's informants had picked up gave tantalizing hints about a weapon in development, but no real information. Not even which demons were involved.

Zadkiel with her incredible talent for revealing what was hidden had led them to this spot, which was the last place Remiel would ever have thought to look for demons engaged in delicate work.

Delicate, but secret—and for that, Remiel had to admit, you couldn't get much better in terms of isolation. Maybe Zadkiel was on the right trail. Or maybe they were enduring this nasty blizzard for no reason whatsoever.

Zadkiel touched Remiel's arm, and Remiel followed. With her sky-blue wings extended (well, icy silver wings for the moment) and her eyes closed, Zadkiel pivoted a degree, then back, then tucked her wings again and pushed forward against the wind. As long as they kept their angelic signatures suppressed, not even projecting their emotions to one another, no demons would be able to detect them. But that also made it harder to stay in contact, so Remiel struggled to keep her in sight.

Similarly, it would have been a lot easier to go completely incorporeal. Wearing subtle bodies, the angels were vulnerable to wind and weather, but being incorporeal would hamper their ability to search. And that was the reason they were here, the reason their little incursion party consisted of only two angels: a Seeker and someone to protect her.

Zadkiel dropped to the surface and pushed against the snow, raising her wings to provide cover as she dug. Remiel turned her back to Zadkiel, opening her senses for any approaching demons. *You could hurry up whatever you're doing,* she thought.

In her mind, Zadkiel chuckled. *Soon.* And then, *Now.*

Remiel turned in time to see Zadkiel vanish head-first into a hole. She jumped in after.

She hit a solid surface, and her wings flared as her legs gave out beneath her. At her side, Zadkiel was on hands and knees, slush frozen to her clothes, breath heaving.

There was silence. Ice and silence.

Shifting to a stand, Remiel rested her hand on her sword (although for all she knew, the weapon was frozen to its scabbard.) She extended her senses through the cave but felt only distant prickles. There were demons nearby, but not close. Cautiously, she started to glow.

They'd taken shelter in a cavern of ice, barely large enough for two angels and their wings. Drawing her sword wasn't a concern after all: there was no room to use it. Still, she rested her hand on the hilt and projected heat down the blade until the ice melted.

Beside her, Zadkiel flared heat all over her body, dissipating the ice and drying off. *Can you feel their residue?*

When Remiel shook her head, Zadkiel edged to the walls of the cave. *Lots of demons use this space the way we're using it now,* she sent. *That's why the ice is so smooth—they come in, they flare the ice off themselves, and then they head...this way.* She crouched at one corner. *There's a tunnel hidden here.*

Above them, the opening had already sealed over with sleet. Remiel frowned. The pair of them could get jumped very easily, and anything Remiel could think of to improve their chances would only increase the chance that they'd be detected. It would be very easy to cast a Guard in this little hollow, letting her power form the spiritual equivalent of unbreakable walls, but if the demons had any sentries posted at all, a Guard was as good as a signal flare. She and Zadkiel might be able to get free if attacked, but afterward the demons would more tightly protect, or move, whatever this mysterious weapon was.

In other words, if the angels tipped their hand right now, they needed to tip it fully and finish the job in one go. With a strike force consisting of exactly one Dominion and one Virtue.

Stranger things had happened. Remiel sent, *Can you feel how many there are down there?*

In a hundred years, Remiel wouldn't herself have tried scanning outward to detect and count guards who were themselves scanning out to detect intruders. For a Seeker, though, it might be possible, and Zadkiel was one of the best. She rested a hand on the ice. *A half-dozen. One of them...* Zadkiel yanked back her hand and whispered, "Asmodeus."

Remiel grimaced. Asmodeus was one of the Maskim, a Seraph second in power only to Satan. And his involvement pretty much guaranteed the participation of another member of the Maskim: Belior, Asmodeus's bonded Cherub.

Zadkiel frowned at her. *We should bring Michael.*

Not yet. He needs more information than we've got. Remiel considered the ice chamber. Are there any other exits?

Zadkiel pressed against the floor with her eyes shut, then spread her wings. Remiel stood over her, shivering. This position was entirely indefensible.

It took minutes, minutes during which Remiel's wings numbed over from the cold. Then Zadkiel edged toward the opposite corner, put her hand to the ice, and started producing heat.

Remiel clenched her sword hilt. Keep doing this and they were sure to attract demonic attention.

When Zadkiel pulled back her hand, she'd left a palm-sized impression in the ice, as deep as her hand. Beneath that was a fissure in the ice wall.

"Perfect," Remiel whispered.

Zadkiel dissolved her subtle body, making it completely incorporeal. Without any form, she was able to flow down the crack in the wall, pausing just inside. Remiel took a deep breath and then she herself returned to her fully angelic form, losing her pseudo-body's shape and existing as a pure spirit. She attached her attention to Zadkiel, who drew her into the fissure. Before penetrating further, Remiel paused and created heat, melting and smoothing the area of ice Zadkiel had just cleared. Now they were sealed in.

Pulling Remiel along, Zadkiel descended, creeping like water in a steady drip through stone. No, not merely like water. They were water. The two of them were free-flowing energy, etchers of stone and makers of caverns. They were motion and they were slipperiness. And then they were free.

Zadkiel let go, and Remiel found herself in a niche just outside a larger cavern. And there, two wingspans in front of her, stood Asmodeus.

TWO

Asmodeus wasn't paying attention to them, fortunately. His fury was focused entirely on the Cherub before him, shorter and decidedly nervous. Low-level demon soldiers ringed the room, but instead of guarding the location, they were watching their commanding officer. Bad form. When Remiel guarded someone, she looked everywhere but at that individual.

"This isn't going anywhere near fast enough," Asmodeus was telling the Cherub. "I don't care what Belior said to you. We need this finished soon."

"Foreshortening procedure leads to preventable mistakes." The Cherub, for herself, didn't seem fully engaged in the conversation, something Remiel found both impressive and incomprehensible. If this was who she thought it was, then Asmodeus had a primary bond with her. He might be filling her soul with fire right now, and no one else would know it. The Cherub (what was her name?) only said, "We have very little material to work with, so I need to be sure before I commit."

"That's not my fault."

The Cherub narrowed her eyes, still not looking at him. "There's no reason for your defensive response. I'm only stating that given the scarcity of working material, our situation warrants caution. You can infer from that whatever you like. You could also," she added, "send additional units to scour for raw materials."

"We can't get caught." Asmodeus folded his arms, and his eyes burned. "I thought you were better than this."

"Given the importance of this project both to you and to Belior," said the Cherub, "I need to be better than better-than-this. Your harassment doesn't improve my ability to function."

She turned to him at last, and she extended a hand. Remiel could detect nothing, but she knew what was happening because she'd seen it often enough between Gabriel and Raphael: the Cherub was drawing off the Seraph's fire. It would energize her, and at the same time, she'd flood Asmodeus with Cherubic calm. It took a moment, but the flames licking around Asmodeus's wings lowered, then winked out. The Cherub's eyes brightened correspondingly. "I want Belior to succeed. There is nothing I want more. You know that."

Beside Remiel, Zadkiel leaned forward. Remiel followed her focus toward the work area. Oh, for five minutes to explore those containers, the notes, the implements. Not even five. Just get enough of a glimpse so she could report back to Michael. Why did they say they didn't have enough material? What material could they be talking about?

Demons didn't like matter, but they also didn't hesitate to use it when it suited their purposes. The Psalms said God saved His children's tears in a bottle, but that was just a metaphor: Remiel sometimes joked about endless storage rooms filled with oceans of tears separated in thin glass tubes, each labeled and dated. What if the demons were captudring something like that? The blood of the martyrs, for example, since the Roman Empire whipped or even crucified the Christians far too often. Maybe the material was bits of the Holy Bread the Christians used whenever they renewed the New Covenant during their worship.

Well, whatever material they were talking about, they'd been harvesting it without detection, but it was limited.

And it was, apparently, weaponizable.

Remiel steadied herself. Okay, so based on this conversation, Belior was the chief driver of the plot. Asmodeus wasn't saying Satan wanted this done, so that left one delicious scenario. And boy, was this a good one.

Twenty years ago, right after the Resurrection, Satan had demoted Asmodeus and Belior within the Maskim. Although they'd been his top advisors, after everything went down, they'd been put in command of Hell's army instead. And here they were now, were making this weapon in secret, so it must be meant as a gift to Satan. A really amazing gift that would raise their standing and win back that top position. This Cherub what's-her-name must be helping because as Asmodeus's primary, she'd benefit too.

So: highly motivated demons, keeping to something like a timetable, and experimenting with very limited resources. Based on the low number of guards, they were working in extreme secrecy but didn't fear immediate detection. And given the setup, the demons were unable to move everything on a moment's notice.

Well, this could get fun in a hurry. In fact, she had something of a duty to make sure it did.

Remiel squeezed Zadkiel's hand. Zadkiel met her eyes, and she stared her down.

Zadkiel looked unnerved. But even though neither angel had projected anything, Remiel knew she'd understood. Zadkiel would stay put.

Remiel slipped back up the crevice, maneuvering through the walls with the gentleness of an air current until she unsealed the fissure and slipped back into that first small shelter.

Remiel reached for the Holy Spirit. He responded, though faint. Hell didn't want Him here, and God obeyed the laws He'd set for His own creation.

Well, here we go. Sword drawn, she shot down the hidden entrance tunnel toward the cavern.

A demon guard collared her the instant she burst inside, but she slashed him and then detonated with light and heat.

And Zadkiel, Zadkiel who was cautious and brave and so perceptive, Zadkiel stayed hidden. Exactly as she was supposed to.

All five guards rushed after Remiel, but she blew them back. And then she did the dumbest thing she could think of: she charged the work table.

Asmodeus exploded toward her, fire blowing out like projectile vomit. With a shriek, the Cherub encased the work area within a Guard (perfect) and now Asmodeus discharged even more energy at Remiel without fear of harming their work. Remiel fled back toward the wall, and he pursued. The soldiers blocked the entrance, but they hadn't cast a Guard over the whole cavern yet, so she flashed out into the sleet and wind.

Asmodeus followed, and once outside, he called for backup. Again, perfect.

Remiel streaked through Hell, streaming light as she flew. She hurled her sword back at Asmodeus, and it didn't even slow him down. She flashed through multiple spots in the interior of Hell, reappearing in the labs, over the Lake of Fire, in the upper levels, and finally in the entry portal, the only means in and out of Hell.

Asmodeus had filled it with soldiers. With a shout, Remiel emitted a flare of light, then summoned another sword from the fabric of her soul. As a battalion of archers loosed flaming arrows, she gathered herself and flashed out into Creation.

Asmodeus was after her—him and a hundred soldiers—so she fled, pushing as hard as she could. She tucked her head, but something slammed into her back, driving her into the side of a mountain and sending a shower of snow up.

She looked up to find Asmodeus glowing like a super nova, his sword flying toward her neck. She rolled sideways, and he nicked her wing. Again she flashed away, reappearing over a tropical forest. This time Asmodeus reappeared with Belior at his side to fill him with Cherub energy, energy Asmodeus released like a lightning blast.

Remiel tucked into a ball and dropped, flashing out of Creation just as his soul's energy shot through where she'd been.

And then in the next moment, she flashed right up to Heaven's gates and barreled through to the other side, landing on her shoulder and rolling up onto her knees, laughing.

Asmodeus slammed against the gate but couldn't get in.

She pushed her hair out of her eyes. "Nice try, loser."

Archangel guards clustered around her as Asmodeus discharged a blast of flame at the gates, but nothing got through. Remiel grinned.

Belior joined him, startled, maybe even frightened.

"What's the matter?" Remiel got to her feet and dusted off. "Someone got into your super-secret club house?"

Belior shot a look at Asmodeus and must have been asking what she'd discovered, so she stepped closer to the gates. "You had all those little toys and your toy soldiers to go with them. You're so cute."

Remiel ignored the flood of invective from the Seraph and watched the Cherub. *Come on, Belior, give me a clue.* But Belior only put his hand on Asmodeus, who whirled on him and stared him down, and in return Belior fixed him with an equally stony stare.

The Archangel Michael appeared at Remiel's side, so she faced him. "Situation under control." Remiel chuckled. "These two built a snow-fort. Nothing to see here."

At her back, both demons vanished.

Michael was projecting five flavors of surprise and shock. "Where's Zadkiel?"

"Safe." Remiel backed up her words with a projection of reassurance and mischief. "She's the one doing the real work."

From her hiding spot, Zadkiel listened as the demons attempted to batten down the chaos Remiel had created. *She's good at that,* Zadkiel prayed, *but I'm not sure this was really the best way to get the answers we need.* Because in the next moments, the remaining demons, including the Cherub Satrinah, were sure to search the room.

Zadkiel hid herself more thoroughly than before. First she dissociated, and then in her pure spirit form, she released all her thoughts. Every attachment to here and now, including her worries, had to dissolve in order to escape the intensive scans.

So before Satrinah even ordered the soldiers to search the cavern, Zadkiel went deep into herself and brought up the memory of wine. Cana. Jesus at a wedding with her invisible at his side. The simplest of instructions with no light show and no magic words. Just: fill this jar; bring this to the steward; his mother's gentle, *Do whatever he tells you.* The fabric of a miracle looking like everyday canvas.

That was when Zadkiel had offered a trade, and in exchange for something she'd never needed anyhow, he gave her a cup of that wine. *I want to know what it tastes like when my Lord says 'wine,'* she'd said to him. She'd turned her subtle body into a human body, and he'd given her a chalice filled to the top. She'd drunk that cup to the very bottom not for the taste nor the detached feeling alcohol gave a human body, but for the truth it contained.

Afterward Jesus had given her the ability to recreate that taste whenever she wanted, and she did it now. Wine. It had been the unknown hint of a covenant about to be born in a later cup of its own, and she'd tasted it that first day. She alone of all the angels, Zadkiel, not even one of the great ones.

Zadkiel prayed with the memory, dismissed herself in her hiding spot and became nothing more than the truth of what she'd tasted two decades earlier. And there she remained, unaware of the bustle and undetected by the demons.

When at last she returned to herself (a gradual return, so gradual lest she trigger their notice) she became aware of two tense voices: Satrinah and Belior.

"They suffered no disruption," Satrinah was saying. "I cast a Guard over the work area immediately in order to maintain the process's stability because it stood to reason he'd flame her without consideration for the potential damage."

Belior huffed. "No, that would never occur to him, even after some of the material destabilized and disappeared. But are you certain we can't move them?"

Tentative, Zadkiel extended her senses until they encountered a bristling anger at her back: the area now bore a strong Guard, whereas before there had been none. Until Remiel had blown in, therefore, their chief fear must have been discovery by Satan rather than discovery by the angels, and setting a Guard might have attracted attention. Interesting.

Satrinah didn't answer right away, moving about the work area with a rustle of feathers, leaning in, touching the table, focusing closely on the work. "You should reassess my calculations to be certain, but I would prefer not to transport. Stability is the greatest concern. The losses aren't considerable, but given our lack of materials, we need to account for replaceability."

Belior said, "Then we need to prevent her from getting back in. She may not even try. Her sanity is never entirely to be taken for granted."

He called one of the soldiers and gave instructions. The bits Zadkiel caught told her the demons were going to seal off the cavern by destroying the entrance.

Entombing themselves, in other words. With that Guard up, no one would be able to get in or out without their explicit permission, and the Cherubim would be aware of any attempt.

That done, the Cherubim returned their full attention to the project at hand. On the plus side, they felt secure: they'd scoured the room and now no one could get in. Whatever Remiel had done after leaving, she'd managed to convince them her objective was creating chaos rather than a targeted search for a weapon under development. On the minus side, they spoke in voices low enough that Zadkiel had no chance of overhearing a thing.

But they're Cherubim, she prayed. Fallen Cherubim, but still.

So as long as the problem of moving their experiment-in-progress absorbed them, Zadkiel was able to move about the room with more freedom. Still cautious, she nevertheless was able to slip through the corners, slide like a thought around the peripheries, and get closer to the work station.

Whatever they had there, it felt dreadful. The Cherubim regarded it with disgust, and as if it were a living thing, it behaved with repulsion toward them as well. What was it? She couldn't sense any kind of energy signature, but at the same time, the Cherubim handled it as though it contained power.

They weren't dealing with a sigil. It wasn't material imbued with human feeling. It wasn't ensouled. But it was something that, according to them, they occasionally had less of.

She couldn't even gather from the Cherubim's conversation what they'd designed the weapon to do. She'd heard Gabriel get like this before, of course, wrapped up so much in one tiny detail of a problem that he overlooked the chief purpose of the project. If he were part of a construction team, he'd be the one working so hard on a latch that when he finally solved the problem of securing the entrance, he'd be shocked to remember the door was part of a house, and the rest of the house had been built around him. Microfocus was like a Cherub disease. These two needed a Seraph.

Or rather, I'm glad they don't have one around, Zadkiel prayed. *Let them take longer. I'm not going to object.*

Deep inside, she felt the Holy Spirit chuckle.

Who's the target of this thing? With a weapon, you wanted to know that first. Something to kill a human? Microbes, maybe? A weaponized disease could in theory wipe out the human race. Demons tended to warp rather than kill, though, even when they had permission. You couldn't destroy a soul, human or angelic, because souls were immortal. The demons struck greater victories not by killing human bodies but by having the humans strangle off God's life in their own souls.

Maybe the pair were forging something to damage the Earth. The universe had no shortage of materials capable of that, though. Matter was matter. To experiment like this, they must think they had a means of destroying the planet permanently, or maybe just the Holy Land. Gabriel had talked once about unstable elements, and how they were perforce rare.

Oh, that made sense. Satrinah had emphasized stability. That must be what the Cherubim were using.

Zadkiel withdrew on herself and again recalled the taste of wine. Then, steadied, she considered her options. Remiel's escape meant Michael by now knew as much as she did, and therefore help would come at some point. Zadkiel could wait. She'd have to remain undiscovered, but that wouldn't be a problem.

If she were correct, the weapon itself would be of no use on the spiritual plane, and for now the demons had it sealed up away from Creation. Zadkiel couldn't leave, but as long as the demons didn't realize they had an intruder, she had an advantage.

So which demon was projecting the Guard? She doubted it was Belior, given his focus. It might be Satrinah, but most likely it emanated from the only two remaining soldiers, either one or both. Satan or Michael might cast a wide net searching for Satrinah or

Belior's signatures, but no one would know to search for two anonymous soldier demons who probably even Satan wouldn't recognize.

The soldiers watched the Cherubim at work, each in a defensible position on opposite sides of the room, and each on high alert. The one closer to Zadkiel appeared to be an Archangel; she couldn't decide about the other. In a pinch, she could take one down. And if the Cherubim got close to finishing their weapon, she would have to.

But for now, Zadkiel prayed. Prayed and centered her heart around the memory of a cup whose liquid she still could taste.

THREE

"I wish you hadn't done that."

Remiel leaned over the map Michael was creating with light. "You said as much already. I used my best judgment, and I thought we needed to shake things up a bit. You might want to position that a little further down," she added, gesturing to the entry cave. "I didn't get an exact sense of its location, but it felt as if we traveled further."

Saraquael folded his arms, coming around Michael's other side. "I dislike leaving Zadkiel down there for too long. Let me scout it out."

"Asmodeus has the whole army on high alert at the moment. You won't get close." Michael looked up, frowning. "I'm hoping she has the common sense to stay hidden for as long as it takes."

Remiel said softly to Saraquael, "That's a subtle shot at me."

"Nothing subtle about it." Michael looked up, arms folded. "You were reckless, and you cast the die too early. I needed you down there for surveillance, and now in effect we've got no surveillance, and we need to get to Zadkiel."

Michael turned back to his map. "Okay, let's go over this again. See if I'm missing anything."

Remiel forced down her anger while Michael and Saraquael reviewed the basics again, and she reached for God until she could participate without snapping. *He's over-reacting. He wasn't there. You don't criticize a soldier from the observation room when she's the one in the middle of the attack.*

But finally she could focus again as Michael and Saraquael discussed tactics. You couldn't enter Hell except through one tightly-guarded entry point. Satan liked to know who got in and who got out, and while a sneak entry could be done in small numbers, even the lowest level demons would recognize a strike force. Waiting until the weapon was complete and ready to deploy wasn't in anyone's best interests; neither was abandoning Zadkiel in Hell to be discovered.

"So we're going to have to knock on the front door," Michael said. "Flash in, flash deep into the interior, and fight our way into that cavern."

Saraquael said, "And hope they don't move their project elsewhere in the meantime."

Michael said, "Remiel? Any more ideas on the kind of weapon it was?"

She bristled. "Nothing more comes to mind."

Michael turned back to Saraquael. "Suggestions?"

"Not waiting too much longer." Saraquael shook his head. "There are too many uncertainties right now. What materials they're gathering, their intention, their timetable... If they do find Zadkiel, they could use it on her, and we wouldn't know."

Michael said, "Remiel reported that they're not ready."

Saraquael said, "If she's right, though, and this is an attempt to get back into Satan's favor, they're going to rush their timetable now that they've been discovered."

Remiel smirked. "That's exactly what I wanted them to do."

Michael's wings tensed, and then he shook his head. "Saraquael, I want a team of Dominions, maybe twenty. Since Remiel started by distracting them, we're going to continue the distraction tactics. I want you to attack the wrong place. How about...here?" Michael lit up an area of the map. "This looks topographically similar enough to the actual location that Asmodeus might think we're just in error. He'd like to believe we're stupid, so he's more apt to believe it. Make a lot of noise and get a lot of attention."

Saraquael laughed. "Give me a few Seraphim too."

Grinning, Michael pointed at him. "Take five. Burn a few acres. Israfel hasn't blown anything up lately, so set her loose."

Remiel flexed her wings. "Now that sounds fun."

"Not you." Michael turned to Remiel. "You and I are going to be really quiet, and we're going to finish the job."

Although Remiel tried to hide it, Michael knew she was angry, and he reached for God to calm himself before deploying.

She's doing her best, Michael prayed. *I have to believe she didn't actually want to cause harm. But she made my work harder.*

You just do your own best, God replied. *I'm with you.*

Keeping Remiel at his side wasn't the punishment she thought it was; it also wasn't, as she thought, a vote of non-confidence, a way of saying he needed to baby-sit one of his best officers during the mission. No, he just wanted to keep the actual strike force as small as possible, and Remiel knew how to get him back into that cavern.

Prickly as she was, she wasn't talking beyond the necessities, and Michael gave her space during the last minutes before deploying. Then he prayed with her and Saraquael, asked for God's blessing on the mission, and in they went.

Saraquael's team rushed Hell's entry point, creating all the chaos Michael had wanted, and more. Asmodeus had left sentries posted throughout the opening, and the Dominions clashed with them for quite a few minutes without breaking through. Michael was about to order another squad of angels into the opening when finally Saraquael called to his force, and they all disappeared into the ice fields, to the decoy site.

Michael took Remiel's hand, and she flashed them back to where she thought the cavern should be.

In the lashing snow, Remiel dropped to her knees and put her hands on the ground. "It should be near. It feels right."

Michael extended his senses for Zadkiel but felt nothing other than the chaos Saraquael was creating in the far distance. He pushed out harder, and then gasped.

Remiel's head snapped up.

We're in the right place. They've got a Guard. Michael squinted against the wind as he projected his thoughts to Remiel. They'd never be able to hear one another talking. *I thought I recognized it, that's all.*

The Guard tingled against his memories, almost but not quite familiar.

Remiel sent, *Belior's?*

He shook his head. *No, but it doesn't matter. I'm just going to blow through it.*

Remiel grinned, but before she could offer to help, Michael focused all his power into his sword and aimed downward.

Snow blew back in their faces like a geyser, stained with light and sharp like shattered glass. Ice cracked, but beneath them the Guard held. Michael took to the air, Remiel at his side, and tried again, his power this time augmented with hers. The Guard shuddered, and Michael pushed harder, praying for power and channeling every strength into soul energy aimed at that wall.

"They're reinforcing it!" Remiel shouted. "It's not going to be enough!"

Even as she said it, though, the Guard caved inward like a roof with one of its support beams gone. Michael gave one more blast, and the energy structure collapsed.

Zadkiel! Remiel was laughing into the wind. *She must have taken them out.*

Michael shot through the gaping roof of a cavern filling with landsliding snow. At one end he found Zadkiel, her sword locked with a demon soldier's, and in the center were two Cherubim, one of them shouting and the other lifting a metal lid on a black case. It was Belior, and he'd opened their weapon. Opened it and aimed it at Michael.

Zadkiel streaked across the room, in between Michael and Belior, and light exploded through the cavern. Light...and darkness. The light sliced through Zadkiel with a scream, then turned into darkness that sprayed over them both. Michael braced for pain, but it never came. Instead the darkness began swirling around Zadkiel, curling around her heart.

Satrinah flew backward from the table, eyes hemorrhaging hatred.

"Get back!" Remiel charged at the work table in the center to reach Zadkiel. Belior was gone; Michael hadn't felt him flash away. But when light and dark had spewed out of the box, he'd vanished.

Zadkiel slashed at the coiling dark as it tangled in her wings and stuck to her hands. Remiel rushed at her, hands outstretched, but Zadkiel slashed at her with her sword. "Stay back!"

The blackness slipped up Zadkiel, binding her arms to her sides and then coiling down her legs. Remiel went back toward her again.

Michael shouted, "You don't know what that is! You're going to get hurt!"

"Doesn't mean I can't do it." Remiel dropped her sword and reached right into Zadkiel's heart. "That only means it's going to hurt."

Before Michael's eyes, as Remiel reached through Zadkiel's heart to uproot whatever was that dark thing, the darkness erupted from Zadkiel and exploded through the room like vines grasping for anything to strangle. Zadkiel screamed, but Remiel reached in deeper. The whole cavern shuddered with the darkness, slimy and sludgy, but then silence fell, and stillness.

When the darkness cleared, Michael looked for Remiel and Zadkiel only to find they'd disappeared.

In the far corner, the other Cherub stared with wide eyes. "It worked!"

"What did you just do? What was that?" Michael rushed Satrinah, but she didn't attempt to flee. He shoved her against the wall. "Saraquael! I need you here, now!"

Saraquael appeared with several soldiers in time to seize the two minor demons who had been powering the Guard. "Where's Zadkiel?"

Michael pushed his sword against Satrinah. "What did that weapon do?"

She regarded him in silence, her eyes orange and brittle.

"We've got no time. She's calling Asmodeus." Saraquael put a hand on Michael's shoulder. "Give me orders."

"Guard the room. Secure the weapons."

Saraquael cast a Guard on the ruined cavern, then called another Dominion. "I need help. There isn't enough of a structure for a strong Guard."

"Michael," called another of Saraquael's crew, "there are no weapons."

Michael turned. The bench was clear. Where before there had been an assortment of boxes and implements, now there was nothing.

"Asmodeus!" Saraquael called.

His Guard shattered, and Saraquael fell to his knees with his hands over his eyes.

Asmodeus burst into the room, wrenched Satrinah away from Michael, and vanished with her.

Michael rushed over to Saraquael, who murmured, "I'll be all right. I knew that wasn't going to work." He rubbed his temples. "Secure the area," he managed to tell another of his team. "Do a better job than those demons two did." He smiled wryly. "Do a better job than I did, too."

Michael lowered his head and rested his hands on his knees, trying to steady himself. He probed outward into the universe and couldn't detect Zadkiel. True, it was hard to scan for things in Hell, but he should be able to turn up at least her signature. Instead, nothing.

And Remiel—it did no good to scan for Remiel's signature because any scan would turn up another one of her. Her identical twin. Her identical fallen twin, Camael.

Saraquael had grown steadier, and got to his feet. "You can't find them either? Whatever this did might have left them unconscious." He sighed "I'm going to have our team secure the premises and remove everything from this room that they can. Something's going to give us a clue. I don't suppose Belior left us his lab notes, but at least we have his lab rats."

Michael followed Saraquael over to the two demon soldiers they'd seized, the guards left behind when Belior vanished and Asmodeus rescued Satrinah. There was nothing special about either of them until the moment Michael recognized one.

"Hastiel," he breathed.

The demon glared at him. "I hate you," he hissed. "You have no idea what you've done."

"No kidding," Saraquael said, binding him for transport back to Heaven. "But I look forward to asking you lots of questions about it."

FOUR

Heaviness. At first that was all Zadkiel could think of, the clumsiness and heaviness of whatever she was in and wherever she was. She tried to raise her head, but nothing moved the way it should. Her wings wouldn't flex, and she couldn't see a thing.

Was she in Hell's lab areas? What had happened after she'd been hit in the ice cavern?

For a while she rested, waiting for the heaviness to subside. In addition to seeing nothing, she heard nothing that sounded threatening, so she took her time. Eventually she decided she must be on the plane of Creation, probably on Earth. The first sound she eventually recognized was a susurration like leaves brushing against one another. You might hear that in Heaven too, but maybe the heaviness meant gravity.

She pushed up, and her body ached. A body: she was in a human form, solid, and she was on Earth. She traced her hands over the ground beneath her and felt it damp, sharp. Maybe she was in a cave.

Enough of this. She reached for her angelic form so she could shed the solid body, but it didn't come. Instead her head pounded, and the axis of the world spun like a gyroscope, and she had to lie prone again for a few minutes.

This was wrong. Why couldn't she change back? Why couldn't she remember changing in the first place?

And that explained the darkness, didn't it? Because in human form, she was blind.

God, this is no good.

She reached again for her subtle body, but she couldn't transform. She kept pushing, even when a needles and pins sensation shot through her and the dizziness frightened her, and then she reached all the way to try to completely dissociate, but nothing happened. She was stuck.

Now she gathered herself again and prayed, prayed with a fear she hadn't felt even when Belior had opened that box at her. She couldn't be stuck in a human body, could she? Not forever. Not without eyes.

She tried to remember the taste of wine, and it came immediately. Soothing, perfect, the wine steadied her. This she remembered, and it gave her strength.

"Remiel?" she called. "Are you there?"

No answer. Zadkiel sat herself upright and ran her hands over her body. Her fingers gave her information about the form she was in: for one thing, she was wearing clothing. That was good to know. There were sandals on her feet, and when she prodded her hair, she found it bound up with a hair pin.

So not only was she in a human form, but it was the last human form she'd used. That meant she was female, in her prime, and wearing high-class Greek clothing. Good information to have.

Am I in Greece?, she prayed, and then when she heard no answer, she tucked up her knees and stopped praying with words. Instead she prayed with her soul. She offered to God her confusion and her fear, and she tried not to think too much about what she was going to do to help herself. Not yet. Right now was the time to wait and to trust. She'd pray for God to bless her plans, and then after praying, then she'd plan something.

"Zadkiel?"

Zadkiel's head snapped up. "Remiel? Where are you? I can't move."

"Wait, I'll come to you." Remiel sounded breathless and a little shaken. "Keep talking. Recite something. Sing. I need to hear you."

Zadkiel started one of the psalms David had played in the palace at Jerusalem, keeping it slow and trying to steady her voice. Remiel had to get to her by navigating through the intervening space, and that meant Remiel was trapped in a human form too.

Because if she wasn't, she'd have been able to think, *To Zadkiel,* and just flash to her side.

Zadkiel finished that psalm and then started to sing the morning offering prayer. Was it morning? She had no idea, but she'd just awoken, and whatever they were doing had only started, so it seemed appropriate.

Remiel joined her in the prayer, and her voice grew louder over time, closer. Zadkiel pivoted to face the direction of the sound, and shortly she could hear stones scraping against other stones, and leaves snapping, more motion, and then finally felt a touch on her arm.

Zadkiel clutched at Remiel, surprised by how quickly her body reacted to the presence of another. The fear swept through her, and her voice wobbled. "What happened? Where are we?"

"In the middle of nowhere? I can't tell which *nowhere,* though. Are you stuck too?"

Zadkiel's hands tightened into the thick fabric covering Remiel's arm. "I'm in the same form I had the last time I used a human body."

"Yeah, I think that may be me too." Laughter. "That would explain my clothing, at least. Hang on. I need you to let go before I die of heat stroke."

Reluctantly Zadkiel released her grip, and next she heard the sounds of cloth. Remiel stood, and a heap of something fell to the ground. When Remiel spoke, she sounded tentative. "Are you hurt? You said you couldn't move."

Zadkiel said, "I can't see."

"Oh no! What happened to you? Did you land on your head?" Remiel's hands went to Zadkiel's face. "You're not bruised. Do you have a concussion? Are you in pain?"

"No, I'm just blind. In human form, I'm blind. It's part of the agreement." Zadkiel closed her eyes against the tears that sprang up. She'd never figured it would happen like this; she so seldom used a human form in the first place that she'd said God sold her the eternal memory of wine at far too cheap a price. But this?

"What did you agree to? Disagree to it." Remiel's hands went to hers. "Stand up. I want to make sure you aren't hurt."

Zadkiel got to her feet, swaying because she wan't used to poising herself in a body, and especially not when she couldn't correct her position by sight. "Easy," Remiel said. "You haven't got wings, so don't try to counterbalance with them or you'll take me down too." Remiel moved around her, keeping a hand on her at all times so Zadkiel could follow her motion. "You look all right. Your chiton is a bit stained, but you're not hurt."

"You really can't tell where we are?"

"It's a temperate area, lots of vegetation, plenty of water. We're on a hill, and there are trees below us. It might be Mediterranean, but I can't be sure. The ground won't talk to me." She chuckled. "God's not answering explicitly. So..." She took a deep breath and called, "Michael! Are you out there? Saraquael!"

Zadkiel reached inside for wine, for the Vision of God's eyes and the steadiness of His love. She presented her unease and then her gratitude that she and Remiel were at least together; she presented her thanks for the body she inhabited, and finally her need to get home. *Please bless Remiel's call and make it fruitful.*

Remiel had gone silent, praying as well, and then Zadkiel felt a prickle on the edge of her consciousness. An angel had noticed them and flagged them that help was on the way.

Remiel clenched Zadkiel's hand, and then Saraquael's voice came to her: "Thank you, God!" Someone grabbed Zadkiel in a hug. "What did they do to you?"

"Whatever it was," Remiel said, "we're stuck in human form."

Saraquael let go of Zadkiel as if dropping her. "Stuck?"

"Can't transcend back into an angel. Fully human." Remiel sighed. "I have no idea why, but apparently Belior was working on Angel Plaster, and now we've been molded."

"I don't believe that." That was Michael's voice, so he must have arrived too. "Raphael! We need you."

Saraquael said, "What have you tried?"

"What's there to try?" Remiel sounded partly irritated, partly amused. "You return to your regular form. It's not working."

"Whoa," said Raphael's voice abruptly. It was smooth, assertive. But most of all it was calm. "You're all banged up."

Zadkiel turned toward where she thought Remiel was. "You got hurt?"

"It's not a big deal."

"Nothing very deep, but we should patch that up." A pause. "No broken bones. No internals."

Zadkiel said, "How'd you get hurt?"

"Beats me," Remiel said. "I woke up like this."

"Like what?"

"Given the way your clothes are torn over the lacerations, I'd guess you fell onto the rocks." Raphael sounded absolutely unworried. "I'll check you for a concussion in a minute."

Michael said, "Could a concussion keep her stuck in human form?"

"You're stuck?" For the first time Raphael sounded surprised. "Now why would that be?"

From Michael: "You see, we kind of hoped you'd be the one to answer that for us."

Zadkiel said, "But you're not talking to me. Is Remiel all right? What happened to her?"

Saraquael put his arms around Zadkiel again. "She got banged up. She's okay."

"You didn't say anything to me." Zadkiel frowned. "You should have told me you needed help."

Remiel sounded unconcerned. "You needed it more."

"Hmm?" Raphael looked up. "Why is that?"

"She's blind," said Remiel.

"Okay, can we roll the scroll back a few pages?" Raphael touched Zadkiel, and she turned her face toward him. As he traced his fingers over her face, he said, "Why don't we start this from the beginning so you don't keep surprising me. Next thing I know you're going to tell me she's blind because of the dragon that's hovering right over my head with its jaws open, but that's okay because the whole Earth is being swallowed by Dark Matter."

Remiel said, "Dark Matter? I wonder if that's Belior's weapon."

"Stop!" Saraquael sounded tense. "This is too much confusion. Here."

Zadkiel couldn't feel what happened next, but she suspected Saraquael formed up all the facts into one little pellet of information and put it in Raphael's mind. Raphael's hands on her face felt warm, smooth, and she relaxed her neck as he tilted up her chin, then rested his fingers over her eyelids.

"We can rule out your eyes as a problem. Nothing's wrong." He sighed. "This is just the outcome of the deal you made, and it's a bit inconvenient, but also not an illness, so it's not fixable by me."

Zadkiel swallowed. "It's fixable if I turn back into an angel."

"And that's another thing I'm not able to fix right now." Raphael let her go, and it sounded as if he moved back to Remiel. "I'm not picking up anything wrong with either of them. If you gave them to me without any kind of introduction, I'd say they were human beings. There isn't a strong angelic signature on either one, and I'm not detecting anything that blocks them from reaching their true forms."

Remiel said, "I'm pretty sure I'm supposed to be an angel."

"I'm pretty sure too, and the good thing is, if I reach all the way down, your soul feels like an angelic soul. In fact," and Raphael's voice was a smile, "it's a Virtue soul. But everything overtop it functions as if it's human. It's seamless, without any kind of wrongness that feels as if it's locking you down. You're just...human."

Remiel sighed. "Not exactly what I wanted to hear."

Zadkiel said, "By the way, where are we?"

"Eastern part of the Kushan Empire," Saraquael said. "Hill country."

Raphael said, "Tell me more about the weapon that did this. We should get Gabriel working on the problem."

"Trust me, he already is," Saraquael said. "I delivered him the entire contents of the workroom where Belior and Satrinah developed the weapon, and after he finished thanking God for unending puzzles, he called in five friends and didn't even notice when I left."

Raphael was laughing so hard by the end of the sentence that Zadkiel found herself smiling too.

"Satrinah!" Remiel exclaimed. "That's her name. It was driving me crazy."

"Well, I've got these two patched up as much as I can. You," he said toward Zadkiel, "try to stay calm, and don't worry about your eyesight. There's nothing actually wrong. And you," that went toward Remiel, "try not to fall off any more cliffs."

"I was hoping to make a sport of it." Despite the words, she sounded tense. "And in the meantime?"

"I want you somewhere safe," Michael said. "We don't know if Asmodeus or Satrinah will come back for you, or even what happened to Belior. When you've rested and recovered a bit more, we'll move you. In the meantime, Saraquael, you stay with them for protection." For the first time, Michael sounded weary. "And right now, I've got an assignment of my own."

FIVE

Saraquael would have wanted to be with him for this. Saraquael would never complain about being excluded, but he'd register his disappointment and then would resign himself to not having been there.

Michael felt a little guilty about this, but he squared his shoulders and headed to Heaven's holding chambers.

Heaven didn't have a lot, never having needed many. Demons as a rule didn't want to come into Heaven, and Michael wanted them not to be there, so in the rare instances where a demon did need to be held and questioned, and where the holding couldn't take place in Hell itself, they'd constructed a series of buildings. Each building had one room, and each had been designed to reinforce the strength of a Guard.

From the outside, each was identical: a stone structure with no windows and no doors. But the interiors were all different as over time various angels had adopted one and decorated, outfitting each building in a slightly different way to better suit different types of demon personalities. The prison cells were actually comfortable places to be, if you didn't mind being imprisoned.

Of course, the first thing a demon in custody would do was destroy the entire interior. But Michael consoled himself that at least they'd made the effort.

The current two prisoners had been separated, and Michael stood before the building containing one of them. If memory served right, this interior was of Zadkiel's design. Ironic.

But now it was time to do what he'd come here to do. Michael had permission to get through any of the military Guards, so it let him pass with no resistance. That was to say, no resistance other than his own reluctance.

Just inside, Michael took form and stayed against the far wall. The prisoner, one of the two demon soldiers Asmodeus had left behind in the snow cavern, sat against the far wall, knees tucked up and wings folded with the tips crossed over his ankles. He glared up with eyes still filled with ice.

Michael said, "Hello, Hastiel."

"Hastle," spat the demon. "I don't want His name attached to mine anymore. He has nothing to give me, and I owe Him nothing."

Flinching, Michael averted his eyes. The decor did look like Zadkiel's work: the color scheme and the untouched selection of books felt like something she would do, and Hastiel...*Hastle* hadn't bothered torching it.

The demon added, "And you also don't have anything to say to me. Leave."

"As it turns out," Michael said, looking back into the demon's face, "I have plenty of things to say to you, and I'll stay as long as I want." He folded his arms. "Let's talk about Belior's little project, the one you seemed to think was beyond my ability to understand."

"Aren't we pretentious today?" Hastle snorted. "Raise your sword and get a pat on the head from God, and suddenly you're strutting around like the king of the universe."

Michael steeled himself. "You were protecting that lab. Why?"

"You're in command of Heaven's army." Hastle rolled his eyes. "I'm pretty sure you've figured out the purpose of standing guard."

"Belior was building a weapon."

"Congratulations." Hastle sat back against the wall. "You get a gold star."

"But it backfired."

"Not my fault. I was holding up that Guard pretty well against you until your little spy tackled me from behind." Hastle snorted. "If Belior detonated himself with his own weapon, that's his own stupidity at play. Let Satrinah explain it to Asmodeus. Not my problem."

Michael said, "We need to know what that weapon did."

Hastle took a deep breath but said nothing.

Michael leaned against the wall, waiting.

"Look, I don't feel like talking to you. You and everything you do disgusts me." Hastle shook his head. "I should have known from the start you'd be God's little goodie-goodie, running His errands and standing guard in front of Him like a toddler with a stick. The first time I met you, I should have kept right on going."

Michael shivered, but he kept his voice even. "I'm not exactly pleased with how you turned out, either."

"I didn't invite you in here." Hastle's eyes glimmered. "You invited yourself. You can invite yourself right out again whenever you like."

Michael said, "If you cooperate, we can release you."

Hastle regarded Michael as if bored.

Michael shoved his hands in his pockets. "Belior disappeared too. You saw him vanish when the weapon backfired."

Hastle snickered. "I see no downside. I worked for him, but I don't care one whit what happens to him."

Surprised, Michael said, "Then why were you working for him? You were one of a very small group of hand-selected soldiers working on an elite project. Clearly you were chosen for your loyalty."

"Unlike you," said Hastle. "If loyalty is the criteria, you'd never make it."

Michael bristled. "My loyalty isn't in question."

"It's really the only question." Hastle glared at the floor. "Why did I ever think you'd be loyal to me in the first place? Regardless, I don't have to like someone to do my job, and," Hastle added, "I have objectives of my own. Again, unlike you. I have something I want other than what my supposed superiors tell me I should, and this was the best way to get it. Therefore you can feel free to keep me locked up as long as you like."

Hastle smirked at him, and Michael lowered his wings. He prayed, *Those eyes. They're the same, but they're not. It's all wrong.*

Of course it's all wrong, replied God. *Think of his choices.*

This isn't how he was. Michael bit his lip. *How can I appeal to someone like this?*

This time God didn't answer.

Hastle said, "Did you just ask your Daddy what to do about me?" He leaned forward, eyes sparking. "Are you going to give me torture and pain? More fire? It's kind of interesting to see what you're going to try with me. Maybe He could just pull my little puppet strings and make me give you all the answers you want." Hastle's eyes narrowed to slits. "But then again, if He wants to do that, maybe He should just tell you what you need to know without involving me in the first place."

About to reply, Michael stopped himself. This wouldn't be fruitful. The demon was trying to exert control over the situation, and as long as Michael stayed there talking, the demon was going to think he'd in some measure succeeded. They didn't need answers badly enough to let the demon play these games; Remiel and Zadkiel were safe, and the Cherubim were analyzing the remnants of the weapon-making lab.

Hastle grinned, but Michael just stepped back through the cell wall.

Remiel ran her fingers along the skin Raphael had mended, and when she stretched her arms over her head, they rewarded her by not stinging like crazy. She flexed, and her hips didn't complain. The beginnings of a huge bruise had dissolved, too.

"He's good." She turned to Saraquael. "Do you want take a shot at being my wardrobe consultant?"

Saraquael motioned her over to where he sat alongside Zadkiel, and when Remiel approached, he traced the ripped fabric of her clothing. "Given how torn up you were, it's a good thing this is as thick as it is. You'd have been shredded."

While she watched, he rejoined the fibers to one another, then lifted the blood stains from the fabric over her leg and arm. He added, "Stay still. I want to make sure I'm merging the fibers with their correct counterparts."

Zadkiel sounded subdued. "I wish you'd told me you were hurt." She tucked up her knees and wrapped her arms around her legs. "Actually, I wish you weren't stuck like this with me. You're in this situation at all because you tried to save me."

"And you're in it because you tried to save Michael, so don't mention it. Besides, Gabriel's on the case. We'll be home before either one of us gets hungry." Remiel chuckled. "Although maybe we should find a water source."

Zadkiel didn't object to the change of subject, and Remiel put a hand on her. "Come on, let's head downhill. There's got to be a stream near all that plant life, and it'll probably be less windy down there."

Remiel hefted her discarded winter fur and helped Zadkiel to a stand. It was nerve-wracking how Zadkiel stayed frozen in place, afraid to move through a world she couldn't see. So Remiel stayed close to her and said, "Okay, small steps at first," staying on one side with her arm curled around Zadkiel's waist.

Even so, Zadkiel wanted to stop after ever step, so Remiel put a little pressure on the small of her back, and Zadkiel walked with a jerking hesitation.

Remiel looked ahead for even patches of ground and gave warnings as they went. "There's a plant right in front of your feet." Or, "You're about to step down."

Saraquael had fallen silent, scanning the horizon.

"You know, you're supposed to be taking care of us," Remiel said to him. "You could scout out a good location and then flash us there."

"Scouting, sure, but I don't want to risk teleportation. We have no idea what they did to you." Saraquael's eyes darkened. "If there's something about you that's interacting badly with the angelic plane, it makes the most sense to minimize your contact with it."

Remiel helped Zadkiel around a stone higher than her ankle. "Raphael didn't have a problem healing me with angelic power."

"You weren't immersed in his healing energy. That's a huge difference." Saraquael kept scanning the distance rather than focusing on either of them. "I don't want chance that you'll get knocked unconscious and flashed to who-knows-where a second time. You landed in a good spot this time, but two thirds of the Earth's surface is covered with water, and other parts are just plain uninhabitable."

"You're so sweet." Remiel snickered. "You think I'd die?"

"Do you want to take that chance?" Saraquael's voice pitched upward, and he looked right at her. "I don't. We have no idea what they did to you or why this is happening in the first place. Dying should put you back in your angelic form, but if you can't be in angelic form, what then?"

Zadkiel stopped moving. "Wait, really?"

Saraquael went back to scanning long-distance. "Yes, really. You're stuck in human bodies. What if those bodies are dead?"

Remiel didn't push Zadkiel to keep moving. "No, that really hadn't occurred to me."

"A lot of things haven't occurred to you." Saraquael's eyes narrowed. "Let me suggest another one. Satrinah knows you got hit with her weapon, and if a Cherub has an experimental weapon she's never used, guess what she's going to do after the first time she uses it?"

Zadkiel clutched Remiel's arm. "He's right. We have to take shelter. Now." She turned toward where Saraquael ought to be standing, and he obligingly adjusted position to be where she was looking even though she couldn't see him. "You can't stay. She's going to have Asmodeus scouring the world searching for any trace of us she can study, and Asmodeus will know to look for you."

"I agree. I'm keeping my signature suppressed, but that will only work for so long. I want to get you in a safe place, and then I'm going to send another angel to look after the two of you. But for now, move it." Saraquael turned to Remiel, his green eyes gleaming. "This isn't a game. I'm trying to keep you protected."

Remiel nudged Zadkiel back into a walk, and she struggled to keep her hands from trembling. Was this body still injured after all? Everything sounded too loud, and all Remiel wanted to do was hurry. Hurry, but with nowhere to hurry to. Her breathing hurt, and her eyes stung.

Her voice was thin. "This is my fault."

"Let's debate whose fault this is after we stash you somewhere less exposed." Saraquael took to the air overhead. "Please."

Zadkiel kept her voice low. "I can move quicker than this. I'll be okay."

Remiel struggled to focus on the descent, hyper-aware how far away two women on a hilltop could be seen from and how far they had to go until they reached the tree cover. Her foot slipped on some stones, but she caught herself before taking Zadkiel in a slide with her. Saraquael put his hands on her shoulders, a tingly sensation. "Don't panic. I'm still here, and I'll call for help if necessary."

He could call for a legion of angels right now, except that would attract demonic attention. Even guards at strategic locations would raise some demon's curiosity enough to report it. No, they were doing everything right, and yet it felt entirely wrong. If someone's helpless, you protect them. You don't just tell them to hide and hope for the best.

The going got more difficult toward the base of the hill as the vegetation grew denser, but Remiel tried to hurry Zadkiel. A couple of times she stumbled and once she fell, but Remiel rushed her back to her feet and kept them moving.

When they reached tree cover, Saraquael talked to the Earth until he felt which way they could go to find a stream, and he directed them until they arrived at water and a small clearing.

Remiel led Zadkiel to the edge, then helped her cup water into her hands so she could drink. Zadkiel hadn't spoken for a long time now, and her face was smudged. Her Greek tunic (they called that a chiton, right?) had gotten dirty again, and Remiel looked at herself to find her own clothing in disarray. But for now they'd at least hidden themselves.

Remiel looked up at Saraquael. "We need a plan."

"Right now the plan is to reverse whatever they did to you, and as soon as I leave you, I'm going to follow up on that." His mouth tightened. "I'll find out what Gabriel's learned, and then I'll question the two demons we captured in the lab."

Zadkiel spoke softly. "Belior's out there too. Somewhere."

Saraquael said, "Asmodeus probably found him in the first couple of minutes. Since your souls are still angelic, I assume Belior's is too, and therefore he'll still have all his bonds."

Remiel shivered: by extension, there was another angel the demons would find when they looked for her. And then *he* would come looking for her. And if she still gave off any angelic signature at all, he'd find her. How could he not? It would be like not finding himself.

Zadkiel hadn't made that connection, and said only to Saraquael, "I didn't mean we needed to look for Belior, only that demons hate matter, and maybe he's stuck in a human body too."

Remiel tried to shrug off the targeted feeling. "It serves him just fine if he hates what he did to himself. I won't be in any hurry to share a cure with him."

Saraquael folded his arms. "All the same, since you two landed near one another, he might be in the area also. You might want to avoid other humans, at least for the time being."

Zadkiel stiffened. "He couldn't be trapped in an animal form could he?"

Remiel glanced at the trees. "Both of us ended up in the last physical forms we'd taken, so I suppose it's possible."

Saraquael shook his head. "There's no way to shield your presence from thirty million forest insects, so I'm not going to go that far. I'm going to assign you two ninth-choir angels as if you were regular humans with regular guardians. That setup should at least look normal if a demon does encounter you. If you meet a suspicious human...that's its own set of dangers."

Remiel tightened her fists. "As long as it stays in human form, I think I can handle that."

Saraquael shook his head. "I don't like this situation, but we're going to work on things as quickly as possible. Stay in contact."

He vanished, and a moment later Remiel could feel two bright presences on the periphery of her senses. They glimmered momentarily, then faded into the background. Just like normal guardians.

She looked at Zadkiel, who knelt at the edge of the stream with her hands in the water and her eyes staring sightlessly forward. And for a long time, Remiel didn't have even enough energy to pray.

SIX

Michael looked up when Saraquael flashed into his central command office in Heaven.

"I've set them up in a more secure location with two soldiers posted as guardians." Saraquael looked worried and worn, his wings dropped and the feathers dull. "They've got a water source for the time being, and I've stationed a Virtues in the sky about twenty miles westward to make sure the weather holds."

Michael stepped away from the windows ringing the mountain-top room, then glanced at Gabriel's report on the table at the room's center. The document was far too gleeful for what it contained, but he supposed a Cherub faced with an unsolvable problem could respond in no other way. Gabriel's report began somberly enough: whatever that weapon was, it had vanished without any residue upon discharge. Gabriel noted that this behavior correlated with what they'd heard about some of the materials going missing even while the demons were still working on the project. Gabriel then detailed every single test his team had run on the seized materials and the results of each, sounding progressively more intrigued. He offered his preliminary conclusions sounding chirpy (nothing definitive) and the writing was ebullient by the time he discussed the next direction his team intended to take.

Quite a journey for a one-page briefing. Michael handed it to Saraquael. "Nothing from Gabriel. He can't even figure out the nature of the weapon, let alone why it hurt them."

Saraquael emitted a burst of shock. "*Gabriel* didn't figure it out?" He frowned at the report, then steeled himself. "Okay, then we need to question the prisoners."

Michael paced the office's perimeter. He liked it clear and uncluttered, a convenient area for coordinating operations with multiple team heads and choir chiefs while remaining calm and focused like a temple's heart, but really, it also was convenient for doing laps around that desk in the center when he needed to move and think at the same time. As he paced, he stared at the roots of the mountains, his view of the river interrupted only by wispy clouds and clumps of trees.

"I've dispatched a team to hunt for Belior. Asmodeus found him first, doubtless," Michael added, "but any additional information on how it affected him would have to help."

Saraquael snickered. "Remiel thinks it's poetic justice that he got caught in his own weapon."

Michael glanced at him. "You'd know. You're the poet."

"A confused poet." Saraquael gestured one-handed at Gabriel's report. "How bizarre is it that Belior zapped himself?"

"Unless that was part of the point." Michael shivered. "I'm beginning to wonder if the weapon didn't require a sacrifice."

Saraquael snorted. "Hence the requirement to keep two soldiers with the two Cherubim. The Cherub wields the weapon and powers it with his own personal martyr. Poetically speaking it does have a kind of horrific symmetry." He folded his arms. "If that were the case, I wonder if either of the soldiers knew. It's going to take some delicate questioning to get that information."

Michael flinched. "I already spoke to one of them."

"Oh, you didn't. Tell me you didn't." Saraquael bit his lip. "No good comes from that."

"He was my friend," Michael said, a little defensive.

"Precisely why you should have been the last person to interview him. Or even later than the last one. No good comes from that kind of thing, ever. Plus, now you've contaminated my sterile field." Saraquael offered a smile. "So what did you get from him?"

"You have to ask?" Michael sighed. "Nothing good comes from that."

Saraquael refrained from saying anything further. He didn't have to.

Michael added, "He goes by Hastle now, by the way."

"Good to know, I guess. I'll make sure not to use it." Saraquael smirked. "I'll get an interrogation unit together for the other one."

Michael folded his arms as he looked outside. An interrogation unit. They'd probably send in two questioners and have several others posted outside to monitor and make suggestions. But Saraquael knew all this, and he'd handled this kind of questioning before. It just had never seemed quite this important.

Saraquael laid a hand on Michael's arm. "You're not okay."

He shook his head.

"I'm sorry. I've met old friends too. There's just enough there to remind you why you loved them."

As Saraquael wrapped his arms and wings around him, Michael relaxed. "I wish... I know it can't happen, but still."

"That's why no good comes from it. Because it hurts you, and they enjoy it. I've done it myself, and while you're talking to them, you forget they're master manipulators."

Michael chuckled. "Because they're master manipulators."

"That would be my first task if I were manipulating someone." Saraquael let him go and offered a smile. "I'll get two teams of questioners together. Do you want to stay involved with Hastle?"

Not Hastiel. Not anymore.

"No," said Michael. "Right now, though, we've got other concerns and no clear direction. How safe are Remiel and Zadkiel?"

"Not very." Saraquael's feathers went dull again. "The area is isolated, so I'm not concerned about other humans as much as I am the demons." Walking to the window, Saraquael said, "Two humans out in the middle of nowhere with no means of support and no obvious reason to be there is going to attract attention from the enemy. We need them moved."

Michael sat on the edge of the table. "Raphael?" he said into the air.

An answering spark blossomed in his heart.

"Any further thoughts on whether we can transport them?"

Another answer: still unclear.

Meeting Saraquael's eyes, Michael shook his head. "Thanks. Keep working on it."

Saraquael said, "Is that *No, it's dangerous,* or *No, we haven't established its safety?*"

"The latter. It's just too uncertain until Gabriel comes up with what that weapon did." Michael folded his arms. "In an emergency, sure, I'd try it, but right now it's not an emergency. Leave them where they are."

Zadkiel spent her time meditating. While Remiel paced the area where they'd taken shelter, she kept her attention on God's life in her heart and the taste of wine on her tongue.

A human body: a weird little machine, clumsy and limited in so many ways and yet in other ways such a marvel. If she touched her skin in the thinnest places, she could feel her own heart beating. She could manipulate her sensations by holding her breath or concentrating on one limb or another.

The only thing she couldn't affect was her vision, so instead she directed attention to her other senses. She focused on the heat and cold on her skin from the sunlight as it slanted. She absorbed all the information about her body's position and how heavy it felt versus where it felt most energetic. A few stretches seated her mind a bit more in her own positioning, and slowly she became more comfortable moving. She listened to the stream passing nearby and wondered about the volume of water, something she'd never fully considered before but which continuously came from somewhere and moved to somewhere else.

Remiel's footsteps circled again. "Are you patrolling?" Zadkiel asked abruptly.

Zadkiel's cheeks heated up. She was a soldier. She ought to have been on patrol, or at least set one up.

"What? Oh, no, well, I guess maybe." Remiel gave a nervous laugh. "I can't stay still. I tried, but I want to be moving."

Zadkiel said, "Stress hormones."

"Oh. You think so?" Leaves rustled as Remiel came nearer and sat. "That would be a relief. I didn't consider that the body might be doing it to me. Maybe it's not as bad then."

"You're not used to body chemicals. Neither am I, really, but I've felt them before." Zadkiel reached for where Remiel should be, failed to find her, and finally Remiel clasped her hand. Nice job, Seeker. "It's a lousy situation, but I don't think we need to panic."

"I keep wanting to run. I'm not leaving you," Remiel added quickly, "but even though there's nowhere to go, I want to escape."

"That's what physical bodies do when they feel trapped." As she said the last, Zadkiel's mouth tightened, and she steadied herself.

"It's okay." Remiel squeezed her hand. "You're more trapped than I am. But if it's just the body doing this to me, it'll be okay. It's not real."

It was real, of course. Saraquael maybe hadn't needed to scare them quite as much as he had, but the truth behind his words was still in force: if they were stuck in a body, and the body died, what would happen to their spirits? Did Asmodeus know where they were? With the entire army of Hell at his disposal, was he now combing the Earth one blade of grass at a time to locate them? But Saraquael had wanted Remiel to be more serious, and Zadkiel wouldn't argue with success.

She tensed the underbrush rustled with the passage of an animal, but it sounded small and quick. She'd already had to deal with the fear that insects were crawling all over her; she didn't relish the idea of rodents or snakes.

Remiel said, "It's also not real that I'm hungry, right?"

Zadkiel fought a grin. "That's entirely an illusion."

"Good, because when people get hungry, they get snappish." Remiel sounded more relaxed now, as if she were smiling. "I distinctly recall Gabriel bringing food to Elijah in the wilderness when he needed it. I should pester Saraquael. I bet he'd bring us something good."

"We're in a forest, not a wasteland." Zadkiel gestured around her. "It stands to reason there may be something edible nearby. Let's go foraging."

When Remiel didn't reply, Zadkiel started to stand. "I'm pretty good at finding hidden things."

"No, it's not that." Remiel let go of her and got to her feet quickly. "You stay put. I'll look."

Zadkiel said, "I'm not helpless."

"You're not helpless, but there are tangles of vines and rocks and roots jutting up out of the ground. You stay here."

Then she was gone, and Zadkiel stung with uselessness.

Dead weight. Remiel didn't even want to leverage the one talent she actually had.

In the quiet, Zadkiel returned to meditation and that strong pulse of God's love inside her. Remiel did have a point: she'd gotten hungry too, and her regard for the marvel of the human body lessened in proportion to the inconvenience of having to feed it. But that didn't mean she was an infant who needed food handed to her before she could eat it.

She came back to herself at Remiel's touch. "Here, I found this this." Remiel pressed receive some leaves, into her hands, rounded and thick, still dripping with stream water. "It's a bunch of broadleaf plantain plants I found not too far away. I've seen people eating them before. I think they taste green."

They said a blessing over the leaves, and then it had to be done. Tentative, Zadkiel nibbled a small one, and she decided that *green* tasted a little bitter but not inedible.

"I'll keep looking," Remiel said, and again she made crunching noises as she headed off into the wilderness.

Zadkiel moved on to eating the larger leaves, were more bitter, less green.

Before she was done, Remiel crashed back into their clearing at a run. "I found the perfect food," she sing-songed. "Hang on. You'll love this."

Larger splashing sounds came from the stream. Then as Zadkiel swallowed a bite of her last (and most bitter) plantain leaf, Remiel laid something else into her hands. It felt like a stalk of some sort, rigid and smooth. "Bite into it," Remiel said. "It's not what you think."

Zadkiel ran her fingers up to the nubbly edge, then snapped it off and bit into it. "Oh!" It tasted nuttier than the leaves and had a juicy center. "What's this?"

"Asparagus. There's a whole stand upstream, so eat as much as you want."

They stopped speaking while they ate, although every so often Remiel would dump more of the asparagus stalks onto the last large leaf in Zadkiel's lap. The bottom of the stalks was tough, but even that wasn't inedible.

"Thank you," she said at last.

"I'll get some more in a few minutes so we don't have to forage after it gets dark." Remiel sounded abruptly worried. "I hope we're not here overnight. We've got that coat, but I don't like the idea of being exposed to wildlife while we sleep."

Rodents. Zadkiel shuddered. "They'd stay away from us, right? Animals don't like people."

"I'm going to guess that's true, but usually they don't like the implements people have with them. Pointy things or burning things. We have neither of those." Remiel stood. "I should figure out how to start a fire."

Sparks flooded Zadkiel's mind, and in the next instant her heart hammered: high alert. The angels guarding them had spotted demons.

Zadkiel fought her body's useless urge to freeze, as useful to her in this situation as Remiel's urge to run. Instead she steadied her voice, and as she got to her feet, she spoke in Bactrian so they at least had a chance of passing for people who belonged in this part of the world. "Bring me the rest of the asparagus and the plantain leaves. I'll wash them in the stream while you get a fire started."

Remiel sounded surprised. "Oh, I guess you could." She'd answered in the same language.

"I'm not helpless." Not totally helpless, and it was best to be doing the things demons thought humans did rather than looking like a pair of angels waiting for a ride home.

"I didn't say you were. I just wasn't thinking about it."

Remiel guided her to the water's edge, then gave her the remaining asparagus before heading back into the woods. Zadkiel rubbed them under the water, trying to determine by feel when the dirt was off the stalks and leaves. She laid the wet stalks on the broad plantain leaves it in what felt like a patch of sunlight, and she kept working even though her hands grew numb with the cold. When Remiel returned with more plants, she cleaned those as well, and shortly after she heard the sounds of stick breaking.

Eventually the angels signaled Zadkiel: the demons had left the area. She nodded.

Behind her, Remiel muttered, "It's a lot easier to start fires with my mind." Zadkiel smiled. "But I've got some wood together and I cleared a fire pit, so if I can get it started, we should be warm tonight."

As it grew chilly, Remiel did her best to settle them in for the night. Zadkiel prayed but otherwise let Remiel figure it out: the fire proved to be the toughest problem, although Remiel was able to use some tools left in the pockets of the heavy coat. "Good thing my last assignment was in the frozen north," Remiel muttered. "Do you want to maybe wrap yourself in the coat for now?"

In contrast to Remiel's clothing, Zadkiel's was lighter, so she took it gratefully. After a while, Remiel positioned her closer to the fire, and they said another meal blessing. The leaves were still bitter, but Remiel had rigged up some way of roasting the asparagus, and the flavor markedly improved. *Thank you for making edible plants,* Zadkiel prayed. *These are amazing.*

After dinner, the angel guarding them sent another alert, and Zadkiel knew demons were scouting again. The alert lasted longer this time, but Zadkiel stayed close to the fire while Remiel worked in silence across the clearing.

The worry and tension passed: the demons had gone.

"Glad that's over." Remiel sighed. "Well, I cleared out an area that looks like we can keep warm in."

"If we huddle together, with the coat, we should be all right," Zadkiel said. "I think."

"I'm not sure how cold it gets here." Remiel shook her head. "But we'll do our best. I have to believe that if we're about to die of exposure, Saraquael will come back and do something even if it risks detection."

"Even so, shouldn't he have by now?" Without being able to see the sun it was hard to tell the time, but her body told her time had passed. They'd eaten twice. The air had gotten chillier. She was tired.

"We don't know what they discovered." Remiel's voice dropped in volume. "If it's dangerous for us to intersect with the angelic plane, maybe we can't even talk to them. We might be on our own." Zadkiel started, but Remiel added, "Whatever they decide, tomorrow we're not staying here. We'll find a human habitation. We'll insinuate ourselves into some kind of normal existence, and we'll wait while doing something, not hiding in a hole to be discovered like baby rabbits."

Zadkiel got a handle on the fear creeping up her spine. "I think you're right. The scouts passed over us today, but if we stay in one place, they're going to start asking questions."

A moment later, Remiel added, "Let's pray evening prayer."

So the sun had set. Saraquael should have returned.

Zadkiel swiped her hand over her eyes, and she tried to compose herself while Remiel led off with the prayer and she gave the responses. Halfway through, though, another voice joined them: Saraquael's.

At last. Oh, thank goodness. Answers.

They finished up because no one interrupts a conversation with God, but as soon as they ended, Remiel said, "Well? What have you got?"

The tension in her voice told Zadkiel what the answer would be. She must have detected it from Saraquael's expression or his posture, something Zadkiel could re-create in her own mind after so many years of working with him as her commanding officer and fellow standard-bearer for Michael. He wouldn't look defeated, but he'd be missing that hint of mischief in his eyes, and he'd look more business-like than playful.

Sure enough, he said, "Nothing yet."

"Nothing?" Remiel's voice broke. "What's Gabriel doing?"

"Oh, trust me, Gabriel's doing something. I've got a list as long as my arm of tests Gabriel has run on every scrap we pulled out of Hell." Saraquael was trying to sound upbeat, but Zadkiel heard it as frustration. "Every test comes up as *nothing,* which he assures me is in and of itself a clue as to the nature of the weapon, but when I ask him what kind of clue, he can't begin to guess."

"This isn't supportable." Remiel got to her feet. "We can't stay here. We've already been scouted twice."

A pause: Saraquael must have been conferring with their Angel guards. "You've got a point. You're a curiosity."

"So we need to get out of here. Extinguish the fire." Her voice had dropped in pitch. "Zadkiel, take this." The coat settled over Zadkiel's shoulder, still warm. "Saraquael, you're going to have to move us. Now."

"It might be dangerous."

"So move me first and come back for her after you know it works. Or, if it doesn't work, then at least you know for sure." Remiel's voice grew insistent. "This is my fault to begin with."

Saraquael's voice pitched upward. "I'm not willing to take the risk."

"You're not risking anything." Remiel's eyes would be tight, and Zadkiel knew she'd be standing with her hands clenched. "It's my risk to take, and I'm willing to take it. Move me first. Come back for her. It's better than freezing out here or getting discovered and kidnapped into Hell." Her voice sharpened. "How many seconds do you think Satan would hesitate before transporting us once he knows who we are? Do you think he's going to worry one jot about our safety?"

No answer from Saraquael.

"So help me, I need you to do this." Remiel sounded more intense. "Extinguish our fire. Take me away. Come back for her if it works."

More silence.

Zadkiel raised her head. "Where would we go?"

"We've already figured that out." Saraquael sounded subdued. "Raphael suggested we take you to one of the Christian communities in Greece. They'll shelter you and feed you, and if you do get attacked, they'll have the authority to fight back demons as well."

Remiel sounded outraged. "Why aren't we already there?"

"The risk of moving you."

"Then do it."

The silence stretched so long that Zadkiel wasn't sure if they'd gone. "Guys?"

"I don't like this." Saraquael was barely audible. "I want to register my objection. If something awful happens, I don't want to regret participating forever."

"This isn't your fault. I'm the bully. It's my fault." Remiel sounded steady, relieved. "Let's go."

An abrupt scent of smoke told Zadkiel the fire had winked out. "I'll be back for you in a minute," said Saraquael, "no matter what happens."

Zadkiel forced herself to sound brave. "I'll be right here."

A chill settled over her, and she huddled beneath Remiel's coat. With the fire's sounds gone, she could better hear the small motions of the forest: leaves and little creatures and insect calls.

Then Saraquael's voice. "We can do it. Barely. I want you to hold tight to me, and keep your eyes closed."

"Keep my eyes closed?"

He laughed. "Oh, right, that shouldn't matter as much to you. Remiel's really disoriented, but she's intact, so if you want to take the chance, I'll move you as well. Be prepared for a monstrous headache on the other side."

Zadkiel reached forward, and Saraquael's subtle hand met her own. "I remember what Remiel said before." She forced a smile. "That only means it's going to hurt. It doesn't mean I can't do it."

SEVEN

"It's called a migraine," Raphael was saying, "and I'm doing my best with it. You're still a bit of an enigma."

It had been dark when they left their hiding spot, dark and silent. Remiel wanted the darkness back.

She lifted her hands from her eyes, squinting in the blinding sunlight and harsh gleams off every random piece of metal in the city of Ephesus. The entire city seemed to be talking at once, and her every movement made her feel numb. She was bathed in sweat.

"But the good news is, it's not going to leave you blind too." Raphael crouched before her. "Stay still a little longer. Take some time to regret being brave."

She forced a small smile. "And regret eating dinner."

"You got rid of the dinner just fine on your own." Raphael put his hands against her head, and she could feel the pressure from his subtle body as a series of tingles that threatened to make her vomit again. "Next time you go somewhere, you walk."

She wasn't sure she walking right now was an option either. Gingerly she turned her head to check on Zadkiel, who was also in bad shape but hadn't been as effected by the transfer. Fortunately. Maybe Saraquael had done something to help her transition easier because she hadn't thrown up. Beside Zadkiel, Saraquael sat with his wings over her while she lay curled on the ground.

Remiel tried to stand, but Raphael gentled her back down. "You need to take some time."

"Time is what we don't have. You gained us a few hours, but the sun sets here too, and we need to get to our safe house." She forced herself to her feet and put her hand on the wall. It felt stable—and upright in a way that helped her vestibular senses determine which way was upright too. "I should at least scout our way."

"I'll be all right in a minute," Zadkiel mumbled.

With her head pounding, Remiel braced herself to take stock of their surroundings. The alley to which Saraquael had flashed them was unpeopled, so they hadn't immediately been seen, but in a city of two hundred thousand, it would happen sooner or later. She trusted Saraquael was doing something to keep them invisible to demons, of which there had to be a crowd because of that multitude of people, but his protection couldn't last forever either.

Remiel took a step, and the smell assaulted her again: sewage, human refuse, death, sweat, all mixed in one bouquet that left her wondering if maybe hungry demons in the forest had been the better option after all.

Well, no time for regrets. They were here. With an act of will, she raised her head. "One last thing. We're not presentable. Can you clean off her clothes, at least?"

Saraquael snapped. The dirt fell off Zadkiel's tunic, and her hair styled itself into a twist. Remiel laughed. If he felt secure enough to show off, and he absolutely hadn't in the forest, then they'd greatly improved their safety margin. There he'd been dismal, tense. Coming here was the right choice. Given that it was all her fault to begin with, she'd take a pounding headache to protect Zadkiel.

Zadkiel got to her feet, still pale but otherwise steady. Reaching for her hand, Remiel said to Saraquael and Raphael, "Thank you. I think we've got it from here."

Raphael blessed them both, then vanished. Saraquael said, "If I can do it without compromising your safety, I'll check you later tonight. You've still got your personal guards, although from now on you have to assume there are demons around you at all times, and here's a map of the city."

Abruptly Remiel knew the layout of all the streets, the location of the harbor, the house they needed to go to—and the remaining contents of her stomach. She went on all fours and dry-heaved until tears came to her eyes, and afterward only huddled around herself in misery.

Saraquael hunched in front of her, dismal again. "I'm so sorry." His voice was broken. "I didn't think about that. It's just—"

"Just that you're used to me being an angel." Remiel swiped her wrist across her eyes. "It's okay."

Zadkiel rubbed Remiel's shoulders. "Please don't do that again, if you don't mind."

"Yeah, from now on, spoken directions." Saraquael shivered. "I need to leave. I don't want to undo the good of bringing you here." And with a blessing, he vanished.

This stank. Where they stood literally stank, of course, but the situation itself also reeked of awfulness. It wasn't fair. They were angels, except they couldn't be. They should be able to move around, to transmit knowledge to one another, to face down demons with absolute freedom. Not this. This was imprisonment.

Zadkiel said, "Can you walk?"

"I'd better." Remiel stood. "I'm going to guide you." She put her hand on Zadkiel's elbow. "At least I have the layout of the city in my head now, so I can direct us. We're going first to the commercial agora."

"For what?"

"Supplies." Remiel steeled herself. "For one thing, I need better clothing."

She guided them through the narrower streets onto a larger thoroughfare she suddenly recognized as Curetes Street. She attracted the attention she'd known she would: with shorn blonde hair, strange clothing, and a half-dozen earrings, she didn't look like your standard Ephesian. Zadkiel, by contrast, had olive skin and black hair, plus she wore a chiton and an overtunic, so she fit right in. A half-step behind her, Remiel guided Zadkiel by resting a hand on her elbow and moving it like a tiller, and she kept her own head down.

The smells intensified, as did the sounds. Remiel bit her lip. It didn't make sense to add pain in order to relieve pain, but for some reason it helped a little. As she walked, though, she laughed abruptly. In Greek, she said, "Remember when Paul wrote that the faithful could make up for whatever was lacking in the sufferings of Christ?"

Zadkiel said, a bit hesitant, "I do."

"We've never had a chance to do that until now." Remiel giggled. "So I guess some good comes from this."

"Oh." A momentary pause. "I wonder how we do that. Is there a ritual or a prayer?"

"You'd have to ask Paul." Remiel shrugged. "Okay, this way."

At the market, Remiel found to her surprise that Saraquael's mental map included such information as which sellers dealt in which merchandise. That was helpful. Otherwise, the tumult might have overwhelmed her: if anything, her over-saturated senses were now even more saturated, and her head pounded harder. *Whatever could have possibly been lacking that this is making up for it?* In addition to the sounds and smells, she now had other human bodies to avoid, elbows and shoulders that wanted to slam against her as people rushed to finish their business before the day's end.

And the conversations—even the snippets were too much to follow. Price haggling, arguments, softer thank-yous and how-are-you-doings, and several people gleefully recounting a gory murder that had taken place on the city's outskirts only this morning. That topic came up repeatedly. The poor victim had died in three different and very graphic ways by the time Remiel reached the clothing merchant Saraquael wanted her to visit.

This particular older man with thin hair and a full beard had his tent near the tremendous theater under one of the colonnades. Remiel stopped before him, bowing. When he looked at her, she lowered her head and presented the fur coat. "Sir, how much will you give my mistress for this coat?"

Zadkiel's head pivoted toward Remiel, but she ignored her. The merchant lifted the coat from her arms, examined it thoroughly, grunted, then offered an embarrassingly low price.

Not being stupid, Remiel said, "Thank you. We will move on."

"Wait, wait!" The merchant stepped forward. "You're not getting a better deal anywhere else. This isn't worth anything. It's not the style, and you can tell how warm it is in this country. You think you're still in the North? No one needs this."

Remiel bowed her head again. She said in flawless Greek, "Good sir, you are insulting my mistress. This coat will fetch you an amount five times as much. The workmanship is high-end, and people do travel northward. I'm sure some other merchant will be willing to discuss fair terms for its purchase. May you be blessed all the days of your life."

"Now wait, wait. Don't go cheating your mistress out of what should rightly be hers. By what authority are you negotiating?"

Zadkiel tilted up her chin. "Mine."

Remiel kept her voice even and low. "She knows the garment's value. She owns the garment together with the servant. You are not the first," she added, "to under-estimate the value of these items. We will go elsewhere."

Abruptly the merchant was more amenable to discussing money, whereas Zadkiel had gotten five times as tense. The money wasn't the issue. Remiel didn't care quite so much about the actual value of the garment—let him rip her off if he wanted to; only his own soul would suffer. More important than the price was her need to blend in, so she required an entirely new wardrobe, and the pair of them needed at least a little money. So the bartering continued: he said such a price was too much; Zadkiel said it was too little; Remiel said, "What if we also sold my boots?" which led to the merchant's examination of her footwear, followed by him asking if she'd sell her tunic.

Now they were getting somewhere. "My mistress will not permit me to walk naked through the market."

The merchant laughed. "Now that would be a sight! I'd purchase you myself for that, but you're right, you're right."

A deal was struck: everything Remiel was wearing at an agreed-upon price for the mistress, plus new clothes for the slave. "Serviceable clothes," the merchant assured Zadkiel. "She won't be dressed more fashionably than you."

Maybe he attributed the horror on Zadkiel's face to the notion that Remiel might be more beautiful than herself. She said, "Let it be done."

The merchant produced a tunic and sandals, plus the money, and then sold them a bag to keep the money in. He ushered Remiel into a nearby alcove where she made sure he wasn't watching and then changed clothing. While there was nothing to be done about her hair and skin color, she emerged looking marginally more Greek than when she'd gone in.

"Now you look like a decent woman!" The merchant turned to Zadkiel. "Sell her to me too. I'll reimburse you for twice her value."

Zadkiel's eyes flared. "Absolutely not!"

"No offense, no offense." The merchant handed Remiel a pair of sandals. She removed the hot, heavy boots, and he watched her fumble with the sandal straps until finally he made a show of how to put them on. Her skin crawled at his touch. He said, "Did you hear about that foreigner who died over at the magician's house?"

Remiel edged back her foot. "The one they found decapitated?"

"Nah, he got burned to death." The merchant barked a laugh, and Remiel made a note to question Saraquael about what exactly qualified this merchant as desirable. "That's what happens when you mess with the gods. I know the magician he was dealing with, though, and he deserved worse than he got."

"Don't we all?" said Remiel as she backed away from the merchant and strapped on the second sandal by herself.

Ten minutes later, two angels were back on their way through the streets.

Horrified, Zadkiel whispered, "You're my slave?"

"You can't see me, but trust me there's no other conclusion anyone could reach." Switching to a Gaelic tongue, Remiel patted Zadkiel's arm. "I look like a Northerner, and from my hair it's pretty obvious that I'm a prisoner of war, probably a gift from your father or husband. It's not a big deal. I'm sure you're a good owner."

Remiel stopped at a food vendor shutting down for the day and bought his last two loaves of bread at a discount, plus some dried fish. Zadkiel ate the bread as they walked, but after one nibble, Remiel decided her stomach didn't want to be occupied again quite yet. She tucked the rest of the food into their bag and hunched her shoulders. *Exactly what are we making up for again?*

Zadkiel said between bites, "I'm sorry you're in this position. You outrank me."

Remiel made a strangled sound. "No you don't!"

"Absolutely you do." After a moment, Zadkiel added, "And as my slave, you're not allowed to contradict me."

Remiel lowered her voice to a soft, smooth Greek. "My mistake, Mistress. You are correct in all ways."

Zadkiel grinned.

Correct or not, Zadkiel didn't know how to get to the Christian community in Ephesus, and Remiel did, so once again she walked a pace behind and steered her supposed mistress with a hand on her elbow. The sun had begun setting on the pair for the second time that day, and as it grew darker, Remiel's headache lessened.

They walked for a quarter hour, the streets getting narrower and the people farther between. Voices moved from the streets into the buildings, and a smoky scent choked the air. The structures changed from temples and monuments to personal dwellings, smaller and more crowded-together. Eventually they reached a home that called out to Remiel as their destination. She stopped at the front gate, then steeled herself.

Zadkiel's head lifted. "Is something wrong?"

"Not more than usual." There wasn't any point in delaying. It would hurt, but that didn't mean she couldn't do it.

They went to the entrance where an elderly woman was already standing. She wore a striped tunic and a tan head-scarf over her grey-streaked black hair. Her eyes meet Remiel's with warmth, and in that moment Remiel knew the woman had been warned of their approach.

Remiel dropped to her knees and crossed her arms over her chest. "*Chaire,*" she said, "*Kecharitomene.*"

EIGHT

Michael stood outside Hastle's cell, arms folded, eyes dark.

"It's not as if we didn't try," Saraquael said, being overly generous with that *we* in taking the blame because Michael knew he hadn't actually been part of the questioning team, only an observer. Still, Saraquael had picked the best questioners to go in there and start their work with the idea of keeping Michael out of the process, and here he was anyhow.

A little chagrined after the incident with Remiel, (unnecessarily so,) Saraquael said, "They pulled back before the situation got irredeemable, but I don't think further interaction is going to change the situation. He'd demanding to talk to you."

The second demon had given very little information because he didn't have much. He'd been brought into the experiment solely for his expertise in stealth; as such, he knew it was in his best interests not to know anything more about what his superiors were doing. That demon's information had centered around who worked in the lab and how often Asmodeus stopped by, why they'd chosen that location, and how he'd structured the cavern to make the Guard harder to detect should he need to put one up. They'd verified that there was only one lab location and the identities of the entire staff working on the project. (All the others were unfindable right now. Not a huge surprise: Asmodeus must have them under triple Guard.) The interrogation team had determined their detainee wanted to leave, and they'd ensured his cooperation by promising that once the situation was stable, he could go. It was in his best interests to hasten his own departure.

Which left them with only Hastle, whom they hoped had more information. Michael sighed. "Let's review it again."

Saraquael opened his hands, and a light box formed between them. The scene unfolded just as before: the two direct questioners entering Hastle's cell, Hastle saying, "The only one I'll speak to is Michael," and then making no further response. Saraquael helpfully included a timer at the bottom of the re-enactment, and it would run for a further twenty-three minutes while the interrogators tried speaking with Hastle, then bantered with each other, then prayed together. (Hastle at least obliged them there by moving to the room's farthest corner.) Michael skipped ahead, at times focusing the recording in on Hastle's face, his eyes, reaching into it to detect whatever emotions he'd let stray, except there were precious few. He noticed the first at the fourteen minute mark. Disgust. Determination.

It was, sadly, the Archangel he'd known way back when, and whatever game he was playing, he wanted Michael to play it with him.

"Before I go in," Michael said, "I want you to stop second-guessing your decision to move Remiel and Zadkiel."

With the color still bleached from his wings, Saraquael stared at the ground. "It could have worked out a lot worse than it did."

"And yet it didn't. You did fine." Michael gestured to the cell. "You can go now. I'll get the team back together."

Michael met the interrogators. One was an Angel and the other a Principality. They'd worked together before, and even the way they stood near one another in total comfort displayed the rapport they'd developed.

Michael said, "You're the experts here. I'm going to follow your lead as much as possible, so don't hang back. I need you to drive the show. I'm only there enough to get him to open up."

"Even with you present, he's not going to open up," said the Principality. "We're going to have to pry him open."

The Angel added, "Although he won't realize at the time."

The Principality gestured to the other four members of the team, a mixture of Angels and Archangels. "They're going to be listening in the whole time, and if they want us to push on a particular subject or back off, or if they want us to use a particular phrasing, they'll advise. But it's always the questioner's decision whether to accept the suggestion, and given your greater history with him, I suggest you trust your judgment."

Michael shrugged. "My judgment wasn't all that great with him before."

Either before, when they'd spoken in the cell, or before the Winnowing, when they'd been friends.

Michael loosened his shoulders and relaxed his wings. "Well, let's begin."

They began with a prayer, and after God's blessing settled over them, he went with the other two questioners back into the cell.

Hastle hadn't changed position since the last time Michael had met him. He sat against the wall, knees tucked up, eyes without any warmth. "Oh, look, the good little servants fetched you."

Michael said nothing. The Principality led off. "You said you were willing to talk if he was present, and we want you to be as comfortable as possible."

Hastle laughed out loud. "He's an idiot," he said to Michael, "and he must think I'm an idiot too. That isn't what I said at all. I won't talk to any of them. I said I'd talk to *you.*"

Michael knew that was a lie, but he didn't bother to correct it. "I'm here, so let's talk."

The demon shook his head. "Only you. Dismiss your entourage."

From the other side of the wall, Michael could feel the rest of the team giving an assortment of advice. The Angel moved nearer to Hastle. "Your name used to be Hastiel, right?"

The demon raised a hand. "Tell her to get back." He glared at Michael. "Make them both leave."

The Angel sent, *Our presence is escalating his defensiveness.*

Do you mind if we go? sent the Principality.

A thousand times yes, he minded if they left. The plan was supposed to involve two highly-skilled questioners luring Hastle into a sense of trust and cooperation, obtaining the information they needed, and then leaving him secure but otherwise unharmed until this situation resolved. Having two others with him gave

Michael the ability to use the group's dynamics to help with the questioning and kept Hastle's focus divided amongst three questioners. But that was in an ideal reality, so Michael instead indicated it was fine as long as they continued their backup.

Of course, sent the Angel as if that were never a question, adding a sense that their presence offended Hastle, but Hastle couldn't stop their contributions.

The pair flashed away.

The Angel's voice appeared in his mind: *Start by asking questions he'll be willing to answer. That's why I asked about his name.*

Michael sat by the far wall. "So now you're Hastle. Did you come up with that yourself?"

The demon said, "Do you care?"

"I'm probably going to slip at some point and use your original name."

The demon huffed.

If you wanted a demon to talk, of course, there always was one way to do it. Michael hated his, but he said, "And I take it you're still fine with your decision to leave God's service."

Hastle laughed out loud. "I thought you were smart!"

Michael shrugged. "You're here, and we've got plenty of time. No one's ever crossed over from your side to ours, but if you wanted to try, I'd get a prayer team together and start begging God for mercy right now."

Hastle stared at him a moment, then gathered himself. "There is no mercy."

"There's plenty of mercy. You just don't want it." Michael sat back. "Besides, you've got that plum job working for Asmodeus."

Hastle folded his arms. "Asmodeus is a monster. Every so often I remember Raphael hog-tying him out in Egypt after the Sarah incident, and I want to bring him a crown of laurels."

Michael leaned against the wall. "I thought Raphael did great with him."

Hastle snickered. "I wasn't the only one of us hoping Raphael nailed him, either, but it was dicey there for a while. Raphael's nowhere near as strong as he is."

Momentary silence. The Angel prompted Michael, who said, "So how did you end up working for him?"

Hastle grinned. "Oh, you want to know so many things."

Michael's eyes narrowed. "Only a few very pointed things."

"But you're going to soften me up first. It's a good technique." Hastle's eyes brightened. "Down in Hell they just beat you until eventually you give in and say everything, even things that maybe never happened but you know they want to hear, but I figured that wouldn't be the case up here. Instead you gave me a nice comfortable room, tastefully decorated in an Indus Valley style. Harrapin, is it?"

Michael said, "Zadkiel's the one who decorated this room. You could tell me about what happened to her."

Hastle didn't appear phased. "Poor thing."

The Principality sent, *Close the distance between you.*

Michael would have preferred to lengthen it—maybe a thousand miles would have sufficed. Instead he got to his feet and started walking around the room, touching the designs on the walls. "She liked the Harrapin. They had interesting pottery and a clever social structure." He picked up a vase, then moved back toward Hastle, stopping again at about half the distance of before. "Why are you working for Asmodeus if you dislike him that much?"

"I have my own reasons. They're not his. Maybe he knows that, but I carry out his orders." Hastle smirked. "You taught me well. All that garbage about integrity and fulfilling our duties, it sunk in enough that I know the basics. I made them think I'm reliable, and here I am."

Michael didn't need an Angel to prompt this question. "What were they relying on you to do?"

"Everything." Hastle rolled his eyes. "The great Asmodeus wouldn't want to soil his hands, and the magnanimous Belior was too invested in his latest science experiment. Interestingly, they were never too busy to give orders." Hastle grinned. "And I'm efficient. I got things done when they wanted."

Michael traced his fingers over the vase in his hand. "And not one second faster?"

"Oh, sometimes." Hastle's eyes glinted. "That's the interesting thing about Seraphim: if you beat their expectations, it doesn't pay to let them know because they'll just increase your workload for the next time. Instead you buy yourself some wiggle room so you can do your own thing in those spare minutes here and there."

Michael nodded. "And what did you do?"

"My own game." Hastle leaned forward. "Yes, I know what that weapon did, and and I know what it's made of. I was one of the ones collecting the materials you haven't yet identified, and I know why you can't find Remiel or Zadkiel."

Couldn't find? Now that was an interesting assumption. The questioning team lit up inside his head, and Michael pushed on that line of questioning. "We really want your help." He put more urgency into his voice. "Tell us what happened to them. Your commanding officers might be nasty, but we take care of our own."

"No." Hastle folded his arms. "You don't."

Flat-voiced.

Push him, sent the Angel. *Find out why he wants you rather than us.*

Michael said, "If you're not going to help me help my officers, then why do you want me at all? If the point was you talking to me, then talk to me."

Hastle smirked at him.

The Principality sent, *Leave. Now.*

Michael flashed from the room.

Outside, he gave in and trembled, face in his hands. "I'm sorry," said the Angel, "but we want you in control of the situation. You needed to consequence his refusal to talk. You can try him again later, but I want him to have enough time to process his mistake."

Michael's feathers spread. "Speaking of mistakes, what was that about us not being able to find Remiel and Zadkiel?"

"He gave us a clue as to what that weapon does," said the Principality. "I've already reported it to Gabriel, and we'll see if that helps us turn a corner.

NINE

Zadkiel hadn't heard Remiel this subdued in a long time. *"Kecharitomene,"* she said, "we need your help."

"Come inside," said Jesus's mother Mary, "and please, don't feel you need to use a title. It was confusing enough when Gabriel said it to me the first time, and I still haven't quite figured it out."

When Remiel touched her elbow, Zadkiel started forward. "One step," Remiel said, and Zadkiel stepped up, wobbled a little, then kept going.

"Is she hurt?" Mary's voice was wrapped in concern. "John is leading the covenant meal now, but I can get him."

"She's blind," Remiel said, as if Zadkiel couldn't have answered perfectly well for herself.

Zadkiel said, "We're sorry for bothering you. You can leave us here and rejoin the covenant meal yourself."

"I'm fine here with you," Mary said, leading them through the house. "At the breaking of the bread, I'm worshipping God, and when I take care of others, I'm also worshipping God. One way or the other, I'm with Him, and I want nothing more." Mary's hands were gentle on Zadkiel's shoulders. "Here, let me take this, and you two can sit while I bring you food."

Remiel said, "You've no need to wait on us, *Kecharitomene.*"

"You are my guests," Mary said, "and I do mean it: no title."

Remiel sat on a low couch, and Zadkiel groped her way down beside her. A moment later, Mary returned with a basin of water. "Here, let's get you cleaned up. Have you been to Ephesus before? I was quite impressed with the aqueducts. No more trips to the well."

Zadkiel heard Remiel splashing and did her best to get the dirt washed off her feet and legs as well. Mary brought them a towel, and then she escorted them to a table. She poured wine and laid out a plate of bread and some cheese. Remiel prayed over the food, then passed it to Zadkiel.

Zadkiel sipped the wine, but it wasn't as good as Jesus had made. She found she was hungry, though, and made quick work of the food. Mary gave her more, but she forced herself to slow down.

Mary said, "I remember you. You're the one from the wedding."

Zadkiel smiled. "I am."

"That's why you're blind. I'd forgotten all about that." Mary sounded confused. "Have you tried rescinding the agreement?"

"Why would I do that?" Zadkiel shuddered. "I've had the benefit of the agreement for twenty years. Is a day's inconvenience, or a week's, enough to break me down?" She drew up the taste of wine in her mind, and she clenched her fist. "It's a matter of integrity. This is the bargain."

"I'm sorry," Mary said. "I didn't know whether you hadn't asked or you'd asked and been refused."

Zadkiel said firmly, "I haven't asked."

"And you..." Mary hesitated. "I never spoke to you."

"With good reason." Remiel sounded tentative. "I didn't want to harm you. I still don't. I have...I had a twin. He fell at the Winnowing, but we're still identical." She picked up speed. "You might not have been able to tell us apart, and if Camael came to you, if you thought he was me, you might have believed his lies, or he might have harmed you."

Mary said, "Oh! That's why you're using the title. Because you think a demon wouldn't do that."

Remiel said, "A human's title? Never. Your title? Twice never. So it's a litmus test." A rustling: had Remiel put her face in her hands? "But he'll know by now. He'll know they're looking for me, and he may be looking for me too. You could be in danger, so you need a way to know I'm me."

Zadkiel detected a soft sound as Mary reached across the table for Remiel's hand. "I'm not worried. You're in my house, and you need me. If I doubt it's you, I'll ask the Father for help, but based on what Uriel told me, your twin—well, any demon—would never willingly take on a human form. Didn't they rebel because they hated the idea of ensouled matter in the first place?"

Remiel sounded bitter. "He'd do it if ordered to. I can't imagine Satan putting on a body, but he'd command one of his underlings to do it in a half second if he thought it gained his side an advantage."

Zadkiel added, "And if God allowed him. Aren't we being a little too obvious in this conversation? We came here trying to escape detection, and instead we're talking about angels and demons."

"We won't be overheard inside this house." Mary sounded certain. "Outside we need to be careful, including the courtyard, but John sealed the house. Demons have no permission to enter here."

Remiel sounded shocked. "You can do that?"

Zadkiel smiled. "You've invented the Prayer Guard."

Mary chuckled. "I don't know that we invented it. My Son gave us authority over demons, and John decided binding them out was a good use of that authority."

"In that case," Zadkiel said, her voice sharpening, "does it really appear that Remiel is my slave? Because nothing could be further from the truth."

"It does." Mary sounded a little surprised. "I thought that was your disguise."

Zadkiel folded her arms. "If anything, I should be her slave."

"I don't outrank you." Remiel sounded disbelieving. "You're Michael's standard bearer and the chief of the order of Dominions."

"And you're one of the seven Archangels of the Presence."

"Because of what my brother did, not because of what I did." Zadkiel imagined she could hear Remiel rolling her eyes. "He rebelled, and I got rewarded. I'm not saying God isn't fair, but you have your position because of what you *did*, whereas I have mine because of what I *didn't* do."

Zadkiel said, "I didn't do enough, not enough to keep with my station. That much should be clear."

Remiel said, "What are you talking about?"

Mary laughed. "John tells me the disciples used to argue about which of them was the most important, and here you two are, arguing about who's the least. It's a refreshing change." Her chair scraped as she stood. "Now, sweetie, turn to me."

Zadkiel shifted toward her, and then Mary's hands rested on her head. As Mary began to pray, it felt right to close her eyes even though that changed nothing. Mary's prayer began in Greek and then shifted to Aramaic, and then it shifted back to Greek as Mary praised God, recited a segment of one of the psalms, and then asked God as the healer to settle His power on Zadkiel.

Zadkiel joined the prayer in her heart, relaxing into the embrace of the Holy Spirit as she felt His warmth shooting through her. Her eyes burned, and in her heart she went back to Cana, to the wedding. Wine filled her to overflowing, as if she were the stone jug of water to whom Christ had said, "Wine."

All the uncertainty lingering from their transport had left her, and Zadkiel had the vague thought that Mary should pray over Remiel as well and lift whatever burdened her. The human body felt more solid now, more grounded than it had been only moments ago. Wine's flavor filled her mind and her soul, and she held tight to it.

A warmth built in her spine and traveled up to her throat, a simultaneous peace and electricity she associated with God's presence. The rightness of the moment filled her, and she knew she was being protected by Him. He loved her.

She opened her eyes, and still couldn't see.

She leaned forward, face in her hands.

Mary hugged her.

"Pray over Remiel," Zadkiel whispered. "It helped. I know God answered you, even if it wasn't the way you wanted."

"Of course He answers." Mary kissed Zadkiel's forehead. "I wasn't asking for your sight to be restored, and I would never ask for an agreement God made with anyone to be broken. I asked for His blessing, and He knows what blessings He wants to give."

Blinking to stem her tears, Zadkiel listened as Mary prayed over Remiel. No, Mary wasn't asking for anything specific. She was calling on God to remember His healing touch, and then she was touching Remiel, but it wasn't targeted. In a way, it was as if Mary were entirely indifferent as to how God acted once she invited Him into the situation, because she trusted that He'd act for their benefit. Zadkiel groped for Remiel's hand and felt her relaxing progressively as Mary continued. The prayer over Remiel was shorter, and when it ended, Remiel said nothing. Zadkiel squeezed her hand, but Remiel didn't squeeze back. If anything, she sounded shaken. "Thank you. If you don't mind, I'm actually hungry now," and Mary gave her time to finish the meal Zadkiel hadn't until this moment realized she'd left untouched.

Afterward, Mary led them to a room in the back. "You'll be sleeping here. There are several others from our community who share this room, and I know they'll welcome you when they can." She sounded cheerful. "When we first arrived, one of our newly baptized members offered us his possessions, and one of those was this house, so a group of us moved in here. I say it's John's house," she added, "but it's really for the whole community to use together. Therefore think of it as your home for as long as you remain."

Mary escorted them through every part of the house that they needed to know, then gave them a chance to get settled for the night. Zadkiel trailed her hand along the wall, tracing the smoothness of the tiles as they alternated with empty spaces between. The ceramic pieces must have formed pictures, but of course her fingertips couldn't tell the difference between red tiles and white or green, so she focused on the texture. The room had very little by way of furniture, plus the windows were shuttered against the heat, so it carried a faint echo. She wondered if human ears could use the echoes to navigate, like a bat or a whale, and whether she'd be in this body long enough to learn.

Mary said, "The covenant meal will be ending soon, and I know you're exhausted. You should get some sleep now, and we'll talk again in the morning."

"If we're still here," Zadkiel said. "They may find a solution overnight."

Mary said, "I love having you here, but I do hope you're right."

Remiel said, "Join us for evening prayer," and Mary did. She must have learned the prayers from Uriel, because she was able to do all the call-and-response and then recite the evening blessing.

Remiel helped Zadkiel get settled in her bed. "Rest well, my lady."

"If owners are allowed to beat their slaves," Zadkiel mumbled, "I'm going to thrash you once we get back into Heaven."

"Only if you can catch me." Remiel chuckled. "I have it on good authority that slaves sometimes run away."

She settled herself at Zadkiel's side, and in the dark her breathing deepened, and she was asleep.

Sleep eluded Zadkiel, however. She prayed for a while, then meditated in a hazy kind of slip-in-and-out of consciousness. She'd be contemplating God and then find herself thinking about something Saraquael had said a few days ago, then she'd startle back to awareness and focus again on God only to realize she'd been thinking about the taste of asparagus. Every so often she'd startle awake at other noises in the room and realize other community members had gone to their beds. Remiel never stirred.

Finally the dark felt right, so Zadkiel relaxed into it. She puzzled on and off about why when Mary had prayed over her, why her eyes had burned when there hadn't been any healing.

And then Remiel gasped awake. "No!"

"Remiel?" Zadkiel hissed, but there was no response, only rapid breathing. "Are you okay? What's wrong?"

She groped for her, but when her hand made contact, Remiel jerked away "Don't touch me." She sounded frightened, and she was speaking in angelic language, not Greek.

"Are there demons?" Zadkiel sat up. The Angels guarding them weren't on high alert, although she detected concern. "What's gong on?"

"Leave me alone. Stop." There was a rustling as Remiel moved away. "Just stop."

There were assorted sounds as Remiel got to her feet and left. And once again, Zadkiel found herself alone. Blind and alone.

TEN

Remiel sat in the front room, her legs tucked to her chest and her forehead downd on her knees. Moonlight cast a triangle on the tiled floor.

For the moment, she couldn't even pray. She kept her eyes focused on the moonlight triangle and wondered how long until dawn and what she could do until then.

Mary came into the room. "What's wrong? Can I get you something?"

Remiel couldn't answer.

"I'm sorry," Mary said, "but at my age I'm often awake during the night, and I heard you get up." Mary approached. "Do you want some company?"

Remiel huddled tighter around herself.

Mary rested a hand on her shoulder, and Remiel flinched as if burned. "Please don't."

"I'm sorry." Mary drew back. "Let me at least get you some wine, and you can get back to sleep."

"I'm not going back to sleep." Remiel swallowed hard. "I'm not going to sleep anymore."

Mary waited, and when Remiel didn't elaborate, she said, "Did you have a dream?"

"Don't say it like that, like I'm a kid who doesn't know nightmares aren't real." Remiel hugged her knees tighter against her chest, and if she still had wings, she'd have closed them around herself like a cocoon. "Sometimes they are real. I don't want that to happen again. If I don't sleep, it can't."

Mary said, "What was it?"

Remiel's jaw clenched. Eventually she said, "Please."

"I'm going to be awake for a while praying," Mary said. "I can pray with you."

"I want your prayers." Remiel closed her eyes. "But I want to be by myself. I'm sorry."

"You don't have to explain." Mary got to her feet slowly, as if stiff. "God hears each of us just as well in separate rooms. But if you want someone with you, call me."

She left the room. Remiel again pressed her face into her arms.

The night crawled. Why hadn't Gabriel found out what that weapon was yet? Why wasn't Michael interrogating those two demons until one of them confessed what they'd done? Why had she rushed ahead and gotten them into this mess in the first place?

When she calculated the time, it wasn't that long she'd been trapped in a human body. Longer than she'd at first thought she'd be stuck, yes, but not terribly long overall. It had been early morning or mid-morning when she'd first regained consciousness, and they'd gained a few hours when they transported to Ephesus, so it might be coming up on a day. Sometime soon Michael ought to be returning with a report about what had happened and what they were going to do to fix it. These things took time, but the Cherubim were on it, and Gabriel had proven repeatedly he could figure out anything. He'd come through for her. Or Saraquael would.

The room grew lighter, and shortly she realized a shape sat across from hers. Gradually it became apparent that the shape had wings, and then Remiel could make out a face.

Remiel squinted. "Nivalis?"

The figure smiled, and yes, it definitely was her. She wore the uniform she'd worn these past twenty years since the end of her guardianship over Judas Iscariot, but despite the drab colors, Nivalis's eyes were bright and her face animated. Her wings picked up a mother-of-pearl-tone in the early sunrise, and she carried them high.

Remiel scrambled forward. "Did someone die here last night?"

Nivalis shook her head. "I'm not here on business, don't worry. No one's lost."

Remiel blinked. After the Resurrection and the judging of human souls, Nivalis had asked God's permission to form a team she called the Grief Squad. There hadn't been a need for them before, but once some human souls were a confirmed loss, their former guardian angels needed support. In need of support herself, Nivalis had taken charge of meeting the need.

Remiel's brow furrowed. "Then why are you here?"

"I'm here for you, silly." Nivalis's shortish hair curled around her face, and her black eyes glinted as she moved. "I have a perfectly capable team to handle my regular work, and for the time being, I'm stationed with you and Zadkiel."

Remiel frowned. "As a grief counselor."

"As whatever you need." Nivalis looked unperturbed at Remiel's tone. "I've had experience as a guardian, as a soldier, and as a listening ear."

Remiel pursed her lips. "What awful thing did you do to get stuck with me?"

"Don't be ridiculous. I asked to be with you." Nivalis cocked her head. "In prayer for you two, I had a strong urge not to be on the sidelines. I wanted to help, and I asked God how I could. He asked what I wanted to do, and I told Him I wanted to be here, with you, helping directly. I don't know what I have to offer, to be honest, but I'm at your service." She smiled. "I've gotten permission for you to see me, too."

Remiel stared at the floor. "So you're not here because of my dream?"

"Oh, tell me about your dream." Nivalis flashed right in front of her, and Remiel's skin crawled from the residual angelic energy. "I didn't know about that."

"It's not that I don't appreciate your coming, but this isn't going to work." Remiel didn't look up from the tile floor. "Saraquael has to stay away because we need to avoid detection. You've already been a guardian, so the demons know you're not with one of us. And that's not even addressing the fact that normal humans can't see angels."

"Apparently these objections don't bother God." Nivalis sat back. "We'll work out the details as we go along, but for now, I'm assigned to you and Zadkiel. She's still sleeping, though." Nivalis got a concerned look. "You don't need to stand guard over her. I'll do that so you can get some more rest."

Bristling, Remiel said, "I'm not going to sleep. Why is everyone so concerned about that?"

"Because you're tired and you're making stress hormones." Nivalis looked momentarily sad. "That can't be comfortable."

"I'll handle it." Remiel smirked. "Maybe I'm doing that *making up for what's lacking in the sufferings of Christ* thing."

"Meritorious suffering has some benefits." Raising her wings, Nivalis rested back on her hands. "But you don't need to look for additional opportunities. I think you've had enough already."

Remiel shook her head. "It doesn't matter. Saraquael put us here because we're somewhat safer in this house than out in the wild, and they're working on finding an answer for us." She pivoted her head. "Or are you here because they don't have any answers?"

Mary entered the kitchen then. "You didn't get back to sleep, did you?"

"No, and now I have a new companion. Are you able to see her?"

Mary looked around the room, then shook her head.

"Well, she's waving hello."

Mary bowed her head. "Hello to you in return, my guest." She turned to Remiel. "Please don't be offended by my working, but I need to set the bread to rise."

Remiel stood. "Why would I be offended? I'd prefer you put me to work. Tell me what you need." When Mary hesitated, she took a step closer to her. "Last night you told us to consider ourselves members of the community. Don't your community members do things for one another?"

Mary rewarded this logic by letting her help make the bread. As they mixed and kneaded, Mary kept the conversation light, and Remiel watched Mary's hands to figure out how to work the dough. Her loaves were nowhere near as expert as her hostess's (Mary could justifiably have taken them away and redone them all) but

Mary was gracious and didn't comment on their flaws as she set them to rise and later as she put them in the clay oven.

By turns the rest of the household began to rise, and Remiel introduced herself as Remaya. Zadkiel slept through most of the awakenings, but when she awoke, Remiel called her Key, and everyone was glad to have her as well. Remiel busied herself bringing bread and olive oil to the table as the men ate, and when the men began heading out to do their work, she served the women.

A muscular man in rough clothing came to the door with three girls, and Mary ushered the children inside. After the man had left, she said, "He's a fisherman. His wife died of a fever, so he brings us his girls during the daytime."

Remiel said, "Is he a part of your community too?"

Mary chuckled. "No, but he's willing to take advantage, and the girls are learning the Good News."

The middle girl of the three walked with a pronounced limp, leaning on her youngest sister. "Can she be healed?" Remiel said.

"John won't pray over her until the father allows. The father has so far refused, so we're waiting." Mary patted Remiel's arm. "Don't worry. We're all praying for him every day. When he's ready for faith, he'll ask, and when he asks, God will respond."

The girls settled at the table near Zadkiel, and the younger two chatted with her while the oldest went to a storage room in the back. Shortly the girls were taking Zadkiel by the hand out into the courtyard where they were going to start their work for the day.

Mary said, "Key, I'm going out, and I'm going to take Remaya out with me. Can you supervise them?"

Zadkiel raised her head, startled. "Can I?"

"They're good girls," Mary said. "They've plenty of work to do mending the nets, and you can stay with them. You should come in from the courtyard before it gets too hot, though."

"We'll tell her!" the girls asserted.

Mary loaded Remiel with two baskets of bread, and she took a third. "With your help, I was able to get a lot more done this morning. Thank you. But that means we're going to be busy if we want to finish our visits before the heat peaks."

They walked through Ephesus, Mary in the lead and Remiel following with her head bowed the way a slave should. Mary strode without hesitation through some of the narrower streets, to certain smaller houses and specific crowded apartments, and in every one she left food, and in some she checked bandages and sent Remiel to fetch water, and in every one she prayed over the residents. "That's the temple of Artemis," Mary said at one point, gesturing to the most magnificent building in the city. "Artemis doesn't take care of the people, though, so the Ephesians are willing to let a few of those odd Christians help out."

Remiel said, "Well, other than the silversmiths going after Paul. Do they still give you trouble?"

"Not since the riot." Mary sighed. "I'm glad I wasn't here for that, but I heard it was chaotic. The Romans might have gotten involved, and that would have been a disaster. For now, they're leaving us alone. And so is Artemis." She straightened. "One last house. This child is very sick, so I understand if you don't want to stay."

They'd already gone into several houses with sickness, and Mary hadn't warned her before those, so Remiel only said, "I'll accompany you, *Kecharitomene*."

Mary tapped her on the head. "You're a sweetheart, but you're being stubborn about the title."

At a spacious house with a landscaped courtyard, Mary entered. A servant led them through several rooms until they reached a small one at the back.

The stench hit Remiel before she even entered, and with her eyes watering, she halted in the doorway. Mary walked right inside with a bright, "Good morning!" and then went directly to the child's bed.

In the windowless room lit only by an oil lamp, the child's mother looked drawn, her eyes sunken. As she raised her weary head, Mary said, "Go take a break for a while. You should nap if you can. I'll care for her."

Beside Remiel, one of the household's servants whispered, "It's horrible, eh?"

Horrible in so many ways. Remiel had done so many sick calls that one more shouldn't have bothered her, but the stench from this room was like a miasma.

"I can't see that she's going to help her much." The servant grunted. "You'd be better to get your mistress out of here."

Instead Remiel stepped forward. She didn't know why: the smell, the scene, the surroundings ought to all make her want to run, and instead she found herself moving toward rather than away. Mary turned, but Remiel didn't meet her eyes. Instead she took another step closer to the child.

"Remaya," Mary said.

Remiel stared only at the child, and again she stepped closer.

"Remaya." Mary's voice grew firm.

And then came the voice of Nivalis. "Remiel!"

Remiel started. Her eyes focused, and she looked at Mary.

Mary said, "Don't come closer."

Nivalis appeared, looking urgent. "Back off. Now."

Remiel looked around. The room was small, close. The smell was still there, and it burned the back of her throat. Mary was washing the child's shrunken limbs with a basin of water and a soft cloth, and Remiel's eyes stung: she couldn't tell whether it was the stench or actual tears. And still her heart wanted to move just a little bit closer even though her body hungered to run. Run away even if it meant knocking over that servant at the door or the lady of the house in the hall, run until her limbs ached and she couldn't breathe and she collapsed in the day's rising heat.

Mary shooed her. "Go. I'll take care of her. Go."

It took more effort than it should have. She'd been acting the slave, and she'd made herself Mary's guest, and she kept using Mary's title. And despite that all, Remiel wanted nothing more than to defy her and move right up alongside that child.

Instead she backed away a step, and that first motion made it easier to take a second, and then a third. Finally she left the room. In the diminishing shade of the courtyard walls, she waited.

The servant came out to dump water from the basin and get new.

Remiel struggled to find her voice. "What's wrong with the child?"

"She's wasting away. I don't know what else." The servant shuddered. "Her skin's the wrong color."

"What was the smell?" Remiel said. "Gangrene?"

"They don't tell me anything," said the servant.

"Death," said Nivalis. "I don't have a body, and even I could tell she smells like death."

The servant carried the basin back into the house, brimful with clean water. Alone, Remiel closed her eyes against the sun and prayed while she waited. The air smelled like flowers, and flowers didn't smell like death.

ELEVEN

In the courtyard with the three young voices, Zadkiel wondered how exactly she was supposed to be supervising them. Any one of the three could wander off without catching her notice.

So the better to keep track of their voices, she started asking questions, starting with their names, and she quickly picked up their different cadences. If she kept them talking, she'd at least know where they were. They wanted to know about her, why she was blind, if she'd always been blind, and what things look like when you're blind. They told her about people they knew who were blind, and that got Zadkiel's attention. "What do those people do?"

"Oh, they do all sorts of things," one girl said.

"There's that old man who begs," said the youngest girl.

"But he has only one foot," said the middle girl. "That's why he begs. Otherwise he'd do stuff."

"Mary said you're not from Ephesus, right?" The oldest girl had a sensible voice, very steady. Zadkiel couldn't guess her age, but she might end up married off in the next couple of years. If her father hadn't remarried by then, he would expect her to take her sisters into her home. "Tell us about where you come from."

Zadkiel wondered how she'd pull that off, and when no way out presented itself, she said, "I've got an idea. I'll tell you some stories about where all of us come from."

So while the morning crawled on, she told them the story of Joseph from the Torah. They hadn't heard it, so they peppered her with questions, and they were oohing and laughing when Joseph ended up saving his brothers in Egypt.

At one point the middle girl handed her work to Zadkiel and asked the youngest to help her go fetch some water. "She has trouble walking," said the oldest.

Zadkiel fingered the work that they'd dumped into her lap. "What is this?"

"We're making nets. Here." The oldest manipulated the ropey fabric until Zadkiel felt an oval wooden object in her hands. "That's the shuttle. You use that to make the knots so you can have a net."

"Oh, for fishing." Zadkiel ran her hands over it, noting the pattern of knots and strands. "Would I be able to make a knot?"

"That's easy. Watch." She couldn't watch, but the girl sat beside her, resting her hands on top of Zadkiel's and moving the shuttle in her hands. It took two or three passes, and then she tugged it tight. "See, that's a nice knot. You need all the knots to be strong like that so if any one of them breaks, the rest of them hold. That way the whole net isn't ruined and all the fish don't get away."

Zadkiel said, "Teach me again."

The oldest must have taught her younger sisters how to do this, because her instructions were simple and to-the-point. After she'd demonstrated a second and third time, Zadkiel tried on her own: bring the shuttle up through the loop, toward herself. Then bring the shuttle back through the middle of the loop, wrap it around the back, and run the shuttle again in front of the loop. She tightened it, and the girl said, "It's a bit large, but it's good!" The girl gave her a rounded stick to gauge the size of the loop she made, and Zadkiel tried again.

By the time the younger two had returned, Zadkiel had made three more knots, so the oldest handed her work off to the middle girl, and she started repairing one of the broken nets.

"We sell the new ones," said the middle daughter. "And when Dad's nets get broken, we repair them for him."

Mixing knot-making with story-telling, Zadkiel spent the morning. She needed some help when she reached the end of a row, but the girls would get it turned for her and then ask for more stories.

When Mary called a greeting, Zadkiel proudly showed off her work. "I'm very slow," she said.

"But she told us about a man named Joseph who got sold as a slave into Egypt and then ended up just like a king!" The youngest giggled. "Have you ever heard that story?"

"I have," Mary exclaimed. "Come with me while I make more bread, and you can tell me your favorite parts."

Remiel dropped down beside her. "At least a net is something useful," she said.

Zadkiel's nose wrinkled. "You didn't spend the morning being useless. You spent the morning helping Mary."

"She didn't need me." Remiel yawned. "Did I tell you we have a visitor?"

"We're in the courtyard."

"Oh. Right." Remiel got to her feet. "Later, then. Oh, hello, sir."

Zadkiel hesitated, and then came John's voice, "Hello, Remaya. And Key, is it? Have you met Ignatius?"

A deeper voice said hello, and then both men went into the house.

"It's getting hot," said one of the girls. "Let's work inside where it's cooler."

Zadkiel gathered up her net-in-progress, and the middle girl took her by the hand, jolting as she led her with limping strides. They both stumbled over the one step into the house, and they ended up laughing. "I didn't warn you," said the girl, and Zadkiel said, "I shouldn't have leaned on you."

They were setting up their work in a corner of the main room when a tumultuous shouting drew closer. Remiel rushed into the room, and Zadkiel grabbed the smallest girl, shoving her into the corner at her back.

A crowd of men dragged in another man who was screaming in Latin, Aramaic and ancient Sumerian. And what he was screaming—it was all blasphemy, all the most hateful things Zadkiel could have imagined someone shouting about God. "Get back," she urged the girls, but the man's ranting swallowed up her voice.

Remiel pushed up alongside her. In the next moment, John's voice cut above the man's raging, and he started ordering repeatedly, "Out of him!" and "In the name of Christ!"

The hair rose on Zadkiel's arms.

"Possessed," Remiel whispered.

That much was obvious from the languages alone, but in case that wasn't enough, the scuffling and thumping told Zadkiel the man had a preternatural strength as well. John was trying to get command over him, and the man reverted to hissing and thrashing.

"He's a wreck," Remiel whispered. "His tunic is torn. It's taking five men to keep a hold on him."

"We was knocking over merchant stalls in the agora," shouted one of the men, loud enough to be heard over the tumult. "He was threatening you and cursing you by name. We knew he had a demon, so we brought him to the house."

Zadkiel whispered, "Belior!"

Remiel's hand clenched her arm.

She'd no idea why she'd said it, but Zadkiel nodded. It felt like him in the way she always felt right when she was Seeking an object and it revealed itself to her.

The man screeched, and John shouted, "Be silent!"

A long, long hush followed.

Shaken, Remiel said, "Girls, come with me. I want you out of here."

Zadkiel stood uneasily, unsteady until she heard in her head, I'm with you. *I'm Nivalis*, said the voice. *Remiel didn't get a chance to tell you before, but I've been assigned to you.*

The angelic speech left her a little dizzy, so Zadkiel pressed herself into the wall.

John's footsteps moved around the room, and then he said, "Out." The man howled as a demon left him, and John's the footsteps continued again. The second demon he cast out sent the man into thrashing convulsions on the tiles, and the men held him down.

"He's still got one," Zadkiel said to herself, and Remiel surprised her by replying, "At least one."

Mary's voice broke through as well. "Are you sure?"

All these people sneaking up on her, when she was supposed to be a Seeker. Zadkiel tried to get a grip on her frustration. They weren't sneaking; it was just so noisy with the exorcisms.

"John needs to hold him down for the last one," Remiel said. "It wouldn't surprise me if he kills his host on the way out. This demon's powerful enough to do it."

"John!" Mary's voice ticked up a notch. "John, wait."

Another long quiet passed during which Zadkiel figured John was consulting with Mary. Then she felt a firm hand on her arm. "Mary tells me you recognize the demon. Are you really angels?"

"All praise to God the Father of our lord Jesus," said Zadkiel, bowing her head. "Yes, and the demon remaining in him is extremely powerful."

John took her hand. "Beloved, God is more powerful still."

Zadkiel smiled. "I never doubted it."

Remiel said, "But he may do a whole lot of destruction when he comes out. His name is Belior."

"The possessed man is a magician. He's not unknown to me," John added, "and we've debated in the past. It was in his house that a foreign man burned to death yesterday. Maybe that's when the demon got into him."

It was now so quiet that Zadkiel could count John's footfalls as he walked around the room, and she imagined how it must appear. Multiple strong men would be holding down the possessed magician. He'd fought them the whole way here, but had he really? No, he'd done exactly enough to get into John's presence.

John prayed over the demon, who shifted but didn't cry out.

Zadkiel whispered, "He's stuck too."

Remiel said, "Do you think so?" And then she gasped. "You're right. Belior got hit first, but he's never been in a human form. So he ended up in possession of this soul..." Her hand tightened on Zadkiel's arm. "No, he ended up in possession of that other man, the foreigner who died. Demons like to throw people into fires, and that guy burned to death. But instead of freeing himself, Belior just got trapped in the next nearest soul that could accommodate him."

Dizzy, Zadkiel said, "John has authority to cast out demons, and Belior is betting that John can do the job."

"Cherubim are supposed to be smart. Won't he just get stuck in another host?" Remiel sounded tense. "But he must figure it's worth the chance. If he doesn't try this, then nothing changes." Her voice lowered. "Then what did he do to us? If we're right, he can't even figure out how to get himself out of it."

John kept praying over the demon, but other than soft whimpers followed by rapid movements and grunts, Zadkiel heard nothing. Then John said, "Out of him!"

A wind hit the house, and in the kitchen, pottery shattered. Zadkiel hunched down, and Remiel pushed her into the corner, pressing her own body over Zadkiel's face and chest. The floor shook, and as John shouted, "In the name of Christ Jesus, out of him!" there were popping sounds one after the next, dozens of them. Men shouted warnings, and someone called, "Keep a hold on him!" and John ordered one more time, "You are subject to the name and authority of the Son of God! Leave this man!"

The possessed man screamed and then pitched up the scream until his throat must have bled. Even with her hands to her ears, Zadkiel cringed at the sound. Eyes clenched, she prayed with tears on her cheeks.

Finally John shouted, "Enough," and then silence fell.

"Is it out?" said on man.

"It's still there. Keep holding him."

Remiel took Zadkiel by the arm. "We're following John," she whispered as she led her out of the room. As they walked, the floor crunched underfoot.

In the back room, John sounded weary. "Our Lord said some of these only come out with prayer and fasting."

Mary sounded urgent. "Our community does plenty of both."

Remiel said, "It may be that he can't come out at all, not for lack of faith but for other reasons."

Zadkiel held back while Remiel gave an abbreviated version of their story. Throughout it all, Ignatius broke in several times to ask questions, shocked and more than a little delighted to be in the presence of a pair of angels. Mary added what information she had, and John finally said, "We can't turn him loose if he's already killed a man. The demon is likely to kill the man he's in now as well, and then the next. If your theory is true, it's best to keep him here until this resolves."

Zadkiel felt John's hand on hers. "Come, Beloved. Let's learn how well he can talk."

Back in the main room, John said, "Let him sit up. You will answer my questions, and by the authority of Christ's church you may not lie to me, but you will say nothing other than the answers to my questions."

Zadkiel tensed in case the demon struggled, but instead there was no motion, and the demon said nothing.

John was firm. "Tell me your name."

"Belior."

The magician's voice was raspy, as if the demon had torn the man's throat to shreds in an attempt to scream himself free.

John said, "How many of you are in there?"

"Can't you count to one?" Belior snapped. "You already got rid of all the rest of them."

John said, "A number, please."

Belior said, "One."

John said, "And why haven't you left this body?"

"Inconclusive," Belior said, "My bet would be on incompetent exorcism technique."

"I'm not the one who exorcises," John said. "Christ is. Answer: why haven't you left this body?"

Belior said nothing.

"Answer."

"I don't know."

The way Belior spat it out, that admission sounded almost painful.

John said, "Are you trying to keep him?"

"No!" That was pure offense, taken to heart. "Keep your foul magician. Do your job. Impress your sycophants and cast out the bad demon."

Beside Zadkiel, Remiel started laughing. "Oh, Belior, that's so sweet! You came to your enemy looking for help?"

She stepped away from Zadkiel, and the floor crunched beneath her feet. Had Belior shattered the tile floor? Had he brought down the ceiling plaster?

"You expected John to help you?" Remiel added. "Christ isn't fooled. Christ knows who you are. And now you get to regret having put yourself into that body in the first place."

Belior snapped, "Do you think I wanted to be a monkey like you?"

"Silence," John said. "You are forbidden to harm the body you're in. You're forbidden to harm anyone in this house or who is under my protection. The man you're possessing is now under my protection."

Belior growled, an animal sound that should never have come from a human throat. The hair stood upright on Zadkiel's arms, a feeling she'd never experienced before.

John said, "You will stay on the premises. And," he added at last, "until you're given permission to talk, you are to remain silent."

Belior didn't respond. No, he wouldn't, not now.

"Tie him up," John said. "Then carry him to the back room and leave him there."

TWELVE

Feeling Saraquael appear at his back, Michael finished up his work with the guardian angel of Rome, then turned. "Please tell me you've got a solution and it's already in process."

Saraquael's eyes were dull. "I was going to tell you we found Belior."

Michael thought a moment. "Okay, that could be good news. Where, and in what condition?"

"He's in Ephesus, and he's in possession of a man I would have wanted on the other side of the city from Remiel and Zadkiel." Saraquael's mouth twitched. "By all accounts, it looks as if Belior got trapped in possession of a human soul. We've questioned the guardian of that person, and apparently once Belior got sufficient control over his host, he brought the host into Ephesus, to a magician. The magician used a series of amulets to cast him out, and it didn't work quite as expected. When he was partway out, Belior murdered his host and took up residence in the magician instead."

Michael's eyes widened. "Belior had the authority to kill?"

"Once the host gives control to the demon, the demon can do pretty much what it likes. This one seems to have given him the seals to a blank contract." Saraquael shuddered. "At any rate, the magician now has him, except Belior seized complete control and managed to get the attention of the Christian community. The citizens of Ephesus brought him to John, and now Belior's there."

Michael frowned. "In the community's house?"

"Not the first place I'd have wanted him, but yes." Saraquael's eyes darkened. "He hasn't recognized Remiel or Zadkiel yet."

"Not until the minute Asmodeus enters the building and hears them talking."

"They're aware that they need to be circumspect. Nivalis is now stationed with them." Saraquael's head picked up, and some of the teal returned to his eyes. "And Zadkiel is making fishing nets. She's already learned two kinds of knots, and she's quite excited about that."

"But Belior." Michael shook his head. "Since he's in, Asmodeus can get in too."

"I don't doubt it. John's denied demons permission to enter the building, but he brought one in, and because of the bond, I assume he's as well as invited in Asmodeus. What he'll be able to do once he's inside isn't entirely clear, but I'm nervous." Saraquael pulled his wings closer. "I consulted with the interrogation team, and we need you to try again with Hastle."

Michael shuddered. "I hope we have a better script than last time."

"They're going to prep you more extensively." Saraquael shook his head. "I have no way of telling you how little I like this. Hastle is manipulating the situation so well that I'm wondering if he didn't intend to get captured."

"I doubt it, to be honest." Michael sighed. "He valued his freedom over anything else. That's why he's in Hell in the first place."

"He's pretty insistent that he was following Asmodeus in order to forward his own agenda," Saraquael said, "but has never been clear what that agenda is."

"Well," said Michael, "perhaps we need to find out."

Hastle looked annoyed as Michael entered the room, but then he resumed his normal smirk. "You can't stay away from me, can you?"

"It's your magnetic personality." Michael sighed as if bored. "I'm between jobs and wondered if you felt more like talking."

Hastle shrugged. He was in his usual position, seated against the wall, eyes narrow, wings up.

Michael folded his arms. "You have an agenda. You've told me that often enough. You also have information we want. I'd consider a deal with you: we might be willing to help with your undisclosed agenda if you're willing to give us the currently-undisclosed information."

Hastle cocked his head. "Maybe, but how do I know you'd cooperate?"

"I can't guarantee anything at this stage." Michael met Hastle's eyes, and although the gesture seemed friendly, he used the time to calculate Hastle's intentions. "Obviously it depends on your goal. If you're trying to unseat Satan, have at it. If you want to harm the Christian communities, we're not participating."

Hastle rubbed his chin. "I'm not sure I trust you even if you agree."

Michael said, "Then we're at an impasse," and drew up his wings as if to leave.

"I didn't say no." Hastle leaned back, folding his arms. "Keep talking. Are you offering material support, or you just wouldn't stand in my way?"

When Michael hesitated, the Principality member of the interrogation team sent, *Lead him on.*

Michael shook his head. "I'm not offering anything specific at the moment, but you understand that if we both want something, there may be a way to meet in the middle."

Hastle's mouth tightened. "Even so. Hey, you didn't bring your entourage this time. Does that mean you're softening up?"

"It means I'd rather you talk than not. I have my own authority to make deals and don't require the consent of *my entourage*." A demon would like that, the whole radical independence thing. "So, your agenda?"

Hastle's face changed so he looked warm and eager. "Why are you in such a hurry? If we don't have a chorus of bystanders here to lecture me, I want to reconnect with you." He laughed, and his eyes snapped back to ice. "Remember when it was just you and me and Danel? I want that again. How about you bring him over and we reminisce?"

Absolutely not, sent the Angel.

Michael said, "How about you and I talk about your agenda?"

Hastle frowned. "You certainly have an agenda."

"You're wasting my time."

"Bring me Danel."

Michael didn't even need a warning from the Principality. "You're not dictating terms here."

Hastle grinned. "Actually, I am."

It's normal for him to try to assert control over the interview, sent the Angel, *but we can't have him involving any more participants.*

Of course not. Michael didn't even like the fact that he was in there himself. Given a demon's general slipperiness and their willingness to twist any kind of truth into a weapon, talking to them got more dangerous the longer you did it. If Remiel and Zadkiel hadn't needed help, he wouldn't be doing it now.

The Principality sent, *I'm not sure why he wants Danel, but keep the focus on what he wants in the long term rather than catering to the short term. He thinks we need him more than he needs us.*

Michael paced the cell while Hastle watched. *And wouldn't that in some respect be true?*

The Angel sounded uncomfortable for the first time. *In some respect. But the situation isn't as dire for our side as he thinks. He may be playing the long game and counting on us to play shorter, figuring we'll crumble before he does.*

Ah. That made the strategy a little different, as far as Michael was concerned. Michael tucked his wings closer at his back. "I've already said there are some terms I won't agree to, and you cleverly went and found one of them already." He rubbed at a speck of lint on one of his flight feathers. "We can do this without you. It might take a little longer, but our Cherubim are reverse-engineering the work of your Cherubim."

Hastle snorted. "Reverse engineering *what* exactly?"

"You left evidence behind in the form of Remiel and Zadkiel." Michael opened his hands, as if to say it should have been obvious. "They were affected by your work, but we can analyze those effects, and we're confident Gabriel will figure it out in short order."

Hastle's nose wrinkled. "You don't have them."

"I know exactly where they are." Michael projected his sincerity. "I swear by Him who made the Heavens and the Earth. I've spoken to them and assessed them, and I know where they are."

For the first time, Hastle looked rattled. His feathers stood out. "That's a parlor trick. If you know their location, why talk to me?"

"I thought you were dictating terms, not begging for information." Michael rested a hand on the wall. "I've got a better idea. Why don't you think a little longer about whether you'd like to cooperate, and if I feel like it, I'll come back in to talk to you. Without Danel."

He stepped back out through the wall, and once away from Hastle, leaned against the bricks and covered his face with his hands and wings.

THIRTEEN

Remiel hauled water from the aqueduct so she could scrub out the main room. Mary joined her, but she demurred with, "I've got this," and just kept cleaning. Some of the tile pieces blown apart by Belior's demonic tantrum could be fitted back together, but the ones ground to powder were hopeless. They'd need to be replaced.

Nivalis hovered, shooting glances toward the back of the house. "I don't like having him in the building."

"He's got to be someplace, and at least here we know where that is." Remiel's nose wrinkled. "It's bitter justice that he's trapped too. You'd think he'd be the first one to know how to reverse whatever he did." Remiel picked up more slivers of shattered tile. "If you want to choose one part of this situation to be unnerved about, that's the one."

When Nivalis didn't reply, Remiel brought the trash bucket into the street and dumped it, then returned to the house. "How's *Key*?" she asked.

"The girls are scared, but she's calming them down by telling them stories. The last time I checked on her, it was Daniel in the lion's den. They liked that." Nivalis's wings flared. "Remiel, now. The storage room. Asmodeus."

Remiel strode through the house, fists clenched, before she realized there was nothing she could do in her current state. Really there wouldn't have been anything she could do in her previous state either, given how much stronger Asmodeus was and the fact that he and Belior were bonded. But she hadn't quite decided what to do about that.

Mary called, "Remaya? What's wrong?"

Remiel stepped inside the storage room, and she let her eyes adjust to the darkness.

Though tied up, Belior had managed to back himself into the corner, and his eyes were defiant as he stared at a spot above and in front of him, but the rest of that human body read terror. Stopped in the doorway, Remiel watched an exchange between him and nothing.

Nivalis came up behind her, and at her touch Remiel shuddered with a sparking headache—but now she could experience Asmodeus's presence and power. He towered over Belior, dark and imposing. Remiel couldn't detect any conversation even though they must have been arguing, but through Nivalis she also could read Belior's physical stress levels, the cascade of fight-or-flight hormones in his host's brain, the anger, the helplessness, and yes, the fear.

Fear. Of his own bonded Seraph.

She should have expected it. Of course she should have, but she'd seen Gabriel and Raphael so often, and so many other Cherub/Seraph pairs as they worked with one another, steadied and supported and encouraged. Even when they argued (and she'd seen it a couple of times) they did it without intimidation.

But Belior looked intimidated. Whatever was going on interiorly, he might have been holding his own, but he was trapped and without means of defending himself.

"Stop!" Dizzy, Remiel clutched the wall. "You, demon, just stop it. Leave him alone."

The darkness that was Asmodeus didn't even acknowledge her, but Remiel staggered between him and Belior. She crouched right in front of Belior and looked up at where Asmodeus was. "By Christ's authority, leave."

A blast like a waterfall struck Remiel, nauseating her and blurring her vision. Information flowed into her human brain like oil from a jug, oil spilled across a tile floor and gathering in slick, viscous pools. Of course he had the right. He owned Belior. She was nothing. She needed to leave. And her body, her pitiful human body overflowed with fear to the point that even if she wanted to run, she couldn't have. Her legs would never have supported her. Her mouth burned. Her eyes watered.

"Stop!"

Mary strode into the room. "In the name of my Son, you are ordered to leave. You have no authority."

Remiel registered that the one she should be protecting was Mary, but the axis of the world wouldn't stop pivoting: Nivalis's touch and Asmodeus's energy were overwhelming her human senses and exacerbating whatever damage Belior's weapon had done. Mary, on the other hand, just stepped forward. "He's my guest. You're threatening my guest, and I'm ordering you out."

That wasn't what you wanted to do, make a demon your guest. Remiel wanted to say it, but she couldn't form any words. The presence of Asmodeus lay like an oppressive blanket over the room, and in the center Mary stood without buckling. It looked for all the world as if she didn't even notice it. "You have nothing to say to me," she added. "You have no claim on me."

Asmodeus actually answered her. "His soul is mine."

"Settle that after he's outside these walls." Mary folded her arms. "For now he's here. Leave."

The presence vanished.

Mary shook her head, then whispered, "Thank you." It was a prayer.

Behind her, Belior collapsed to his side, and he vomited.

Where she still knelt on the storage room floor, Remiel whispered, "Get out of my head. I can't think."

Nivalis backed off, and Remiel closed her eyes, breath heaving. Sweat drenched her body, and her arms trembled as she leaned on them.

Belior wore a bloodless pallor, and his body gleamed with sweat. Mary went to his side and helped him upright, then edged him toward a clean part of the floor. "Remaya, bring me a basin of water and a towel."

Remiel staggered to her feet, leaned on the wall, and then said, "Yes, Ma'am."

Outside the room, it was marginally easier to breathe. She made her way into the kitchen, then out to the aqueduct for water. By the time she brought that and a towel back to the inner room, she felt steady again, but Mary took them from her at the entrance. "I'll do this."

"I'll stay, *Kecharitomene*."

Mary moistened the towel and cleaned Belior's face. He pushed her away with his bound hands, but she kept working, ignoring the hatred in his eyes. Remiel came closer, but Mary said, "I'm taking care of it."

Her hands worked quickly, but there was gentleness in the way she cleaned him up, and Belior gave up struggling. He lay on the floor, limp.

Mary kept her voice low. "I know about Seraph/Cherub bonds, but can't you break this?"

Belior glared at her with disgust, projecting something uncomplimentary about human stupidity.

Mary chuckled. "I never before appreciated the broad degree of subtlety angels can convey without using any words at all."

He dropped back to the floor, projecting irritation.

She finished cleaning the stones, then handed the basin to Remiel to dump in the street.

Outside, Remiel regained her bearings. "Don't do that to me again," Remiel whispered. "I don't react well to angelic contact."

Nivalis said, "I'm sorry. I thought it worth the risk, given who you were facing."

"You nearly incapacitated me. When Saraquael did that, I ended up just like Belior is now."

Remiel drew water from the aqueduct and washed out the filthy towel, then dumped the basin again, rinsed the towel, and brought everything back inside.

In the storage room, Mary was spooning a thick porridge into Belior's mouth a little at a time. "The body you're in needs something. John ordered you not to harm the body. You have to eat and drink."

Remiel said, "He may have a really bad headache too. And don't expect even the slightest gratitude from him for stepping between them."

"I didn't do it for his thanks or any kind of debt. I did it because I will not countenance someone hurting someone else in my house." Mary spooned up a little more, and Belior tightened his lips against the food. "I doubt he'd consent to having me pray over him to relieve the headache, if that would even help him. But I intend to make sure he doesn't kill his host."

A host who apparently hated God every bit as much as Belior did. Remiel sat in the entrance, suddenly aware of her own exhaustion and how futile it all felt. Aware of how intense a tragedy it was that Belior couldn't trust someone who had full access to his soul, and even worse the tragedy that would have been if she and Camael were together on the wrong side.

For the first time, Remiel wondered if Camael would have done that to her if she'd fallen at his side. If they'd have struggled for dominance and made each other afraid and had to stay linked anyhow. Without really dwelling on it, she'd always assumed that if they'd both fallen, they'd have been the same in every way except that they'd both hate God. Not that in some sense, eventually, they'd hate each other.

But it had to be that way. Hating the image of God meant hating yourself because you had His image on you. And the twins were in the image of each other.

Camael. *God, I miss him.* She closed her eyes as she prayed. *I just miss him so much sometimes.*

Demons weren't that hard to deal with when you could spy on them, fight them, irritate them, and run for home. Being in such close quarters, though...being able to see their interactions and their twisted almost-friendships as they almost-functioned: that seared her heart the way an open flame seared meat to a blackened crust on the outside and left a bloody rawness just beneath.

She got to her feet. "My lady?" Her voice came thin. "Should I send John to help?"

Mary waved her off. "Go. He's not going to hurt me."

Mute and tied up, he still might find a way to do it. But Remiel chose to believe her, and she withdrew to the kitchen to start preparing the evening meal.

FOURTEEN

Michael prayed for an hour, purifying himself and growing calm, before he entered the Holy Temple in Heaven. He remained just inside the entrance columns, focused on the angels at the front as they moved through their mid-day liturgy. Censers streamed with a rainbow of fragrances; angels appeared and presented prayers, then disappeared again; several angels canted a psalm in a call-response rhythm; and a number of white-robed angels knelt in adoration with their arms crossed over their chests while a choir of Seraphim sang the holy Trisagion.

After a time, Michael joined in the liturgy, praying, praising, asking, scrutinizing his own actions and intentions in order to bring any imperfection before God for cleansing. Then at the end of the ceremony, Michael flashed to the doorway at the front and joined the other angels as they departed.

He fell in beside Danel, who turned toward him with a smile. "I felt your arrival. Thank you so much." Danel hugged him, then put a hand on his head and blessed him. He still glistened in his white robes, and his lavender wings smelled faintly of myrrh. "Wait for me, please?"

Michael tingled from the blessing. "I came here to talk to you. I'll wait."

Danel reached his wings forward to touch the tips of Michael's, then vanished.

Michael waited outside the white stone structure, soaking in the peace and perfection of its columns and its carvings, the geometric absoluteness graphed out by the Cherubim and then evoked with heart by the Thrones. *Thank you,* he prayed. He wasn't even sure what for, but gratitude swelled inside him. *I love You so much.*

Danel returned, wearing blue and with his hair a tousled mess. "Let's go somewhere quiet. I wanted to talk to you, but it sounded like you were so busy with this crisis."

Danel took his hand and flashed them away before Michael could wonder that everyone thought it a crisis. Or that word had gotten as far as the Sanctuary angels, who tended to stay to themselves.

They reappeared in a deserted spot: literally and figuratively both, as it was desert sand underfoot and cactus plants standing guard all around. Danel started walking at a thoughtful pace. "God told me in prayer that Hastiel was in custody, and I wanted to find you. But I also didn't want to presume that talking would help you."

This whole meeting had gotten away from him already, so Michael abandoned anything he'd planned to say and just followed the conversational stream. "Why wouldn't it help?"

"If you wanted only to forget about it all, then having me show up wasn't going to achieve that end." Danel chuckled. "Some angels who encounter a former friend will choose to pretend it hasn't happened, or that it's not the same soul. I figured you'd face him head-on, but just in case, I waited. Besides, I'm not so different from you. You stayed in the back of the Temple until the liturgy ended, and I also didn't want to interrupt your work." He stopped to crane back his neck and study the sky. Contentment rolled off him, and Michael felt him quickly reach out to God, just a touch, and then return to himself. He looked at Michael with his silvery eyes gleaming. "It must be so difficult for you."

Michael looked at the ground.

"I wanted to tell you how sorry I was that you had to deal with him under the circumstances." Danel's voice grew softer. "He's probably changed so much."

"He hasn't changed *enough*." Michael shook his head. "He's still recognizable. It's there—he's all there, and he even asked me to bring you in like when we were the troublesome trio, and I refused, but for him even to ask that..."

"He asks things like that because he knows you're going to hurt. I'm betting he doesn't genuinely want to engage with you any more than you want to engage with him."

"That's not true." Michael's hands clenched. "He works hard to keep drawing me back. If he didn't want to engage, he'd have talked to the other questioners, the professionals. The ones he never cared about and who are trained not to care about him. To make me go away, he'd either give me the information or make fast on a staunch refusal to say anything whatsoever." Beside him, Danel's light dimmed. "We've had demons before who refused to speak. Hastle could easily be one of them. Easily." He resumed walking, and Danel hurried to keep pace. "He hates what I've become."

Danel chuckled. "I can only imagine what he'd say about my vocation."

Michael muttered, "I don't know if he even believes the things he says. It's a game."

Danel's head picked up. "He always was mischievous. It made him fun to be around."

"This isn't mischief." Michael's feathers tightened. "It's malice."

"Or is his behavior just mischief stood on its head?" Danel flexed his wings. "He's not just hurting you. He's hurting you and having fun at the same time. It wouldn't be fun to you or to me," he added, "but we also didn't reject God." Abruptly Danel chuckled. "You were a mischief-maker too, though."

Michael pivoted. "I was not!"

"Oh, no, of course not. Do you remember when you and Miriael detonated Hastiel's music?"

"That wasn't my fault!" Michael's eyes widened. "Not entirely my fault. I *suggested* it, but I didn't realize Miriael was going to act on it. I mean, that he would act on it too."

Danel's eyebrows arched, and he folded his arms. "Totally blameless, were you?"

Michael closed his eyes. Hastiel had set up hundreds of little Guarded spheres containing specific atomic contents so each of them would glow a different color and make a different sound while burning. The flame of each would set off the next after a specific time, and the overall effect would be a wave of sound and color designed to glorify God. Hastiel had put these together so many times. They were beautiful and so delicate.

Danel said, "And you weren't even a little involved in what happened next."

Michael smirked. "I just thought it would be funny to change some of the contents of some of the spheres so they burned a little differently. It wasn't my fault that Miriael went ahead and did it again after I did it. And I really didn't expect it to go like *that*!"

Danel snapped, and a blue flame shot up from his hand all the way to the stratosphere.

Michael laughed out loud. "How was I supposed to know such a little change was going to have such a huge reaction?"

Danel said, "So instead of one little flame touching off the next in a beautiful string of colored lights and notes, we got in effect a supernova and an entire symphony played in the same two seconds."

Michael covered his face in his hands. "He was so...so angry at us..." He dissolved in laughter. "I felt so bad. I spent the next three days helping him put the whole thing back together, and then he wouldn't even let me be there when he did it again."

Danel grinned. "But no. You were never involved in any mischief."

Michael said, "Do you remember what happened after, though?"

Danel looked puzzled, and then his eyes brightened. "That's right! Miriael had picked out a spot to make his own little domain, and he was so pleased with it and went on and on about it!"

"And on." Michael nodded. "And on."

"So Hastiel followed him to it and then scouted out every last little bit so he could make a perfect duplicate."

Michael said, "And it was perfect. Everything right to the last detail."

Danel grinned. "So then Hastiel brought us all over to the duplicate and summoned Miriael to us and asked for a grand tour of the place, and when Miriael was showing it off, Hastiel just started shrinking the whole thing, smaller and smaller..."

Michael closed his eyes, shoulders shaking. "I don't remember how crowded the place got before you said something, but we were all practically on top of each other, and then Miriael looked horrified, like he'd built his house on some kind of vortex."

Danel said, "And then he ranted at Hastiel for about an hour afterward. The only saving grace there was that I didn't have anything to do with it."

Michael made his voice a little deeper. "I'm sorry, Miriael. I'll never do that again."

"You're not looking nearly smug enough." Danel folded his arms. "See? We don't have him anymore, but we do have the memories, and you can still laugh at the ridiculous things we did. It's okay to still treasure the good times."

Michael shook his head. "That's so hard."

"It is. I'm not denying how hard it is." Danel looked at the darkening horizon. "I asked God to give me this acreage a while ago, as my own special place. He made it mine, but I've never built any kind of structure here." Danel offered a smile. "Not just because of what happened to Miriael. I like it as it is." He turned to Michael, the silver in his eyes glimmering gently. "You've still never staked out a home for yourself?"

"I have an office, but no, no place ever struck me as that special. God's in all of them." Michael shook his head. "I'm sorry for dumping all this on you."

"We carry one another's burdens. That's what friends do." Danel hugged him. "Are you going to speak to him again?"

"Probably."

"I'll be praying for you. Do you think it would help if I were to accompany you?"

Michael shook his head.

Danel projected agreement. "I wanted to ask, in case." He stepped back and extended his hands, projecting an invitation to pray together. Michael reached for him with hands and wings. Together they stretched out for God, but Michael could feel that Danel also was remembering a time when they'd prayed together and there had been three.

FIFTEEN

After dinner, Mary watched Remiel cleaning the kitchen, noticing how sluggishly she moved, how her hands trembled. "Why don't you rest a bit?" she said, and Remiel only shook her head. *No, Kecharitomene, I'll clean up for you.*

Zadkiel had returned to a corner where she appeared to be making enough netting to snare a Leviathan. During dinner she'd told Mary (and anyone else who would listen) about two different kinds of knots and how they felt to her fingers. Mary grinned as Zadkiel worked the shuttle through the loops in her lap. Net-making could be fun, sure, but Zadkiel was more than reveling in feeling useful. For the first time since she'd gotten stuck in human form, she must have felt as if she were doing something. Finally her work mattered.

Remiel, though, Mary wasn't sure how to help. She looked and sounded exhausted, and whenever Mary made the suggestion that she rest, or even slow down, Remiel declined. Eventually her human body would have to crumple and sleep, wouldn't it? She'd been awake now for almost two days with only a couple hours rest. Mary had seen people awake for longer, though. She may have done it herself, assisting at births. Soldiers at war certainly did it. In a body young and strong, maybe Remiel could manage it too.

Remiel looked up, the lamp-light glinting in the rings on her ears. She had a young form, not even fully grown, with her hair shaved so short that her ears showed. "Is something the matter?" she asked.

Mary shook her head, smiling at her. "You look cute, that's all."

Remiel's nose wrinkled, which made her look cuter still. "That isn't how I thought I looked. I figured waif-like."

Mary stepped closer. "One of the women has a mirror if you'd like to see for yourself."

Remiel shook her head. "Mirrors and I don't get along. But that explains some of what happened on my last assignment as a human."

Mary nodded. "And that was...?"

The way Remiel smiled turned her face brighter. For a moment, she wasn't tired anymore. "I came across a calf trapped in a ravine, and it was cold. The mother cow was up at the top, calling for her, but the baby couldn't get out."

Mary laughed. "You asked permission for that?"

"More than that! God *gave* me permission. It was going to snow," Remiel added. "What I really wanted to do was prevent the snow, but He told me I could go down there in a human body and free the calf. So I did. When I got up to the top of the hill with her, two herdsmen came and confronted me, and I told them about the oncoming storm. Turns out they hadn't realized it would be that bad, so I helped them get the whole herd to safety." Remiel seemed amused. "So the assignment was done, and I tried to take my leave, only they insisted on knowing where I was going. I couldn't lie to them, right, and when they realized I lived 'far away,' they wouldn't let me leave because, you know, there was a horrible snow storm coming that would kill a herd of cows and therefore would definitely kill me." She burst out laughing. "So they ended up with this unexpected guest stuck in their family home for three days while they burned peat and taught me to sing rowdy songs and play a weird little flute thing." She bit her lip. "Oh, and they had this amazing wine made from fermented honey. That was really good. After three days, the matron of the house tried to marry me off to her youngest son, but as soon as the snow cleared, I left." Remiel raked a hand through her hair and struck a pose. "Do you think I'd have done well as a young bride in Celtica, milking cows and cutting peat moss to burn?"

"I didn't understand half of what you said," Mary said, "but do you still remember the songs?"

"I am not," Remiel said, "under any circumstances singing any of them to you." She looked startled and a little serious. "I was just really glad Saraquael hadn't gotten that assignment. Or Michael. They'd have walked out, blizzard or no. I taught the family a few songs in exchange, though. Someday, someone's going to be surprised to learn he's been singing the Holy Trisagion in an angelic language while milking the cows."

Mary giggled. "Can you teach me to sing that instead?"

"I could. You can ask Raphael, since the Seraphim are the ones who maintain the song. It's a constant backdrop in Heaven. If you ever want to hear it, you just listen and it's there, thrumming in the background."

Mary moved alongside Remiel and began putting away the cutlery. "And can you teach me how to make wine from honey?"

"Ah, now that stuff was good." Remiel sighed. "I don't know if you could get all the ingredients in Greece. It had an earthy, yeasty taste. It made me think of oak trees. Do you have oaks here?" When Mary nodded, she went on. "It wasn't really like wine." Remiel lowered her eyes. "Maybe if we get out of this situation, someday I'll bring you a jar."

"You'll get out of this."

Remiel's shoulders slumped, and the exhaustion returned. "We'd better. Ephesus will run out of rope for Zadkiel."

Mary was about to retort that they'd send to Corinth when a messenger came into the kitchen. It was a servant from a house Mary had visited this morning, the one with the sick child. "Mistress needs you," gasped the servant, breath heaving. "Please, we need you now."

Pausing only long enough to grab her tunic and a bag with supplies, Mary rushed outside following the servant. Remiel followed her.

"You don't have to come," Mary said. "Remember this morning?"

Remiel again sounded subdued. "I'll go where you go."

They navigated streets that had yet to fall fully dark, avoiding the sewage ditch down the centers. The servant hurried them, and Mary kept checking to make sure Remiel kept pace.

At the house, Mary said, "You can wait outside," and Remiel murmured, "*Kecharitomene*, I'll serve you."

The child had gone feverish, and the mother wrung her hands walking in and out of the room. Mary tended the child, then prayed over her. Remiel fetched water from the aqueduct and then back again. She still got that spaced-out stare whenever she drew near to the child, but Mary thought she was more in control. Whatever had happened before, this time Remiel expected it and had braced herself.

Mary sponged down the child, who lay on a sweat-drenched bed in no clothing. Her limbs were swollen but her eyes sunken. Her breath reeked of sweetness, and so did her sweat.

Mary said to Remiel in Aramaic, "What is this sickness?"

"I don't know." Remiel bowed her head. "Raphael would know, if you called for him."

The child's mother said, "What did she say?"

"Only that a doctor from her homeland might recognize it," Mary said, "but we'll do the best we can without him."

Back during Jesus's lifetime, of course she'd have called for Raphael in a heartbeat. But in the last twenty years, the angels had withdrawn from her everyday life in so many ways. Uriel sometimes communicated with her, but often it was only in different calibre silences, a pressure or a feeling that flitted through her heart and which she might have ignored if she hadn't paid attention for those moments. The Holy Spirit filled her, and she couldn't ask for better than God Himself, but at times she missed the angels and their ready companionship.

At the moment, Remiel and Zadkiel didn't seem to have the ability to just call for the other angels either, although Remiel appeared to have a companion she consulted without too much hassle. Mary didn't ask for details. If they wanted her to know, they'd tell her. So she didn't ask now if Remiel could summon Raphael, and she continued sponging down the child.

The mother's voice sharpened. "Your people claim to heal the sick. Why aren't you healing her?"

"I've never healed anyone." Mary looked up. "I pray. Jesus heals whom he wants, when he wants. He's the one who makes us whole."

The mother's fists clenched in her tunic. "Then why doesn't he want to make her whole?"

Mary said, "Your faith will have to save your daughter."

"Why? Just heal her!" The mother stepped closer, but Mary didn't flinch. "The magicians said they couldn't heal her. The priests at the Temple of Artemis said they couldn't heal her. But people said John and your ilk have healed the sick, and I'm begging you for your help!"

Mary kept her voice low as she turned back to the child. "You can't force God to do something. You ask. You wait. You receive." She reached for the mother's hand, but the mother yanked back. "Healing isn't the final good. If you have eternal life, that's the final good. You need to have life in order for your child to have life."

The mother sounded urgent. "And how do I do that?"

Mary said, "Repent and be baptized. Pray to receive the Holy Spirit."

John spoke to people with such fluidity. He'd preach to crowds and people would press close, asking to become disciples. Why was it so hard for her, one-on-one, to find the right words? The Holy Spirit would move in her too, but Mary always felt this urge to do no more than repeat the things her son had said and then encourage people to do whatever it was he'd told them to do. She liked getting people to the brink where they'd finally pray, and then watching what happened when they reached out and God reached back. She could pray for the outcome, but it always felt so much better when she left off and God took over.

These final moments of struggle, though, when she knew there must be demons active just out of sight to pressure the person to cling to doubt—doubts that would be there in any case because the things Jesus said were so amazing, so true and yet so easy not to believe as true—those were difficult. You couldn't say, "Trust me" because then the person's faith was in you rather than in God. But how to guide them there?

So Mary tended the child and told the mother stories about Jesus, told her the things he'd said and the stories he'd told people whenever he'd traveled. She sponged down the child's body and alternated praying over her with talking to the mother. Remiel fetched water. The household servant brought wine and brought food when they needed it. Mary spooned a little porridge into the child's mouth, but the girl gagged, so Mary didn't try again. They were able to spoon her up a little water mixed with wine, and maybe that would be enough for now.

"Why won't Jesus heal her?" the mother sobbed. It was well after the second watch of the night. Remiel sat at the child's feet, too weary to move, and Mary prayed for strength to see things through until morning. The night felt so long. Just so long now.

"Do something," urged the mother. "Don't you care?"

"Of course I care," Mary said. "I watched my own son die."

The woman leaned closer. "Then you know! Why would you do that to me too?"

Mary wrapped a hand around the mother's. "It's not up to me. I stood there. I watched the Romans execute him, and I knew he was innocent the whole time." She nodded. "Crucified. He was bleeding and gasping too much even to breathe, and I could only watch."

The mother whispers, "I'd trade places with her."

Mary squeezed her hand. "I'd have done it too. But he'd already traded places with me. With you. With your daughter." She reached for the woman, who relaxed into her hug. "I miss him. You know how a mother grieves. We lost him for a few days when he was twelve, and when I found him, he said, *Didn't you know I'd be in my father's house?* He meant the Temple, but now it's real: he's in his Father's house. Waiting for me."

The woman said, "That doesn't help."

"No, it doesn't always." Mary kissed the mother's forehead. "But I know what you're going through."

"Tell me more," the woman said. "Tell me more about him, if he'll heal her."

And so, during the course of the second watch, the mother asked more questions about Jesus, and when Mary answered, the woman seemed to understand, and as the night drew on, she asked if she could be baptized, and her daughter too. They prayed together that the mother would receive the Holy Spirit. And in the hour after, the girl's fever broke and her swelling diminished. Her color returned, and the room air smelled pure.

Mary never presumed to predict how God would answer prayers. God did what He wanted, and that was good. But she'd found so often that healing and conversion worked together, that the healing was secondary to getting the heart where it needed to go. In the end, the healing served only as the catalyst to the spiritual life breathed now into the soul, and then it became that life's physical seal.

At the foot of the bed, Remiel looked stunned. Why? She'd seen healings before. She might even have participated in them.

The mother fell asleep alongside her daughter. Mary would have to come back in the morning to pray with them again, maybe bringing John or Ignatius or one of the others. They would lay hands on the woman and her daughter, and then they'd speak to the men of the house. It would be good, but for now, Mary wanted only to get back home. So as the woman and her daughter slept, they bid farewell to the servant and returned to the street.

In the dark, Mary's voice was small. "Are you all right?"

Remiel whispered, "I felt it. The moment God healed her, even though I wasn't touching her, it was as if she'd been clenching my hand. And then she let me go."

Mary's brow furrowed. "What do you think that means?"

"I don't know. I feel like I don't know anything."

Halfway to home, a light shone before them both. Mary stopped in her tracks. Remiel stiffened, then pushed herself in between the light and Mary.

What appeared out of the glow looked like an angel. She had dark eyes and sun-rich skin, and she wore Greek clothing. Gazing at Mary, she said, "Listen to my words. You have a demon imprisoned in your house. I require access to him."

Mary said, "What is your name?"

"I'm Satrinah." The demon cocked her head. "This means nothing to you, as well it shouldn't. But his freedom is worth a lot to me. Give me permission to enter your house."

"No." Mary looked her dead in the eye. The demon had no readable expression and no body language, and if she had expected

Mary to cower or bolt, she gave no sign of disappointment. "Under no circumstances will I give you permission to enter that house."

The demon said, "The information I need is only to be found in a thorough examination of the demon, and since he's in possession of that human, either you need to let me into the house, or you need to bring him out."

"I don't need to do either." It had been years since she'd dealt with a demon this way, and she'd forgotten how infuriating they were. Gabriel and Uriel had wanted her never to talk to them, so Mary decided to end it. "Leave."

Satrinah put her hands on her hips. "I thought your little community claimed to have power over demons. Why can't you expel him?"

Standing in front of Mary, Remiel said, "Why can't you figure out that you're not going to get what you want from her?"

Satrinah noticed Remiel for the first time, and Mary shivered. Although confident that a demon wouldn't be able to lay a hand on her (well, metaphorically speaking) she wasn't sure what authority it could get as regarded another angel. Remiel didn't look at all afraid. Instead she had her hands clenched and her shoulders squared. But in a girl's body, what did she intend?

Satrinah's eyes returned to Mary, marking the slave as no consequence. "Are you Christians weak after all, then? Unable to set a man free of a demon and unwilling to escort a possessed man even into your own courtyard so a demon can accomplish what you've so laughably failed to do?"

Remiel folded her arms. "Nice try. But go."

The demon looked again at Remiel, and then for the first time her eyes brightened. "Remiel! You got trapped also! I didn't think you could possess a human." Satrinah flew at Remiel, but although Mary tensed, Remiel only stood in place as Satrinah whipped around her like a dust devil. "This is a lovely gift. But you're not actually in possession of a human, are you? You're just wearing a body. Still, I think I can get the data I want."

"Permission denied," Remiel said.

"It's data." Satrinah folded her arms. "I don't need permission to collect data."

Mary said, "Tell us what you did to her."

"Well, that's an interesting proposition." Satrinah's eyes brightened. "Prior to giving any information to you, I demand your assurance that I can examine my comrade."

Remiel said, "Permission denied. How much clearer do you need it? Aren't you a Cherub?"

Satrinah looked at Mary. "She's correct that I'm a Cherub. To be explicit, I'm a Cherub bonded to one of the same Seraphim Belior is—the demon in your care right now. Belior is one of Satan's top demons, as is Asmodeus. Asmodeus has charged me with restoring Belior to his rightful form, and therefore I need to conduct an examination. Give me authority and I'll do that, and then I'll leave your household unharmed."

"I don't believe anything you're saying." Still, it puzzled Mary that God had allowed the demon to talk to her for this long. She'd encountered demons only a few times in her life, and always an angel had worked with her to drive it off.

Remiel didn't have the power either, at the moment, but she at least could talk tough. "Asmodeus doesn't care what happens to Belior."

"On the contrary, from my privileged position I can tell he's extremely concerned. He won't be able to keep up the pretense much longer that Belior is on a private mission." Satrinah's eyes darkened. "Asmodeus doesn't want to lose his standing, and before he'd allow that to happen, he'd get me onto the Maskim in Belior's stead." She tossed her head. "I want nothing to do with that."

Remiel snorted. "Oh, come on. You'd love the power."

"I'd hate the interruptions. I love my work and the access I get to all sorts of interesting problems and materials without the necessity of explaining the solutions to Satan." Her clothes had gotten darker now too. "It's best for all concerned if Belior goes back to Asmodeus and they can make their excuses and be done with it. You don't want him. We do. Hand him over."

Remiel took Mary's hand and resumed walking to the house.

Satrinah called, "I'll harm your others."

Remiel made no answer, just led Mary through the street as though she knew where she was headed. Maybe she even did—she'd been on this route with Mary earlier today, and she'd figured out how to find their house in the first place.

Satrinah flashed to the side of the road. "Bring him just to the edge of the courtyard. That will suffice for my research."

Mary followed Remiel and didn't answer. They were nearly home. And then, as they entered the courtyard, Satrinah appeared once more before them, directly in the doorway.

She lit up the stones at her feet with a blue light. "Position him here. Not out of the house, but not quite inside. I'll undertake the examination from outside the perimeter. I'll find a solution, and I'll set him free. You can have your filthy magician, and I'll have Belior."

Remiel walked right through Satrinah's image without slowing down, so Mary followed. The light dispersed, and they were back behind the sealed walls.

Mary checked on the various rooms. Zadkiel was sleeping in the common dorm with the other women, but Remiel didn't go to her. Instead Remiel followed Mary to the kitchen. Her cheeks were flushed, and her hair was dark with sweat.

Mary squeezed her shoulder. "Go to sleep, bad girl."

"I'm fine. You should get some sleep, though."

Mary said, "What did you dream about that was so horrid?"

Remiel's face lost color, so the flush of her cheeks stood out all the more. "*Kecharitomene*, no, please."

"Is it like what used to happen to me after Jesus died," Mary said, "when I used to wake up and remember every detail of it as if it had all happened over again? I used to be so scared."

Remiel closed her eyes hard. "*Kecharitomene.*"

Mary reached for her hand. How could an angel look so lost, so little? "You said you were in that blizzard for days. You must have slept then."

"I didn't. When they laid down at night, I'd just transcend back into angelic form and shield the house and the livestock. Before they woke up, I'd return, and I'd be re-energized."

"But you can't do that now?"

Remiel's mouth twitched. "I can't imagine it would help, even if I could. Given what happened last time."

Oh, right, the headache and vomiting. Mary said, "Speaking of which, I ought to check on our visitor to make sure he's all right."

Mary had heard of people choking when they vomited in their sleep. To Belior, it made no difference which body he was stuck in. If he killed this one, he'd be no more or less miserable in the next, so it stood to reason someone needed to look after him. Mary took some leftover bread from the kitchen and a cup of wine mixed with water, and she headed into the back room. Remiel followed with a lamp.

Belior sat awake, looking at her. Nowhere near as distressed as he'd been earlier, he instead had an attitude of patience. Patient hatred, to be sure, but a kind of predatory waiting.

Mary held the cup to his mouth, and he drank a little, giving a strong impression that even though he must be parched by now, he was doing it as a duty rather than to slake thirst. Mary fed him the bread, and again he ate while she had an impression of duty.

She knew the man by reputation because several of their Christians had dealt with him in the past. They whispered that he produced healings and rid girls of pregnancies, forged love charms and power amulets, devised storm wards and death incantations. Remuneration was rendered not just in the form of money. Mary had tried not to hear the tales.

The one time she'd seen him in the agora, he'd walked alone— with two companions, but alone, as if even the ones with him didn't want to stand too near. He had tight eyes and a tense bearing, and despite a revulsion Mary couldn't understand, she'd next felt pity for him, and that she hadn't understood either. So she'd prayed for him, and the moment she did, he'd looked right at her with disgust and rejection.

Again now, inhabited by Belior, he watched with his eyes like a wolf's. Mary alternated drink and food for him, and as she did, she knew with certitude that Belior wanted permission to speak. He had a question.

She looked to Remiel, who shone with exhaustion. It was her decision, then.

Mary turned to Belior. "Ask your question."

Belior said, "I know who you are, and I know your power. Why aren't you using it?"

Mary sat back, perplexed. "My power?"

Belior didn't change position. Was it something about demons that their faces didn't change, or was it just that both these demons were Cherubim? Gabriel sometimes had that kind of flatness too, at least back when she used to see him often.

Belior said, "You are the mother of the Word, and that one calls you *Kecharitomene.* By all reports, Gabriel referred to you using that term as well."

Mary shrugged.

Belior remained expressionless. "You had an angel call you the equivalent of *Your Majesty,* and yet you pretend not to know what kind of power you wield?"

Mary glanced at Remiel, who looked aggravated but wasn't making any reply. Mary turned back to Belior. "Why don't you tell me what kind of power you think I wield?"

Belior laughed. "Well, your power isn't intelligence, is it now?"

For the first time, Remiel spoke. "If you insult her, we'll shut you up again immediately. Behave."

Belior fired her a filthy look, then returned his eyes to Mary. They were human eyes, but his face was so tense around them that Mary detected a snake-like presence. "*Ke,*" he said, "meaning perfect or complete. *Charis,* meaning the life of God Himself. *Mene,* meaning having been put into that state by God." Belior looked uneasy, but he continued, "Gabriel, who is not without any little power and authority himself, wasn't even saying something as lowly as *Your Majesty.* He said, *Someone whom God utterly and completely filled with His grace.*"

Mary made herself sound amused. "So I have the unusual power of receiving gifts from God?"

Belior started to reply with heavy sarcasm, then glanced at Remiel and back at Mary. Instead he said, "If I'm right, there's nothing you can ask that God won't grant."

Mary's eyes widened. "What?"

"Since by Gabriel's testimony you're completely and utterly filled with His grace," Belior said, "anything you ask will be granted you. So ask that I be freed from this body."

Mary took him in, considered his posture and his direct stare. He must mean what he was saying, no matter how he might be twisting the truth to get what he wanted. For whatever reason, he thought she could pull a string on God, and like a puppet, God would respond.

In all her life, had God ever refused her anything? And if no, why not?

"You don't understand." Mary smiled. "God didn't pick me and then fill me with power, as if I could be some kind of Artemis striding over the land and working wonders." She shook her head as she gave him a little more to drink. "If it's true that God could never refuse me, it's only because I would never ask for something God didn't already want."

Belior looked at her in disgust. "Are you that enthralled?"

"It's like a marriage. Gabriel said the bond between a Cherub and a Seraph is even stronger than marriage, so maybe that too." She smiled. "If you love someone fully, you want them to be happy, and you want what they want. You're close enough that you know whether the thing you want to ask for is within their means and works with their overall goals. If it contradicts their goals, of course you won't ask. Once you realize, you probably won't even want it anymore."

Belior seemed incredulous, so apparently demons could manage facial expressions. "Isn't your position more like the Queen Mother, able to give orders and make demands?"

Mary shook her head. "If I'm the Queen Mother, then any authority I happen to have stems from my Son and His authority. It's not mine, and it never was."

Belior narrowed his eyes. "Then you're useless. Are you content being useless?"

Mary shrugged. "No one is useful to God. I'm the handmaid of the Lord. If He gave me more, that's only to His credit and not to mine."

"I'll give you more that than." Belior's voice raised. "Free me and I'll give you whatever you want. I'll teach you how to wield the power at your disposal. You'll be able to heal, able to work miracles. I'll make sure you live in comfort and are honored wherever you go. Remember how Gabriel pretended to be in thrall to you? I'll do it. I'll serve you myself!"

"No." She stood. "Do you want anything else to eat or drink?"

Belior frowned at her. "This body can starve and die for all I care."

Mary said, "Then return to silence. I won't force you to eat any more tonight. I'll offer again in the morning. You may not care, but the body will start to care."

As Mary washed the cup she'd used for Belior, she prayed. *Is that really true? You wouldn't refuse me anything?* Demons lied as a matter of course. But as she washed the cup and put it away with the others, she realized that in all her life, she'd never felt as if God had refused a prayer of hers. Even watching Jesus die, she'd either asked God to intervene and work it out for the best, or else she'd just been too numb to pray. It hadn't been, *Get him down from there.* It had been horrible to know what her son was going through, so horrible, and she'd had so many nightmares afterward, and for years fear every time she'd seen a Roman soldier, but she hadn't asked God to end it. Jesus was submitting to torture and death, and therefore she knew it must be what the Father wanted.

Instead as she looked back over her life, she saw prayers answered: souls healed, families re-united, peace among friends, accord among the Apostles.

Well, maybe it's true, she said to God, *but if it is, surely it's because you've guided me never to ask anything that would offend you. I wouldn't want to be an offense to you, and that's the most important thing for my soul: to keep things right between you and me. Even if I were to want something you didn't want, I wouldn't want you to give it.*

Belior's question told her quite a bit about Belior, though. Asmodeus certainly wouldn't have refrained from using any kind of power he had to get control over whatever he wanted. And Belior wouldn't have considered what Asmodeus wanted before making decisions that affected the both of them.

That's sad, Mary prayed. *That's not the way you wanted them to be.*

Glancing at Remiel, who looked even more wretched than before, Mary prayed, *I wish there were something I could do to help her, just so she'd feel better about whatever it is she dreamed. Or that someone could decipher what happened to them so they could work out how to reverse it.*

She hesitated, wondering suddenly if it were okay to ask for things in prayer after what Belior had said. But then she caught herself giggling: as if a demon had any right to get in the middle of her relationship with her Creator. God was still God, and nothing she did could make God less who He was. She loved Him, and in the end, that was the only thing that mattered. So she let go of Belior's insinuations and asked, *Father, if it's all right with you, please let Gabriel figure this out. I know he's already working with you on this. But please, just give him some help.*

Behind her, Remiel said, "Oh, hello there."

Mary spun, and Remiel was facing Gabriel and Raphael.

Nice, she prayed, grinning. She stepped forward, and Gabriel bowed, extending his wing tips toward her. Raphael smiled and gave a wave, and Mary beamed broadly at them both. "Welcome! I haven't seen you in so long."

"You shouldn't still be awake. It's late at night, isn't it?" Gabriel paused, as if figuring out when he was, and then shook his head. "I thought maybe if I got a better look at Remiel and Zadkiel, I might have more of a chance at figuring out what Belior did to them."

Mary said, "You can examine Belior, too. He's tied up in the back room."

Gabriel's feathers flared. Raphael said, "We did tell you he'd been found."

"I didn't realize he was *here*." Gabriel looked more serious than usual. "How did Michael tolerate that?" He turned to Remiel. "Do you mind if I examine you?"

She shook her head. "Anything if you can get me out of this mess."

Mary expected him to walk around Remiel, touch her, move her into the light—and instead he just stared at her. He focused, frowning in a way Mary remembered from long ago as him thinking deeply. Finally he said, "Talk to me. Has anything happened that you think is unusual?"

Remiel muttered, "You mean other than being stuck in a human body?"

Mary couldn't hide the smile when Gabriel missed the sarcasm. "Yes, other than that."

"Would you like the list in alphabetical order," Remiel said, "or chronological?"

Raphael said, "Take it easy."

Gabriel kept staring into her. "Nivalis is with you."

Remiel shrugged. "She got permission."

"It's curious that God stationed her with you. There's something to that." Gabriel kept staring at her, into her. "So you've just been doing regular human things, and except when you intersect the angelic plane, you haven't felt as if anything was odd?"

"There was one thing," Remiel said. "There was this sick kid, and it felt like she was pulling on me. We weren't touching, but there was a perpetual tug, like I wanted to be near her."

Gabriel's eyes snapped back into focus. "Really?" His wings raised. "And did the child die?"

"No, God healed her. That's also odd. I felt the healing take place."

Gabriel's feathers spread.

Raphael stepped closer. "What did that feel like to you?"

Remiel chuckled. "Oh, of course, you'd want to pin that down."

"But it felt like…?"

"Like she'd been yanking my hand, and then she let it go."

Gabriel rubbed his chin. "Okay, this is getting a lot more interesting, and it was already the most interesting problem I'd dealt with in fifteen years. I'm going to make your life more difficult for a little while." He turned to Raphael. "Your turn." Back to Remiel. "You reacted badly to Saraquael's power before, so I'm going to repeat what he did, but with Raphael at your back to make sure you don't suffer too much."

Remiel's nose wrinkled. "You're so nice."

Raphael said, "You're really cute in that form."

"I'm going to thrash the life out of you the minute I'm back in my right form." She turned to Gabriel. "Just do whatever you have to. I'll cope."

Gabriel hovered over her. "I'm not going to overwhelm you, so you don't need to be afraid. I'm going to challenge you by infusing you with a calculated amount of energy while I monitor your response."

Mary reached for Remiel's hand and squeezed. Remiel sounded uncertain. "Maybe we should do this in the back room. That way if I vomit, at least I vomit on Belior."

"Tempting." Gabriel's eyes sparkled. "Okay, and...now."

Remiel's hand tightened on Mary's, but then Gabriel backed off, and she relaxed. "That was good. I'm going try that again, just a jot more." Once more Remiel's hand clenched on Mary's, and she squeezed her eyes tight. Gabriel said, "You're doing great. Can you handle it if I do this one more time?"

Remiel's voice wobbled. "I think so."

Gabriel said, "No, if you're having problems, I'll stop. I may have enough." He paused. "You're physically stressed, too. Would you like me to put you to sleep?"

Remiel sounded bitter. "No. I'm fine."

Mary said, "Can you at least refresh her, Gabriel? Make it as if she'd slept without her sleeping?"

Raphael shook his head. "Infusing her with that kind of energy wouldn't have the effect you want."

Remiel folded her arms. "I'll be fine. I'll stay awake and pray."

Gabriel said, "I dispute that you'll be fine. You're unused to the demands of a human body, and while some human urges require discipline, others shouldn't be fought, and sleep is one such. Ten days without sleep will result in death." He nodded. "Keeping prisoners awake has been a type of torture in multiple totalitarian human states throughout the centuries."

"Then it's a good thing no one's keeping me prisoner." Remiel glowered at him. "Drop the subject."

Mary said, "Can you block her ability to dream?"

"Not without consequences." Gabriel turned to her. "Although it seems like one continuous unit, human brains undergo four separate stages of sleep, and the stage of dreaming sleep is necessary for—"

"I said to drop the subject!" Remiel's voice raised, and Mary jumped. "I don't care about the stages of sleep or what other cultures do to extract details from unwilling informants. This isn't your concern. Just find out what they did to us and figure out how to reverse it."

Gabriel started, then said, "I'm sorry." He stepped forward. "I didn't mean to minimize your feelings. I'll come back later and ask you to forgive me."

He vanished.

Mary stared at Remiel in shock, then looked at Raphael.

Raphael shrugged. "It still takes some getting used to when he does that."

Mary put her arms around Remiel, who had her face in her hands. "Even if there are consequences for not dreaming," Mary said, "whatever Gabriel meant by that, can't you protect her from dreams? I mean, she's not dreaming *now,* so how much worse could it be?"

Raphael shook his head. "In theory someone could wake her up whenever she started to dream, but it's part of the way the brain is wired. If she sleeps, it's going to happen, and the longer she puts it off, the sooner she'll enter dreaming sleep every time. Eventually, she'll just start to hallucinate while she's awake." He reached his hand to Remiel. "Is it that bad?"

"Worse," she whispered.

Raphael said, "I'll pray for you, but I don't think there's anything else I can do about it."

And he vanished as well.

With them both gone, Mary put her face against Remiel's shoulder. "I'm so sorry you're going through this. What can I do for you, sweetie?"

"I don't want to sleep."

Mary rocked her. It was that instinctive part-hug part-motion that came back to her from long nights with her own son. Remiel looked so young. Mary put her hand up to Remiel's soft hair. "Sweetie, I'm not going to tell you what to do, but eventually your body is going to give out."

"Not if Gabriel solves it first."

"Gabriel didn't sound like he was going to. You need rest. You're going to fall apart."

Remiel whispered, "I haven't slept for thousands of years."

"Then you're a few thousand years past your bedtime."

Remiel laughed helplessly against her shoulder.

Mary said, "That title you use for me."

"*Kecharitomene.*"

It was an awful thing, but Mary said it anyhow. "Does that mean if I order you to sleep, you'll do it?"

Remiel deflated in her arms. "Please don't."

Her smallness was frightening. This was an angel. By all accounts, a very high-ranking angel. "You're beyond the end of your rope."

"I can hang on a little bit longer." Remiel shook her head. "I'm not weak."

"I never said you were weak." Mary kissed her forehead. "But for now, you're human." She gave a squeeze. "I won't order you to sleep. But I've been human all my life, so I'm warning you, you need to be careful. The more tired you get, the more clumsy you get, and the worse your judgment is going to be. Your temper will get shorter."

Remiel said, "Is that why Gabriel was more irritating than usual?"

"You're not used to the exhaustion," Mary said, "and you're in a difficult situation where you might need to make quick decisions. So listen to me. Even if you don't sleep, and I won't order you to, please rest a bit. Try to get back some of your strength. Maybe the angel that Gabriel mentioned, Nivalis, maybe she can help out too."

Remiel murmured, "Thank you."

"I'm going to sleep, though." Mary ran a hand through Remiel's hair, so fine and yet so crisp at the ends as if God had shorn her like a sheep right before sending her to rescue that calf. "Wake me if you need anything."

By the time Mary settled herself in bed, Remiel had extinguished the lamp, and Mary hoped that meant she'd at least get a little sleep, even if it was despite herself. And she prayed for God to touch Remiel's dreams. *I don't know what's in there,* Mary prayed, *and I have no idea what an angel's interior life must be like, but clearly something's hurt her more than she ever let on.*

SIXTEEN

Michael and Saraquael answered together when Gabriel summoned him. Maybe...please, God, let this be their breakthrough. Please.

They appeared in a basement room beneath Gabriel's library, currently outfitted like a laboratory and occupied by four other Cherubim. Gabriel looked up with a smile as they flashed in, and Michael swelled with hope. That looked like a Cherub with an idea.

Gabriel rubbed his hands together. "You were quick. We may have an answer."

Michael said, "You detected something on Remiel?"

"Nothing at all," Gabriel said happily. "I also monitored her for adverse responses while I sent minuscule pulses of energy through her. It's fascinating how little I learned from that encounter."

Michael's eyes widened. "But...you have an answer anyhow?"

"Almost." Gabriel leaned back against a table and folded his arms. "Raphael says you'd prefer the short story rather than the long one, but the long story is really intriguing, and I'd love to document it in detail someday. But on the assumption that Raphael is correct about your preferences, the key is Nivalis."

Michael frowned. "She wasn't part of the strike team when the weapon went off."

"I had no idea why God would have pulled her off the grief squad in order to tend to Remiel and Zadkiel. It's not as if we've a shortage of bereaved guardians right now, although I wish we did." Gabriel ran a hand through his hair and flexed his wings. "Anyhow, when I tested Remiel, I pulsed her with energy at a much lower level than Saraquael did when he implanted the knowledge of the city's layout."

Beside Michael, Saraquael flinched. "I had no idea it would do that to her."

"But because of you, I did. That's not normal for a human," Gabriel said. "They feel lower levels of angelic contact as inspiration, or our energy makes them excited. They almost always react to strong infusions of angelic power with fear. But migraines, vertigo, and nausea are nonstandard responses." He approached Michael. "What I found is that Remiel's system is actually intolerant of angelic energy right now. I went to Zadkiel and Belior as well afterward to see if I could get similar responses from them, but they were both asleep, and in retrospect, I believe conducting tests while they're sleeping has affected my ability to gather data. The point is, though, that they're not exactly *stuck* in human form. They're using it to take refuge from their rightful angelic forms."

Michael blinked. "How so?"

"Exactly! What would do that to them? It's amazing."

This was the short story, Michael reminded himself. He'd need to thank Raphael later.

Gabriel stretched his wings. "But Nivalis's presence told me there's another mechanism at play that I hadn't accounted for, and to get the final answer, I needed you."

Michael opened his hands, projecting readiness.

"Just stand still." Gabriel's put his hands on Michael's head and stretched out all six sets of wings around him. "When you modeled the laboratory for me and explained how the weapon detonated, we all ignored the fact that you were peppered with that weapon's energy too."

Michael's head dropped. "Zadkiel took the hit for me."

"No, Zadkiel absorbed the majority of it, but it's quite certain you were hit. There!" Gabriel's eyes glimmered. "Oh, you're brilliant. Just stand still and be calm. Meditate. This won't take very long, and I don't think it should hurt at all."

That wasn't quite the reassurance Gabriel intended, but before Michael could reply, a sensation like cold crept over him. "What are you doing?"

"You're not doing what I said," Gabriel said. "Meditate for a few minutes."

Michael closed his eyes and took his focus off the cold sensation. *What is he doing?*, he prayed.

He's doing what I created him to do, replied God.

Michael focused on God's face, on Love and Creation, and he let himself get lost in contemplation. His inner sight trained entirely on God, and he started dissociating.

"Hey, stay with me," Gabriel said.

God guided Michael back toward himself. *You'll learn what he's doing in a minute. In the meantime, spend that minute with me.*

Michael fought the tension and tried not to be aware of his surroundings until finally Gabriel said, "Okay, here's our answer."

Saraquael exclaimed, "What's that?"

Michael blinked uncertainly as he brought his focus back to the room and the others. The other Cherubim had crowded around him, and he could pick up projections of amazement, gratitude, confirmation, and five flavors of questions. Saraquael tugged two of the Cherubim aside and brought Michael up in front of Gabriel.

On his palm, Gabriel had three jet-black shards. They resembled very tiny blades, elongated points on one end and blunt triangles on the other. "I pulled that out of you," Gabriel said. "Or rather, off you. It hadn't been able to penetrate into your soul, but it had been atomized and was stuck all over your person. Not quite as much as I thought it should be," he added, "but still rather impressive."

Michael shuddered. "How'd that get on me?"

"Oh, it wasn't like this to start with, or you'd have found it. This is the form the material took once it was solo and had only itself to draw in on." Gabriel tapped above it, and his finger struck an invisible Guard the size of a hazel nut. "This is keeping them stable for now. They're very fragile."

Michael gazed into the deep blackness of the shards. "What are they made of?"

Gabriel looked at them in awe. "They're made of Death."

As best as Michael could determine, (after the Cherubim had gotten very excited by the fact that this material existed in the first place, which took a while to work down to a mere tsunami of excitement) this material came from Sheol's shattered walls. Walls the angels hadn't been able to break and only human souls been able to penetrate, but which Christ had broken apart at his Resurrection.

The demons must have scoured the Void where Sheol used to stand, hunting for any stray residue the angels had missed after cleaning up mountain ranges of the stuff.

"But you said it couldn't be Sheol material," Michael said. "You specifically tested for that."

Gabriel projected agreement. "It's not Sheol material as it originally was, no. We were able to move around in Sheol's debris and for the most part suffer no ill effects. But these pieces started out as Sheol material, and Belior weaponized them."

Weaponized. "How did he do that?"

"I have no idea. It's been about two and a half minutes since I confirmed what it was." Gabriel grinned, and his grey feathers shone nearly silver. "You've got to give me a little more time than that to reverse-engineer a process he took twenty years to develop." Gabriel looked momentarily dazzled by the challenge. "But whatever Belior did do has enabled it to escape our ability to detect it. It's not quite the same, and as you recall, Sheol material never had much of a signature to begin with."

That hadn't been Michael's primary concern at the time. The problem hadn't been finding Sheol material as much as navigating within a veritable blizzard of Sheol material. Locating places without it had been more of a priority.

Gabriel looked back into the sphere on his palm. "Because we didn't know it had been changed, it didn't register when we tested for Sheol material. Moreover, it seems to me that Belior or Satrinah altered the material with the specific intention of suppressing its signature further, imparting something of a stealth mode. The target wouldn't be able to feel it coming, and after impact, the target wouldn't know how to expel it from himself."

Michael opened his hands. "And yet you got it off me."

"It wasn't embedded in you. I haven't gone back to check Remiel yet," and here Gabriel hesitated. "Well, I will soon, but not until she's ready. When I do, I'm betting I'll find it's worked its way into the fabric of all three of their souls."

Saraquael said, "Why theirs and not his?"

"That's the perfect question to ask," Gabriel said, pointing at Saraquael, "and that will be one of our next avenues of research. In the meantime, though, I have another question. There wasn't as much on you as I predicted, so where did the rest of it go?"

That didn't sound like as much of a question as a line of research, and the Cherubim must have thought as much, because suggestions began flying around the room: did it destabilize? If it wasn't fully embedded in Michael, maybe it dusted off?

Gabriel said, "Run down where you've been spending your time since then," which could easily have covered the whole of Creation. With Saraquael's help, Michael started an itinerary of places, times, and names, until Gabriel's head picked up. "Hang on. That was it."

A minute later, they stood in Hastle's cell, no support team on the outside, and no intention to interrogate.

Hastle gave Gabriel a bored side-eye. "Michael, why did you bring me a Cherub? Did you think I was missing the opportunity of working with them?"

Gabriel didn't even acknowledge Hastle. "We've got it."

Michael's heart bottomed out.

Hastle said to Michael, "I'm not going to talk to him, you know."

"Good," Gabriel said. "It's easier if you stay silent."

Saraquael moved in close to restrain Hastle, and when he had the demon pinned with his will, Gabriel extended his hands.

Hastle frowned, and then his eyes flared and he screamed. He thrashed and scissored his wings. *Michael! Michael! Don't let them do this to me, Michael! You were my friend! You betrayed me! You sold me out to God and now you're selling me out to them, and for what?*

Saraquael held him still, but the howling went on and on, and Michael didn't listen. Couldn't. Hastle was an animal. A liar. No, Hastle was just a demon, and he hadn't been interested in Michael at all. Not even a bit. He'd been mining Michael to get back little slivers of Death, one atom at a time, all the while stringing Michael along as if he wanted him in there to talk, to negotiate, to parlay, as if still cared about his former friend and everything they'd done together...

Gabriel said, "Silence," and then Hastle couldn't even speak, although he still projected. Projected hatred. Panic. Despair.

When Gabriel stepped back, he was holding four more obsidian arrowheads, and Hastle sagged in Saraquael's arms.

Saraquael released him, and Hastle dropped to the floor, hands-and-knees. His wings splayed around him, and he whined. "Please. Don't. I need that."

Gabriel said to Michael, "I'm finished here," and he flashed back to his lab.

Saraquael fixed a look on Michael. A very pointed, very intent look.

Hastle lay limp, prone.

No, don't think it. Hastle was a liar. He was a user, nothing more. Steeling himself, Michael nodded to Saraquael, and he let his lieutenant transport him out of the cell.

SEVENTEEN

Zadkiel awoke feeling warmth on her face. Sunlight? Perhaps. She stretched, and she whispered, "Remiel?"

"I'm here." Remiel's hand found hers, and Zadkiel squeezed. "We're about to serve breakfast, but Nivalis told me you were waking up."

Zadkiel accompanied Remiel to the kitchen, smelling the scent of new bread and that strange porridge thing they'd had yesterday. "Can I help with anything?"

Mary and Remiel must be exchanging looks. That would have explained their silence. And then Mary said, "Can you carry the bread out to the table?"

The house's layout was simple, and Zadkiel had spent time counting steps and tracing the walls whenever she'd walked from room to room. She tilted her head to gauge the different sounds, and talking voices came from where she figured the men were eating. "I can try."

"Here." Mary helped her get a basket into her hands, heavy with bread. "Remiel, accompany her so we can test how she navigates."

Remiel put a hand on her arm, and Zadkiel said, "Let me try this alone. Just stay by my side." She listened and pivoted by small degrees until it sounded as if she were facing the conversation, then took a step forward. When Remiel didn't correct her, she took another step, then walked with a little more confidence toward the source of the noise. At some point, Remiel touched her arm and she stopped in place. Remiel helped her find the table surface and then settled the basket on top of it.

"Stay with me," Zadkiel said, and she turned to retrace her steps. This direction was harder because Mary wasn't making nearly enough noise in the kitchen (nor really any) to guide her, but she'd counted her steps on the way in and knew approximately how far it ought to be.

A hand grabbed her elbow, and before Zadkiel could protest, she realized it wasn't Remiel's. "Beloved, please," said John's voice, "you have no need to wait at table."

Startled, Zadkiel said, "Jesus served."

"Your desire to do likewise shows your devotion," he said while guiding her in a different direction than the kitchen; she guessed it was back toward the front room, but she'd lost her orientation. "Please consider yourself my guest."

He guided her to sit on a low couch, and he brought the net-making rope to her.

Zadkiel said, "You're letting Remaya wait at table."

But John didn't answer, and Zadkiel fingered the net shuttle. She worked her hands around the rope until she found the last knot, and then she started making more. The only good thing about being blind was that the tears in her eyes didn't blur out the world. She could work with her eyes shut and no one would notice. Assuming they even would have.

Empty spaces. That's all a net was, really: just a bunch of empty spaces demarked by something solid and flexible. Kind of like her own pointless existence: God had made her and you could tell where she was in the world by the empty space she made.

"Hey," said a voice, tentative. It rang more in her head than in her ears, giving her a not-unpleasant feeling like drinking a little too much wine in too short a time. "It's okay."

Zadkiel swiveled her head. "Nivalis?"

"The same." Joy prickled behind the words, and Zadkiel felt a smile come unbidden her face. "You looked so upset."

"Wouldn't you be?" Zadkiel turned her face back toward her lap. "I want to do my part, but I'm too slow and too awkward."

Warmth settled over her, as if Nivalis were hugging her. "John wasn't criticizing you. He didn't want to see you struggling when you didn't have to."

Zadkiel's fingers crept to the next loop, then repeated the wrapping, twisting, pushing motion until she had another firm knot under her fingertips. Another empty space. She tugged and went on to the next. "You're here, and you don't have to be. You could be reclining on a couch in Heaven, meditating on the song of the Seraphim."

Nivalis sounded unphased. "Your situation is temporary. You'll be at work again as soon as you're able."

"Or before," said Remiel's voice. "Here, John wanted me to make sure you had something to eat. Beloved."

Zadkiel put down the net and felt Remiel put the warm loaf in her hands. Remiel said, "There's a bowl of olive oil for you to dunk it in, too."

"I'm just going to have the bread, if you don't mind. Mary makes this so well."

"She's had a lifetime of experience," Remiel said. "I think that counts for something."

They shared the loaf. Zadkiel said, "Nivalis, are you hungry?"

Nivalis laughed. "No, thanks."

"You're missing out."

"No doubt." Again the warmth passed over her, and Zadkiel turned her face toward it, as if toward the sun. "Saraquael wanted me to let him know when you awakened. Should I do that now?"

Zadkiel shrugged. "What did he want?"

"Gabriel figured out what the weapon was while you were sleeping."

Zadkiel straightened. "We can go home?"

Remiel said, "Nope. He figured out what it was. He didn't figure out how to reverse it."

"Yet," added Nivalis.

"I got examined and probed a lot during the wee hours because I'm an easy target, and I got a heartfelt apology from him for my own misbehavior, but now it's your turn to be his experiment." Remiel snickered. "He's going to examine Belior too, and I want to be there for that."

Zadkiel groped for Remiel's hand. "Did you get any sleep at all?"

"I'm not going to. You don't need to keep asking."

She ruined the effect by yawning. Zadkiel said, "I can tell."

"I'm fine." Remiel sounded miffed. "Everyone keeps saying I'm cute. Am I cute?"

"How would I know?" Zadkiel sighed. "Sure, we might as well call Saraquael now."

The world felt emptier suddenly, as if Nivalis had flashed away. A moment later she returned, projecting success.

Remiel handed Zadkiel the rest of the bread. "Here, you finish. I'm going to help Mary clean before morning prayer."

Zadkiel said, "Will you let me help?"

"I'm not sure you can." Remiel yawned again. "Mary was up most of the night, though, and I'll let the other women know so they can convince her to rest today."

Zadkiel made a mental note that while sleep was optional for Remiel, apparently it wasn't for everyone else. She didn't think Remiel would appreciate that observation, though, so instead she made another knot in the net.

Three knots later she felt Saraquael's presence as he projected a greeting. She projected a greeting back at him, then realized she couldn't do that in human form. Instead she whispered, "Hi," feeling her cheeks grow hot with embarrassment. Stuck. Blind. Utterly useless.

A momentary vertigo washed over her as she felt that Gabriel was with him too, and Gabriel wanted to conduct a couple of tests on her (she felt it as "challenges,") so she should just relax and keep working.

As she registered this, the vertigo intensified, then withdrew. It pulsed like this periodically, so Zadkiel avoided thinking about it and just stayed seated, eyes closed because that made the most sense under the circumstances. With nothing else to hold her attention, she kept making knots. Wrap the rope. Wrap the shuttle. Pass it through. Wrap again. Tug. Wrap. She concentrated on her hands, and then when she ran out of loops, she turned it around and started going back.

The vertigo intensified through one of its regular pulses and then kept going, stronger, longer, and Zadkiel clutched the shuttle. She couldn't finish the knot, couldn't even remember where she was in the process. She didn't move, her body numb and distant, the sounds around her a muffled whine, and then she felt Saraquael urging Gabriel to stop.

It took a few minutes for feeling to return to her fingertips and her lips. When finally she could detect herself breathing again, she leaned on her knees and gasped until her ribs hurt. Her hands stung like needles pushing through the skin, and her muscles ached as if she'd climbed a mountain.

"What did you do to her?" Remiel was asking. When had Remiel come back? But there she was, kneeling in front of Zadkiel, arms wrapped around her waist. "I left her alone with you for five minutes! Aren't you the ones saying we can't chance what happens if these bodies die? Well maybe then the thing to do is *not to kill her* for crying out loud!"

Zadkiel leaned into her. "Are you okay?" Remiel said, pressing Zadkiel's head to her shoulder. "What do you need me to do for you? And if you suggest I give these two a good thrashing, trust me, I'll give it a try."

Remiel smelled like olive oil and flour, and Zadkiel breathed it in. This was earthy. This was home. Everything about Remiel was solid and true, and she could lean on her.

I never wanted it to be like this, she prayed. *I should be able to do this on my own. I shouldn't have to be depending on her all the time for everything, but it's like I'm her child and I can't do anything to help myself. I can't bring bread to the table, and I can't mind the children, and I can't do anything other than make nets they can sell to maybe cover the cost of feeding me while I'm here. I'm sorry. I'm so sorry. You made me to be better than this.*

The despair felt overwhelming. She reached for the taste of wine, and it steadied her.

"I'm not going to try that again," said a voice Zadkiel recognized as Gabriel's tenor.

"No, you're not going to try that again because I'll have fifty thousand Virtues standing between you and her before you get a chance!"

"I'm not going to try again," Gabriel said, "because something's blocking me from being able to extract the shrapnel from her heart, and any method of extraction won't make any difference until we clear the blockage."

Zadkiel rasped, "What's the blockage?"

"I can't determine," Gabriel said.

"Are you okay?" That was Saraquael, and he was very close to her. "I didn't think it was going to affect you that way. The stuff slid right off of Michael without any problem. In fact, that demon had been drawing it off him without him even noticing, so I figured it would work on you about the same way. You should have said it was hurting."

"I didn't realize it wasn't supposed to." Zadkiel tried to sit up, but her head still rang from the vertigo.

Gabriel said, "Anything affecting you that much isn't something I intended to accomplish. Feel free to ask me to stop or slow down if you're uncomfortable. I know," he added sharply. "You don't want me to try it again. I've already said I won't."

"You'd better not." Remiel sounded unamused. "Okay, so since you're here, talk. What's going on?"

While Zadkiel got back her bearings, Gabriel talked about Sheol material and weaponization, about death and about some strange kind of stickiness. "I've interviewed all the Cherubim who worked with me to clear the field of Sheol debris, and we're analyzing the material we drew off Michael. Any material the demons had in their lab is gone, but we're searching for more. We're also mining for any other Sheol raw material still in existence."

Zadkiel frowned. "There was a planet-weight of that stuff. What happened to it?"

Saraquael said, "That's exactly what I asked. Apparently they transformed it into the building blocks of the Heavenly Jerusalem."

Remiel said, "And you didn't even keep a small sample of it for memory's sake in a museum case in your library?"

"It's Death," Gabriel said. "It's not something that should have existed in the first place, so we changed it all. It's remarkably plastic," he added, a little more energetic than before. "I'm not surprised Belior and Satrinah were able to weaponize it."

"Oh, about Satrinah," Remiel said. "She approached us last night. She demanded entrance to the house so she could examine Belior and potentially free him."

"Oh, now that's intriguing. I'd love to see her notes." Gabriel sounded thoughtful. "Did she sound confident she could do it?"

Saraquael said, "She didn't actually gain entry to the house, did she?"

"Mary refused her flatly. Satrinah got all stroppy about that and threatened us and everyone we love. Then she tried to at least have us bring Belior into entrance so she could see him from the courtyard, but Mary walked inside and stripped her off."

Gabriel said, "Satrinah wouldn't be able to reach through the entrance, so she just wants to examine him. That means she's no further toward a solution than we are."

Remiel huffed. "It's not a race. She wouldn't fix us even if she did know how. In fact, she recognized me. She wanted to examine me too."

Gabriel said, "I wonder if we should give her a chance."

"What?"

Zadkiel trembled. "A chance to do what? Examine us? Enter the house?"

Saraquael said, "No. A thousand times, no. We do not grant her access to any of them."

"But we might bring Belior to the entrance and let her look him over while I observe her actions. I suggest we have him talk to her. He must be dying to compare notes."

"Dying isn't the right word." Saraquael had gotten a sterner tone. "He's *homicidal* to compare notes with her so he can eviscerate the body he's in and get free again. He killed his first host already, and I'm not interested in taking that kind of chance with the second."

Zadkiel offered, "I know nothing about that magician other than the rumors people carried to us, but given that Belior went into him so easily and that the magician doesn't seem to be fighting for control, his soul might be in jeopardy if he were to die now."

Remiel said, "That's a given."

"Not always," Gabriel said, "but I agree that with what we know, it would be risky to the magician's soul to let him die in this state." He paused. "I wonder if human minds retain any awareness while possessed."

"I wonder if we can stay on the subject," Remiel said. "Zadkiel and I are stuck in human form."

"The more correct phrasing," Gabriel said, "is that you're avoiding angelic form, and yes, it's an important distinction because the object of the research in light of this discovery isn't to get you to shed your human bodies. It's to get your souls to accept your angelic forms the way they ought to."

Zadkiel tightened her fingers on the net shuttle. "We're actively resisting angelic form?"

"I can't figure out why, but yes." Gabriel's form must have touched hers because she felt a bit warm, and she called the flavor of wine into her memory ground her senses. "The closest metaphor I can come up with is an auto-immune response, or an allergic reaction. When your souls in their current state interact with angelic energy, they automatically resist it. That's why you can't access your subtle bodies and why we can't implant information or transport you without passing through the intervening space. This reaction is extreme and total. Again, I don't know why. Your souls therefore had to take refuge in a material form because the material form mitigates the effect of whatever reaction is taking place."

Zadkiel trembled. "Wait, is this a progressive reaction? Does it increase over time?"

Gabriel didn't even hesitate: "I haven't determined that yet."

Zadkiel went cold.

"We could end up stuck in statues," Remiel said, her voice pitching upward, "and you're worried about how much awareness a possessed human soul retains?"

Saraquael said, "Remiel, stand down."

"We need to stay focused!"

"He's working on it," Saraquael said. "He's tackling every aspect of the problem, and he's made progress."

"Here," Gabriel said. "Look."

Silence for a minute. Zadkiel said, "What am I supposed to be looking at?"

Saraquael chuckled. "The shrapnel he drew off Michael pulled itself into a group of little metal triangles."

"They're cute!" Remiel said, and Zadkiel burst out laughing.

"Like you?"

"Far cuter." Remiel actually sounded amused. "They're all lined up pointing in the same direction, like a school of fish."

"To be exact," Gabriel said, "when I hold them near Zadkiel, they're pointed at her. And when I bring them near Remiel..."

"Oh! They swivel," Remiel said. "They're pointing at me, Zadkiel. Like a compass magnet."

"Exactly. And that's telling me something. Sheol material had a natural attraction to itself." Gabriel's voice had taken on that fascinated tone again, as if he couldn't possibly have thought of anything better to do than puzzle out an unsolvable mystery. But for the moment, Zadkiel found his wonder comforting. He'd work on it until solved not because he needed to save them, or rather not *only* because he needed to save them, but also because for him it felt good to be solving a problem. Every little discovery was a victory that fueled him enough to reach the next one. Cyphering was his taste of wine.

"The fact that the shrapnel orients toward the two of you when it's near serves as confirmation that there's additional material embedded within you. I attempted to use this material to draw out the shrapnel in Zadkiel, but it didn't work, which leads me to believe there's more of it embedded in her than there is within this Guard. That's why we need to either obtain more of the raw material or else we need to draw the substance out of Belior in order to have a greater mass outside than inside."

"Can't you go grab a brick out of the New Jerusalem?" Remiel said. "Transform it back?"

"I can't," Gabriel said, "but I've got a team working on it."

Remiel said, "Fair enough. Have you tried extracting it from Belior?"

"I'll do that next, as much as I would rather not deal with him." Gabriel sighed. "But bear in mind that it came off Michael with no concentration on the outside. That leads me to believe there's another undetermined mechanism keeping it bound to you, other than just magnetic attraction.

EIGHTEEN

Michael put a hand on Hastle's cell wall with no energy in his heart, and his wings sagged.

Danel leaned against him, his presence warm and comforting. He was again wearing blue, and Michael kept his eyes closed. *I know*, Danel was projecting. *I know. It's difficult.*

He didn't want to go back in there. Knowing…no, it wasn't Hastiel anymore. It never had been Hastiel. It was just Hastle now.

The interrogation team stood at the ready, and Michael longed to send them away. They hadn't figured out Hastle's multilayered deceptions any more than he had. They'd been sending Michael directions through the wall, but they hadn't realized any more than he had that Hastle hadn't wanted anything more than Michael's presence. Hastle had intended to keep the interviews going as long as he needed to get all his weaponized material back, and the team had played along with it, but who took the blow? Not them. They were on the outside.

The Principality said, "You shouldn't have gone in there before without us."

Michael's head snapped up. "This is my detainee and my operation. I'll make decisions as to strategy and the advisory committees I require."

The Angel straightened even as Danel put a hand on Michael's arm. Michael continued, "He's been asking for me, and I'll head back in now with your guidance, but I'm the one who determines whether your team is called in. Thank you."

The Principality said nothing else. The Angel said, "I understand what you're feeling, and I hear your frustration. We appreciate remaining involved, and we'll try to lower his resistance level to make him more cooperative for you."

Michael wanted to fire back that he understood de-escalative language as much as she did, but instead he turned to Danel. His friend watched with a haze over his eyes: praying while being supportive. Danel touched a wing to Michael and said, "I'll be right here."

Michael braced himself and flashed into the chamber.

Hastle had destroyed everything. Now, finally now, he'd acted like the demon he was and torched the entire interior. The decor he'd so condescendingly judged before was in ashes, and smoke filled the windowless chamber because it couldn't leave. Between the darkness and the smoke, Michael could sense Hastle in the corner but couldn't see him.

He gathered the smoke off to the sides but didn't light the room. There was nothing to see anyhow, other than the destruction wrought by flame.

Michael backed against the wall. It was gritty.

He imagined feeling Danel's palm pressed against the wall on the other side. An ally. Comfort. Someone who wasn't pressuring him to do anything.

The interrogation team listened in his mind, but so far they'd given no advice. Good. Let them ponder for a while. Maybe he'd even take some of their advice when they dared to offer any.

Michael kept his voice low. "They told me you asked for me."

Gabriel himself wouldn't have been able to make that great an under-statement. Hastle hadn't *asked* for him. No, Hastle had battered the Guards and torched the room and screamed for him. He'd opened a sinkhole beneath the foundation and shattered the windows on nearby buildings. He'd rained lightning strikes over the land around him, and when he'd finally spent himself inside these unbroken walls, he'd begged for anyone to come in, anyone at all.

The interrogation team had then located Michael kneeling in the Sanctuary, at the back clothed in white just as the Sanctuary angels were at the front. He'd been absorbed so fully in God that he hadn't been aware of their presence until the Liturgy of the Hour had ended and he was trying to decide whether to stay for a fourth one. He'd been angered by their presence at first—just a flash of anger, but there nevertheless—and that flash was just enough for Danel to come to him. The interrogators had asked for his help, and when he'd accompanied them to the holding cells, Danel had followed.

The buildings were reinforced to hold Guards, but Hastle had cracked the stone. The angels would need to research stronger structures. Or maybe desperation could do that to a demon.

So with Danel at his back and his advisors quiet in his mind, Michael waited for Hastle to speak, and Hastle didn't make him wait. "You don't know what you did." Hastle sounded broken, and he pushed to his feet in the far corner. He wobbled, as if he'd expended all his strength and had nothing left. "I needed that. That was mine. I wasn't doing Belior's work. It was my work, and you took it all, and I need it back."

Whether or not this was an act, Hastle wanted him to feel pity, so Michael decided not to feel it. "Tell me what you want to do with it."

"I need to save myself." Hastle's voice cracked. "You don't understand what it's like. I needed it. I saw the opportunity, and I took it because that's what it was going to get for me. I don't care what Belior does. I don't care if they're in charge of the army or if Asmodeus is Satan's advisor. Satrinah never hurt me, but I don't care about her either. Give her a lab and she does her own stuff and I don't care. But when they recruited me, I realized immediately what I could do, and I wanted to make sure I got in on it."

Behind him, Danel's presence would be warm against the outer wall. It wasn't going to penetrate the Guard, but Michael didn't need it to. He didn't even need Danel in his head because he knew Danel was holding Michael in his prayers. It was good, and Michael steadied himself. This wasn't Hastiel. Their friend was flushed into time.

"You're not making sense." Michael steeled himself. "I need you to speak clearly if I'm going to understand what you're talking about. I have two angels in need of the answers you're not giving me, and you seem to need the shards we took out of you."

My shards. Michael shivered. *They were shards you took out of me first.*

Hastle sagged against the wall. "I was Belior's collector. Belior and Asmodeus prepped me to harvest the bits of Sheol they were going to use to make their weapon, and I made sure I was the best at it. It's boring work and stupid, to be honest, so none of the other demons ever got good at it. I made myself the best one. It takes a while, which is why Belior couldn't do it himself. He'd be missed. Asmodeus couldn't do it because he's a Seraph and they're too impatient. Satrinah couldn't do it because her presence in these odd places would have called Satan's attention to what they were trying."

Hastle couldn't see him, so Michael projected the prompt: *Go on.*

Hastle slid to the ground, making crumbling sounds as if he'd left a trail of soot in his wake. "They'd send me out into the Void, just to the edge where Sheol used to be. If I combed the outer layer of Hell, I could locate those little bits. I learned to call them, and they'd gather. It took weeks at a time to get just a pinpoint. But then I'd bring the fragments back, and Asmodeus would berate me for not locating more. So I'd venture out again and find another batch."

Michael brought up a low light in the room and squatted so he was closer to eye-level with Hastle. "You've been doing this for years."

"Years." Hastle projected emphasis. "Right after the Word destroyed Sheol, almost, Belior wanted whatever leftovers your guys had missed. Your Cherubim were thorough. I cursed them for combing it all out like that, but I was able to find some, and once I caught on to where the pieces usually got missed, I became the best harvester." He trembled, and his distress went through the air.

Michael pressed back against the wall toward Danel's unreachable presence.

"It was so quiet. Michael, you have no idea." Hastle looked up, eyes liquid. "No other demons. No one. I couldn't feel them. They were on the other side of everything, and I was alone, and I could work without thinking, work and just hunt for this stuff, and I didn't have to deal with them."

Was he crying? Did it matter if he was? Michael said, "Go on."

"I want that." Hastle swallowed hard. "That's what I want."

"You had it," Michael said.

"Not forever. I had to keep going back. Sometimes they'd flash out and harass me, right on the edge of nothing. They'd seize what I'd already found and tell me to find more because it wasn't enough. It's never enough. You know that, and they know it."

Michael's head lowered. *God, this is awful. Strengthen me.*

Hastle waited a long time.

Michael said, "But being so good at collecting it, you started collecting it off me once you realized I'd been sprayed."

"I need it," Hastle said. "I wasn't going to use it on you."

That would have been a lovely turn of events, wouldn't it? Bring the demon who held the angel-crippling weapon right into the heart of Heaven and then give him unfettered access to the head of Heaven's army and one of the Seven Archangels of the Presence. This was a brilliant idea Michael had come up with. Saraquael had been right to scold him. He'd only been wrong in not scolding more.

Michael said, "Then what were you going to use it for?"

Hastle didn't reply.

Michael said, "You want something. You've been straightforward about that all along, that the only person whose agenda you care to advance is your own."

Hastle still said nothing.

"You wanted me to come back here. I'm sure by now you've verified that there's no more on me, and that's fine." Michael drummed his fingers against his arm. "So let's just get on with it: what do you want?"

Hastle shifted in his huddle against the burnt wall. Probably Hastle was also shifting around in his head: playing various scenarios against one another, trying to work out which way he could manipulate the situation in order to get something he wanted, or at least get within striking distance of it. Michael had dealt with that mentality all too often in his vocation, and he'd accepted it always as the price of doing business for God. Dealing with God's enemies, you had to deal with creatures that wanted what they wanted and not what pleased God, helped anyone else, or forwarded communal goals. No, for Hastle it would be Hastle on the throne of his intentions, and no one would unseat him.

But at the same time, they might be able to get facts. Gabriel had a list of things a wingspan long that he wanted more information on. If Hastle was that good at gathering this substance, could they convince him to share those techniques? What had he done to keep it stable during transport? What had Belior done to weaponize it?

Michael's list of questions was nowhere near as long. He wanted to know Hastle's long-term goal, because that would tell him what Hastle wanted in the short-term, and knowing those would give him options for leverage. Secondarily, he wanted to know Belior's goals, or rather what his goals had been. (Right now his goal was escape, for which Michael couldn't blame him really, considering the intel he had about the state of that magician's soul).

Hastle picked up his head. "Why are you still here? What do you want from me?"

It was an opening. But before Michael answered, he felt the Principality suggest he ask about Belior, since that was not something Hastle felt sensitive about. It made sense to go for the less emotionally-charged material first, so Michael said, "I want to know what Belior wanted that weapon to do."

Hastle's wings crossed over his body. "Would you be surprised to learn it didn't do it?"

Michael said, "Not really. It wasn't mature." Gabriel had used that term, as though Sheol material were a fetal animal that needed to grow hair and bones before birthing itself into the world. "But the reaction your weapon had on my officers and with Belior isn't giving us much of a hint as to what it was supposed to do."

Hastle sounded surprised. "You found Belior?" And then disappointment. "It figures."

Michael said, "Did you think we wouldn't find him because Asmodeus would find him first and carry him away?"

Hastle said, "It doesn't matter now." He sounded defeated in a way Michael didn't understand but which made him press back against the wall where he knew Danel waited.

He's manipulating you, sent the Angel.

"Since it doesn't matter," Michael said, "there's no harm in telling me. What was the weapon supposed to do?"

Hastle's voice emerged softly from beneath his wing. "It would disappear its target. It would incapacitate and then it would hide the target. You shouldn't have been able to find any of them, and then…"

He cut himself off. "But it didn't work. You said it was *immature*? That sounds like something a Cherub would say. *Oh, the poor little weapon, needing its mommy's milk a little longer.*" He snorted. "It was a pipe dream."

Michael didn't wait for a prompt. "But the incapacitating part: how?"

"Paralysis," said Hastle. "I'm not sure if the victim would still be able to think. The three of them kept all their little conferences to themselves, but I overheard enough to know it would end up with the victim stuck and motionless, and the secondary effect would be to wrap around them and make them disappear."

Gabriel had said that about Sheol material back when it had detonated: that you could hide something inside it and it wouldn't be detectable. That was why they'd gathered all of it up (well, thought they'd gathered all of it up). Gabriel had said it almost as an afterthought back then, but Belior must have seized on the same thought with jaws like a pit bull.

Paralysis, though. That must be the effect of the weaponization. And that might be what was keeping Remiel and Zadkiel pinned in human forms, actively resisting angelic energy.

Michael said, "How long would the effect last?"

"Ideally? Forever. They were playing a long game." Hastle sighed. "God's playing a long game, too. He knew this was going on. He never stopped me on my little harvesting trips. He never made it so Belior got caught."

"Of course he did." Michael chuckled. "We're here having this conversation, aren't we? Who was the intended target of the weapon?"

Hastle projected a shrug. "I figured it was you, but they didn't share that information with their little peons, only frustration that they didn't have more of the stuff to work with. Because it's my fault

Sheol didn't have bigger walls or that you didn't miss more in your cleanup."

Michael drew his wings around himself and reminded himself this wasn't Hastiel. The demon was cooperative for the moment, but it was just manipulation. The triage team should have reminded him of that, so he did it himself: this wasn't Hastiel. Hastiel was gone.

Michael said, "Belior and Asmodeus didn't treat you well, but you were with them for your own reasons. What did you want to accomplish?"

Hastle shook his head. "It's not going to work. Go away." He wrapped his wings tighter around himself and suppressed his signature until Michael couldn't feel him anymore. "It's useless. Just go."

The Principality urged him to stay and ask more about Hastle's goal. Michael thought of Danel at his back, and instead he left.

NINETEEN

As Remiel worked in the kitchen, her thoughts still jangled from what Gabriel had learned, she tensed at the sound of footsteps.

So many people shared this house that one more person moving about shouldn't have surprised her, but the hair stood up on her neck, and she didn't know why. Her mind flew through the house: Mary was resting in her room; Zadkiel was in the front with the girls and her net-making equipment.

Remiel went to the doorway and found herself facing Belior.

Remiel shouted an alarm, but Belior looked just as startled to see her. He jumped backward and then ran toward the front room.

"Zadkiel!" Remiel called. "Watch out!"

Oh, dumb—now he knew who they were. She raced after him, hanging onto the kitchen knife in case she needed to defend Zadkiel or the girls.

Belior ran past the other women and into the courtyard—and then stopped in place as a demonic fire erupted before him.

"What do you think you're doing? Get back in there!"

Remiel wouldn't have been more surprised if...actually, Remiel couldn't have been more surprised. Because that was Satrinah, no doubt about it, and she blasted Belior right out of the courtyard and back into the front room.

He crash-landed with a cry, tucked tight, arm to his ribs. Battling vertigo from the demonic energy, Remiel stumbled to the entrance. "What are you doing?"

"He's to stay in the house! He knows that." Satrinah brandished a sword engulfed in flame, leaving Remiel terribly conscious of how small and dull was the knife in her own. "His only job is to get out of that body, and he's not going to accomplish that if he leaves."

Remiel exclaimed, "He's not going to accomplish it if he stays, either." She tucked the knife into her belt and crouched beside Belior. His hands were swollen, and one dangled at a bad angle. He must have broken his own wrists to untie himself. She touched his flank, but he shoved her away, so she left him on the floor. "What's your deal? I thought you wanted him in the courtyard so you could examine him."

"You're so ignorant. Listen to what people actually say rather than what you assume." Satrinah called her sword back into her soul and put her hands on her hips. "I said I wanted him *there*, in the entrance. I'll position myself in the courtyard and examine him from *here*. That keeps your little hide-bound rule-following self happy, and it gets me what I want."

Remiel said, "Well, I'm about to drag his should-be-bound, should-have-been-following-the-rules self all the way back into the recesses of the house, so say goodbye to your buddy."

Satrinah straightened her wings. "Look, I find it repulsive dealing with you too. It's like looking at what Camael would have been if he'd enslaved his intellect and whored out his will to the Creator. But I'm willing to do it if I must."

Remiel's eyes narrowed. "You're so generous. Will it break your heart when I refuse?"

"You're trapped too," said Satrinah. "Don't you slaves pride yourselves on your compassion?"

A sudden lurch of her stomach informed Remiel that Michael had arrived. He planted himself between her and Satrinah, and next she felt Saraquael's presence.

Satrinah's eyes glimmered. "Oh, lovely, your superiors have arrived. They'll have authority to parlay."

Michael glanced at Remiel. "Are you all right?"

"I'm fine. Our guest tried to escape, and now he has a broken wrist and I think a couple of broken ribs."

"Not nice," Saraquael murmured, moving toward Belior. "There's a human involved here too."

Remiel's eyes flared. "I didn't do that!"

Satrinah tilted her head forward. "If you're done coddling him, I have a perfectly reasonable request."

"Of course you do." Michael didn't have his sword drawn, but as someone who'd served under him since the Winnowing, Remiel could tell he was on high alert. "After experimenting for decades with weaponized Sheol material, and getting one of your own caught in the backlash, you're a paragon diplomat."

Satrinah's eyes widened. "Oh, so Gabriel deciphered it for you? That's a relief. It saves me the rigors of using small words to explain a concept I figured well beyond your ability to understand."

With a tight smile, Michael said, "We're all consideration. You can leave now."

Satrinah sighed. "You let Gabriel study him. I can feel Gabriel's power all over him. What are you doing?"

Remiel turned to see Saraquael bent over Belior, who was squirming to get away. "I'm patching him up. We don't actually want him to die."

"I don't either. But I need him to stay put, and a couple of broken ribs seemed like the most efficient way to keep him in place. A compound femoral fracture is too likely to get infected." She drummed her fingers against her leg. "If you keep doing that, he's going to be able to leave."

Saraquael was whispering, "Stay still. You're still going to have bruised ribs, but I can fix the fractures at least."

"Get his wrist too," Remiel called. "We're going to want to tie him up again, and that'll hurt."

"Listen, you barbarians, he's not going to leave the house. You don't have to restrain him." Satrinah sniffed, and she moved closer to Michael. "I thought your pet humans had authority over our kind. Why hasn't John cast him out yet instead of displaying him like a trophy?"

Michael said, "Tell me why John hasn't cast him out. You're the genius."

Satrinah shivered with tension. "I could make another weapon and destroy you."

Michael shook his head. "You don't have the raw materials to do that. I've had scouts checking out the field where the Sheol material was, and they're not coming up with anything."

"They wouldn't. I counted it, molecule by molecule as it came to us." She tossed her head. "Even with the most careful handling, bits would disappear without any explanation. The way your goons tromp all over the place," (and here she pointedly glared at Remiel) "you'd never gather any of it. Not the way we can."

"You can stop with the threats." Remiel met that look and raised the bet. "Here's the situation as I see it: you messed around creating a weapon you didn't really understand, and then it backfired and trapped your buddy, so you brought him here to his enemies so we could help you out."

Satrinah flared with indignation, but Remiel went on. "You had him make enough of a racket so the disciples in the city would bring him into John's house and John would allow him in. And now that he's inside, you've got the gall to use John's Christian community as a safe house for a demon in order to keep your boss from finding out one of his top guys has humiliated the whole team by getting trapped in a human body."

Michael exclaimed, "Oh, you're right, that would probably be really bad for him, if Satan were to find out."

Remiel said, "But because John sealed this house to keep demons *out,* Satan can't get *in,* and your boss can't detect where Belior is. You need us. And I think it's hilarious."

Belior got to his feet and stalked toward Michael, but Remiel got between them. "Sorry, bud. You can't go out and play with your friend."

Satrinah was vibrating with anger. Remiel said, "We're not wrong on this. You need us. We don't need you."

Michael said, "If, on the other hand, you'd like to talk to us about what your weapon's done to these three, I'm willing to listen."

Satrinah clenched her teeth. "You have nothing to offer me."

Remiel laughed out loud. "Weren't you listening? Michael just said it would be a crying shame if your boss found out where Belior is."

Michael, to his credit, fought back the shock that flashed across his face. No, of course he wouldn't have planned on blackmailing Satrinah. But in the same position, Satrinah would already have been planning an extortion and disinformation campaign, so she backed away a step. "What do you want from me?"

Saraquael's voice was mild. "You came to us. Would I be correct in that?"

"I'm here for Belior."

"And so am I."

The new voice, the deeper voice, sent chills up Remiel's spine, and she retreated a step from the doorway.

Michael glanced at Asmodeus. "I was wondering when you'd show up."

Asmodeus smoldered, and Satrinah focused on him until the flames around his head lowered a bit and she'd brightened. At her side, Belior clenched his fists, and his eyes were riveted to Satrinah.

Asmodeus glared right past them at his other Cherub. "Are you hurt?"

Belior focused on him but didn't even try to speak. Asmodeus said to Michael, "Your people are treating him worse than an animal."

"I'm not getting into a discussion of his treatment with you. Anything he's suffered has been at his own hands." Michael folded his arms. "Satrinah, you can go. You're not getting a chance to examine him. Asmodeus, you can go. If Satan wants to figure out where he is, then your presence here is just as good as a beacon. And if I were to clash with you," Michael said, lowering his voice, "Satan would be sure to come, wouldn't he? And he'd want to know what exactly was going on. You don't expect me to lie for you, do you?"

Asmodeus glared at Satrinah, and although Remiel couldn't see any outward sign that they were communicating, she could make a pretty good guess at it because he erupted in flames. Next he turned on Belior, but when Belior didn't back down, he turned to Michael. "You can carry a message back to those two prisoners who gave in to your torture: I will not forget that they broke loyalty to me and told you what they know."

For the first time, Michael sounded a little uncertain. "Actually, Gabriel was the one who decoded your work. I'll give him your regards."

"Gabriel didn't figure this out. Hastle can look forward to a long, long reckoning." Asmodeus whirled on Satrinah. "I told you I'd examined him myself and found no clues. I don't want you getting caught because you'll lead Satan straight to him, and he'll wonder how you got here in the first place. Is that clear?" Asmodeus turned to Belior. "And you—even if they free your mouth, keep silence. For your own good. Stay in this house. No matter what, you stay in this house."

He vanished, taking Satrinah with him.

Saraquael said, "He really has a certain charisma, doesn't he?" He turned to Belior. "I think I got the bones back together, but wrists are tricky, and I'm not Raphael. Let your host know I did my best to make sure he can still use his hand after he's freed."

Although Remiel wouldn't have bet he could do it, Belior managed to make himself look even more hateful toward Saraquael.

Belior then stepped toward Remiel, but it wasn't in a threatening way. It was the first time since they'd met in Ephesus that Remiel had seen him with a Cherub's natural curiosity. He recognized her now after that standoff with Satrinah, and he was putting together the pieces of their interactions, the fact that this slave girl had been Remiel all along, the fact that she'd been using a title for Mary, and maybe comparing her to her brother. Did he interact with Camael? Did she sicken him too because of how similar she was to him?

But instead of looking sick at how closely she resembled her brother, he seemed fascinated by her. Then he turned toward Zadkiel where she was in the corner with the girls, standing tall and not giving any indication of her blindness other than a hand on one girl's shoulder—and that could have been a protective gesture. He couldn't speak, but Remiel could see him working up an explanation for their presence.

Michael said to him, "We're not going to leave you stuck like this. If we can work out a way to help them, then we'll restore you as well."

Belior kept staring at Zadkiel. Maybe he was imagining those dark fragments working through her blood stream, pinning her into a body that wasn't rightfully hers. Maybe he wanted to figure out if they'd possessed a potential saint the same way he'd possessed a magician. Maybe he was just considering how good it would be to slit her throat and find out what happens to an angel who can't be an angel when you kill its borrowed body. In the name of research, of course. Remiel could never forget that: he hated them, and even if it benefitted him not to bring them harm, he couldn't be counted on not to do it anyway.

Remiel got between them. "Come on." She touched him only to have him sidle away. "You need to be back in that room."

Belior followed, but he didn't at all hide the way he stared at her.

Also not hidden: the way Saraquael high-fived Michael. Now what could that mean?

TWENTY

Michael watched Saraquael at work and wondered again how Dominions pulled off whatever it was they did when they searched out something. He wasn't complaining: if Zadkiel could find a snowflake out of place and trace it to an underground lair where Belior was designing a doomsday weapon, that was fine by him. The Dominions loved doing it, the most expert at it calling themselves Seekers, but right now Saraquael was foundering because whatever he was searching for, he wasn't entirely sure what it was.

They'd gone from John's house directly to here, the ice fields of Hell (well, they'd had to sneak in, but as directly as possible) because of what Asmodeus had let slip: his team had an entrance of their own into Creation. The highest probability was that they'd had an entrance in their secret lab, so to there they went. From the ice fields, Michael and Saraquael had descended into the cavern that used to be Belior's lab, now abandoned and cleaned out of all the equipment. In the past day or so, Asmodeus must have blown off the cavern's ceiling and allowed it to fill with snow.

There was nothing left to find, and yet Saraquael had insisted. "I want to know what they're hiding. And at any rate, if they can create a secret entrance, I want one of our own."

Michael had laughed, but the greater point stood: the demons might still have some of the raw material stashed, and if they'd constructed a secret network of passages between Creation and Hell, he wanted to search it.

Better still, he wanted to use it.

It always gave him a warm glow to consider that although Satan had taken down a third of the angels out of disobedience to God, he demanded those same angels' obedience to himself. Generally he got it, but sometimes, as with Hastle, they obeyed only inasmuch as it furthered their own agendas. And sometimes you ended up with secret passages to circumvent his control of who got in and out of Hell.

They'd gotten into the snow-choked lab in dissociated form, and once inside, had heated the air until the snow sublimed but the ice floor and walls remained. At that point, Michael made light images to re-create where everything had been positioned, and Saraquael began an inch-by-inch search of the ice.

Michael didn't ask, but he'd always thought of this process as Saraquael "talking" to the ice and the ice "talking" back to him. He'd done that with the Earth, palms pressed flat to the soil so the information flowed to him about where he was and what was nearby. This was a much more difficult process, though, seeking out something far finer and fifty times more ephemeral. Rivers and mountains wanted to be found. If Asmodeus had a passage, he wanted it secret.

So while Michael kept watch, Saraquael combed the room, feeling through the structure and learning its internal harmonies and listening for any sense of wrongness, like a comma misplaced in a sentence. Or maybe a single comma misplaced in an entire library full of stories.

Saraquael's head picked up, and he projected that Michael should come closer. Saraquael put both hands on the floor beneath where the table had stood at the room's center, and then he shifted to the right. He lay flat against the snow, and finally he smiled. He projected a question.

Michael shook his head: no. All he felt was that he didn't really want to be here right now.

Saraquael sandwiched Michael's hand between his and the ice. "Wait a moment," he said, and he sent a very thin pulse of energy through him into the ground.

Everything seemed normal enough, except that Michael felt nervous and tense. "Why don't you just open it for me?"

Saraquael shrugged. "I'm not entirely sure this is it. But I'll give it a try." And in the next moment, he'd dissociated and began drawing Michael into the passage.

The passage itself didn't want them moving through. Somehow the demons had lined their tunnel with emotional resistance, and Michael felt a distinct dread that made him want to turn back. Oh! They'd added that: the low-level aversion was designed to keep someone from finding the entrance by accident, and his realization that they must have added this sense was all that kept Michael moving forward with Saraquael. Clever. Still, Michael stuck close to Saraquael, and Saraquael led them forward through a tunnel Michael could barely perceive even while inside it.

At one point Saraquael hesitated, marked the spot in Michael's mind as a place where he had to choose which direction to go, and then continued. Michael wondered momentarily how they'd know if they'd picked the right side or whether Asmodeus had designed a labyrinth to trap anyone who didn't know the right path to take between realms.

Michael drew marginally closer to Saraquael, who sent back a sense of nervousness. Well, at least they were together.

Saraquael hesitated again, then moved forward without marking the spot as a branching tunnel. Michael tried to probe outward, but he sensed that whatever kind of network they were in, it was Guarded like a tube. Once inside, you could go forward or backward, but not communicate through it. The perfect hiding spot in some respects.

Saraquael kept pushing forward, and then they found themselves in a forest.

Michael formed back into his subtle body and dropped to the ground. "Earth," he said. "The Indus valley. We're..." His eyes widened. "We're not far from where Remiel and Zadkiel landed!"

Saraquael flared with joy. "This makes sense! They got hit with the shrapnel and their souls couldn't stay in angelic form. They got funneled through to the nearest place capable of sustaining human life, and they ended up on the other end of the tunnel."

Michael said, "And Belior...does that mean he ended up near here too?"

"He ended up in possession of someone, and I have no idea how possession works." Saraquael's wings dropped a bit. "They can't possess just anyone, but did his soul only get trapped in the nearest potential host? Did he go into someone he already had an established relationship with? I can't begin to guess, and to make matters more complicated, he's not in his original host. He did end up in the next-nearest potential host when he killed the first one, but I'm not sure if that was by choice or by force."

Michael said, "I'll send someone out to question that man's guardian. Maybe someone from Nivalis's team. We ought to find out how and when it happened." He rubbed his chin. "But this tells us part of how they're evading Satan's notice. And potentially how they intended to utilize the weapon."

"It could be." Saraquael's eyes were bright like stars. "I'm impressed with the amount of secrecy they've employed. You'd think Satan would be pleased with having them develop the thing."

"I get the impression he's not really the guy you want to be working for." Michael smirked. "If they promised this weapon and didn't deliver, think how bad it would be for them."

Saraquael said, "A long, long reckoning?"

Michael flinched.

Saraquael lowered his voice. "I saw you tried to deflect it from him, but there was no chance you could."

Michael shook his head. "The irony is that Hastle wasn't the one who revealed it was Sheol material."

"Asmodeus is going to take it out on someone. By all accounts, he's already laced into Belior. Hastle was going to get the backlash eventually." His wings dropped. "I don't think there's anything you could have done about that. Or can do," he added. "Let's start moving. If Asmodeus wants to use his little back door, I don't want him to find us or our energy signatures."

They spread their wings and took off, Michael silent as he glided. Hastle. This wasn't going to end well for him at all.

At last Michael steeled himself. "He chose his side. And he knew whatever game he was playing with Asmodeus was dangerous, but he thought it benefitted him somehow."

Saraquael rolled onto his back and glided while watching the clouds. "Did he ever tell you what his ultimate goal was?"

"He said it didn't matter anymore, that it wasn't going to work. It upset him that we were able to find everyone."

Saraquael frowned. "What do you think that means?"

"Overall? I've tried not to guess, to be honest. There may be all sorts of politicking going on down in Hell, and you'd never unravel it all in a thousand years." Longer than a thousand years. Eternity would last a long time. "He might have wanted that weapon to take out one of his personal enemies for all I know."

Saraquael said, "But really, knowing him, what did he want?"

Michael closed his eyes and let the wind stroke over his face. It was so calm up here, miles above the Earth. Time and space just to glide and let the world take care of itself for a minute.

Saraquael said, "He was working you up for something."

"He was working me up so he could gather the Sheol material off me."

Saraquael said, "And what did he plan to do with it?"

Michael shrugged. "Give it back to Belior as tribute, I guess."

Saraquael said, "Unless he planned to do something with it himself."

Michael shook his head. "Not in a cell. Think about it: even in a lab with highly controlled conditions, Satrinah said that material was fizzling away."

Gasping, he cupped his wings and stopped in mid-air.

Saraquael drew up in front of him, but Michael was shaking. No. No, he couldn't have.

Saraquael waited him out, projecting a question.

Michael's fists tightened. "He *was* gathering it to use it. That stuff wasn't fizzling away. He'd been stealing the processed material back from Belior all along."

TWENTY-ONE

Remiel lay alone in the dark long after everyone had fallen asleep.

She listened to the outside world, so very quiet in a way that felt unnatural to her ears. The last time she'd been human, she'd gone through that snow storm: the whine of wind and snow, the creak of the building, the snap of the fire. Here the air lay heavy and still.

Insects—there should be insects, and maybe night creatures calling to one another. In the city, though, there weren't that many. The animals stayed distant from the humans, and without dense vegetation, the insects themselves weren't dense.

As if in reply, thunder sounded in the far distance. With no windows in the room, Remiel hadn't seen the lightning. But at least it was a sound.

She waited for more, but no more came, and her mind started drifting.

So instead she prayed, and she ran her mind back over the conversations from earlier that day. She prayed about Belior breaking his own wrists to escape a place where he was protected and fed, and then prayed about Asmodeus threatening two Cherubim who by all measures appeared personally loyal to him in every respect.

Loyalty. It wasn't often she saw glimpses of the demons' old selves through the new, but in Satrinah she'd seen personal loyalty to Belior and to Asmodeus. She had a bond with Asmodeus, and maybe that explained it, but she didn't appear to be maneuvering to supplant Belior nor even to make him look bad in the eyes of

Asmodeus. By all accounts, she appeared to have disobeyed Asmodeus in order to help him (although to his credit, Belior looked to be nourishing an insane amount of jealousy toward her whenever she interacted with the Seraph.) If you could believe what she said (and granted, you never wanted to trust a demon) then apparently she wanted not to be on the Maskim in Belior's place but just to keep running Belior's experiments for him. And through their every interaction, it seemed never to occur to her that the two demons giving her commands were both jerks of the highest order of magnitude.

Again the thunder rolled, and again came the silence.

What if there were still something of their original souls inside all of the fallen? But of course there was. They hadn't lost who they were. They hated God, and because of that they hated themselves, but those selves were still there.

And that meant Camael...

Remiel felt her eyes getting heavy, and she whispered, "Nivalis?"

Nivalis showed herself, casting a bluish glow that didn't make Remiel squint in the dark.

"I was thinking, remember how Gabriel infused me with some of his energy?" When Nivalis projected assent, Remiel said, "You could do that to me too. Just enough to wake me up without making me vomit."

Nivalis recoiled, projecting negation with all her feathers spread.

"It is not a bad idea," Remiel replied. "You're here to help me, and I need help."

Nivalis touched Remiel's hair and gentled it back from her forehead. Remiel tingled where her fingers passed through. Nivalis kept her voice soft even though no one else could hear her. "You need to sleep."

"I'm not going to sleep," Remiel hissed. "I've said that."

Thunder. And then thunder again.

"What if you're in this form for months?" Nivalis's glow faded to a deep purple. "I can see into your body. Your stress hormones are pegged, and at some point you're going to start making really bad decisions."

Remiel curled around herself, fists tight in her blanket. "I'm not asking you for your opinion. You came because you wanted to help."

"I do. I'm not sure this helps." Nivalis ran her fingers over Remiel's hand, and Remiel made it unclench. "Even if it's only a little, you say our energy hurts."

"I know it will hurt." Remiel smiled wickedly. "That doesn't mean it won't work."

The thunder claps were sounding closer together and louder. What would it sound like when the rain began pelting the tile roof? When she'd weathered out that blizzard, the wind had been her constant companion, singing and puffing and sneaking cold air through the walls like warriors entering a besieged city. Would there be wind? Would rain send its droplet spies through the tile roof?

Nivalis's mouth twitched. "I'll make a deal with you. I'll do it, but first I want you to answer a question."

Remiel's eyes narrowed. "It depends on the question."

"And I promise to do it no matter what your answer." Nivalis wrapped her fingers around Remiel's other hand. "What did you dream so horrible that the certitude of pain is preferable to the possibility of dreaming it again?"

Remiel tucked down her head. "You know."

"I don't know. I'm asking."

Nivalis waited in silence while Remiel tried to think of the words. Don't answer—that was the thought that kept ricocheting around her head there in the dark, surrounded by a half dozen sleeping human women. Don't answer because it was so much more real if she did.

Nivalis cuddled around her.

Thunder again. The rolls were coming almost on top of one another now, and Remiel could smell the ozone. If it wasn't raining already, it would be soon. "Camael," she whispered into one of the booms. *Camael. Camael. Camael. My brother.*

Nivalis tightened around her. "As he is, or as he was?"

Remiel shook her head. "That's two questions."

Nivalis said, "I know you miss him."

"How would you know?" Remiel jerked up her head, scattering Nivalis like motes in the sunlight until she gathered herself back into form before her. "I'm the only one."

"I lost someone too." Nivalis's eyes clouded. "You're the only one with *this* loss, but you're not alone."

Remiel said, "Would you dream about him?"

Nivalis said, "I've never dreamed. But I don't want to forget him."

"Dreaming isn't remembering." Remiel kept to a whisper, although if the thunder hadn't awakened the other women then surely her voice wouldn't either. "It's different. You're there. You're with him. He's in your heart and you're feeling him, and he fits so perfectly." Her voice broke, and there was rain in the room but it had come from her rather than the sky. "And it's right even though you suspect it's wrong, but you don't care because of how right it is. And then—"

Remiel pushed her face down onto her forearms. And then you woke up. And then he was gone. And then you were totally alone in every way that ever mattered, swallowed by darkness and aware of how much distance there was between yourself and everything you ever intended to be and because of that how wrong the world was. Because you were alone.

Nivalis said, "And then he changes?"

Remiel tucked her head closer. "And then *you* change." She was whispering into the little space made between her chest and her arms and the bed, so faint even her own ears couldn't pick it up. Nivalis could hear anyhow. "You're empty."

Nivalis cuddled her. "And you miss him even more."

Remiel didn't move. "You don't know. You don't know."

"I know some of it."

Remiel whispered, "The denial. You don't know that. They won't speak about him."

Nivalis moved closer. "I've seen that. I mention being a guardian, and other angels will tense up and change the subject."

Remiel shook her head. "No! Not like that—they won't speak about him, but back then, he was *me*. We were *identical*." She fought to keep the hysteria out of her voice. "Don't you see? It's not the same at all. The other angels won't speak about *Judas*. But they'll talk about *you*. Back then we were the Irin together, or if we weren't, then they can't figure out which Irin they were dealing with, and they won't talk about Camael because he's fallen, so—"

Remiel ducked down her head.

Nivalis whispered, "Oh. No."

"I didn't have a name before the Winnowing. And they talk like I didn't exist before it happened. They don't want to talk well of him. They don't want to talk badly of me. You're grieving for Judas, but the one who's dead isn't Camael. It's me." Remiel blinked hard and pressed the heels of her hands into her eyes. "And then you want me to go back to that, after I've spent all this time not being Irin anymore, and exist in full again, and then wake up and get that stripped off *again*, and be dead again, and for what?" Her voice broke back to the inaudible whisper only Nivalis and God would be able to hear. "I'd rather stay awake a thousand years. I can't do that again. I can't."

She fell totally silent because nothing remained inside her. There was everything, everything lying out there in full view as if she'd vomited again and instead of the contents of her stomach it was her heart spewed all over the floor, reeking and disgusting, a wild and living thing that had clawed its way out and now everyone could smell it for what it was.

She curled tight, struggling to breathe regularly. Nivalis felt close, so close. The thunder sounded so far away, but getting closer. And somewhere closest still in all this was God: in her, in Nivalis, in the thunder. In her past. In her future. In the angel she was made to be and never would be again.

And then Nivalis let go of her and moved away because why would she stay? Seeing that, why wouldn't she go?

Only instead, Nivalis slipped around in front of her and rested her hands on Remiel's shoulders. "Thank you for talking to me. It sounds awful." She was warming up against Remiel's skin, or maybe Remiel was just tensing. "You're right: it's not the same. No one pretends I didn't exist before Judas. But I'll carry your burden with you. You never get over it. You carry forward. It's right to be sad sometimes." Nivalis breathed over her neck. "It's your heart that got hurt, and you have a beautiful heart."

Remiel knew she didn't have a beautiful heart. She had a heart sawn almost in half and then ripped apart the rest of the way, cast off on the roadside and feasted on by vultures. Where was the beauty?

"Breathe deeply," Nivalis said. "Let your body relax. You tensed when Gabriel did this, and that may have made it harder."

Before Remiel fully registered that Nivalis was about to make good on her promise, the energy already flowed through her. It seeped in like the cold wind through the walls of that winter-strong fortress, and her ears rang, but she tried to relax and let it happen. Nivalis was being so gentle, and her natural power was a hundred times less than Gabriel's. It felt like the sting of extinguishing a candle by pinching the wick rather than the prickles of an entire body deprived of oxygen. So she waited, and Nivalis kept the flow gentle, monitoring her and feeding her and killing her with an energy her body cried out against in protest.

And with the energy came something else: came Nivalis's assurance of the presence of God even in the loss of Camael. God was with her in the grief, with her in the regrets.

No, she never regretted staying with God. She loved Him.

Yes, it was as if Nivalis's heart replied, she loved God more than Camael. That had been her choice, but she regretted the necessary sequel of that choice, and God was at her side in that.

Remiel's head pounded, and when the pain got sharper, Remiel tensed up. Nivalis backed off, then whispered to her, "Relax your shoulders. Relax your jaw. Now your eyes."

When had she curled up around herself like this? But it was good: she felt so much more awake than before, and now she had hours in the dark to work down the headache and wait for the nausea to subside.

"Thank you," she whispered.

Nivalis projected back her own thanks.

Sure, thank you for sharing what a freak you are. Thank you for not masking the truth.

Thunder exploded overhead, and Remiel started. One of the other women awoke with a gasp, and Remiel reached for Zadkiel's hand in the next bed.

Zadkiel sat up. "What's going on?"

"It's just a storm. It's been coming on for a while." Though dizzy from Nivalis's power, Remiel squeezed her hand. "It's finally gotten close."

Another crash shook the house, and Remiel's head pounded harder. She knew what thunder was; she'd ridden storm fronts. And for goodness sakes, she'd been in that blizzard for days and never felt the same kind of fear this one innocuous rainstorm was causing just because it had the nerve to be loud. *Poor thing,* she mocked herself, *frightened by a noise.*

One of the children started crying across the room, and in the dark, the mother made soothing sounds. Remiel rubbed her arms and tried to settle back down on her bed. Her head still hurt, and because of the headache she saw sparks along with every loud sound.

Again came the thunder. Again Remiel reminded herself it was just a noise. Trying to sound confident, she said, "You should get back to sleep."

"I don't suppose you'll sleep." Zadkiel settled back down.

"Nivalis figured out how to help." Remiel fought her own dizziness as she helped Zadkiel straighten the blanket. She said in Gaelic, "I asked her to run a low stream of energy into me, the way Gabriel did. It's just enough to energize me and not enough to flatten me."

Zadkiel replied in the same language. "That's probably not healthy. If she misjudges how much energy to put into you, you're going to be worse off than before."

But not as bad as it could be. Camael. Saying it to Nivalis had brought it all back in ways Remiel never anticipated it would, or rather, had known it would do all the time and had wanted against all hope never to feel again. Wanted not to feel that oneness, that simple comfort in her own self that she hadn't enjoyed since the

Winnowing. Because she'd always had it back then, just being together with him, and now she'd never have it anymore.

Unless she fell asleep. And then she'd have to give it up all over again.

More thunder. Zadkiel whispered, "Pray with me. I don't like this."

Remiel moved closer to her, and in the dark they prayed with hands joined, silent. Remiel remembered Jesus calming the storm over the sea of Galilee and prayed for it to happen again. *It's silly to be scared.* But the more she prayed, the more she found herself repeating, *It's wrong. This feels wrong. The storm smells wrong.*

She'd harnessed storms and ridden the crash of storm fronts against one another. She knew their power. *So why doesn't this one feel right?*

Remiel's throat tightened as she reached for God and listened to the thunder three times in a row.

She didn't get a chance to hear the next one before someone in the street screamed, "Fire!" And then the thunder slammed overhead again, and Remiel raced to the front of the building.

TWENTY-TWO

Five Angels rushed to Michael in fewer than two seconds, all urgent and all with the same alarm: Ephesus was under attack.

He went without thinking, calling four squads of Archangels to himself and putting all the rest on high alert before he'd even finished flashing out to Mary and John's house. He arrived in the midst of flames.

People hollered in the streets, calling for help and rousing their neighbors to leave their houses. Michael flashed to the heart of the flames and ordered three Archangels to start calming the winds before they carried the fire.

"Lighting strikes," reported one angel. "Two hit the roof of that house, and one hit the tree."

Both targets were immediately adjacent to John's house.

Michael flashed to the courtyard where Mary was helping the other Christians bring their children out of the home. Remiel was leading Zadkiel by the hand. "Keep the flames off the roof!" he ordered, but the winds were so strong, and even the lashing rain wasn't helping extinguish the fires. The trees between the houses had ignited, reaching toward the sky with branches like fingers of flame, and the bushes were engulfed as well. Men were fighting to douse them with water, but the rooftops were too high and the flames too hot to get close.

Roman soldiers charged in, shoving pedestrians out of the way.

Remiel handed off Zadkiel to Mary "Stay here!" she shouted, then ran back into the house.

Michael flew alongside her. "Are people still in there?"

"Yes," she gasped.

Before Michael could focus through the walls to see how many and where they were, Satan appeared before him.

Michael drew up short. With his twelve white wings flared around himself, Satan said, "You took one of my officers prisoner. I'm taking your house. Fair exchange, no?"

How did he know about Hastle? Why did he even care about such a low-level demon?

Michael manifested his sword and flared his wings. Satan waved him off. "I'm not stupid. I can't get in there, so I'm having them bring him out."

And then Satan turned his back on him and drove up the wind higher and peppered the ground with lightning strikes.

The human crowd scattered. And as John's house ignited, Michael reached inside with his heart to find Remiel racing for the only souls still inside: the magician's human soul, and Belior's demonic one.

Michael flashed inside. The roof beams were burning. The walls were already hot, and thick smoke choked through the windowless rooms. "Remiel! You've got to get out of here!"

"Come on!" she shouted, but Belior was bracing himself in the doorway, his eyes white-ringed and his body shaking. "You can't stay! Your host will die!"

Michael manifested to both of them. "Remiel! Leave him! You're going to get trapped."

"He'll be trapped too! He'll end up in another body and we'll lose him!"

Michael shouted, "I don't care! We'll find him!"

Remiel yanked Belior by the arm, but he wrenched free of her grip and fled to the back corner of the room. Michael shouted, but Remiel pursued him.

From another part of the house came a crash as the tile ceiling caved in. Broiling air rushed through the building, drawing a startled cry from Remiel and finally breaking Belior's hold over his host. In panic, the human host's survival instinct overcame the demon's instinct to hide, and the magician bolted for the front entrance.

Satan appeared before him in what used to be the front room. "Look, the walls are down. No building. No protection." And he snapped.

Belior was gone. Satan pointed at Remiel. "You too."

Nivalis barreled in between Remiel and Satan. He swatted her into the burning wall, then blocked a blow from Michael's sword. Sparks flew through the angelic realm, and Remiel crumpled to the broiling hot tiles.

Satan grabbed her around the waist and flung her into the air. A demon appeared, snatched her, and vanished.

Michael rushed him again, but Remiel was gone. Satan blew him into the wall beside Nivalis, who pulled herself onto hands and called her sword back to herself.

Michael flashed to a stand, but Satan only looked him right in the eye. "Don't try to protect my traitors from me. I'll take care of them myself."

He vanished too, leaving Michael standing, horrified, in the ruins of the house.

Zadkiel couldn't stop crying. She knew she shouldn't be crying. She needed her head together, and she needed to do something to help Remiel. Anything. And instead tears kept welling out of her useless eyes, and this body she'd never wanted to be wearing in the first place kept dictating how she responded: with tension, with shaking, with salt water on her cheeks and a continuous tremor in her chest and stomach.

Mary held her as she walked. Nivalis was all around her. They were being nice, but Zadkiel didn't need anyone to tell her: she'd failed everyone. Failed by getting caught by the weapon in the first place. Failed by being the reason Remiel couldn't just leave her. Failed because now the Christian community had nowhere to call home. Failed, failed, failed.

Failed because she couldn't see. Because she'd made a deal with God and because God had kept His part of the bargain. Maybe as a punishment. Maybe to show her that what she wanted had been bad for her all along, and she should never have had the nerve to ask for it.

She couldn't even reach for the taste of wine. She didn't deserve it.

The heat on her face. The smoke. The children's sobbing. The smut in the air. The shouts of the Romans and the yelling of the men hauling water to the fires.

As soon as the building had come down, the wind had died. The fires were being contained, and the Romans had ordered everyone to clear the area.

There was no reason to stay here anyhow. The house was destroyed. Zadkiel had heard it crash down, had felt the rush of heat as it collapsed, and then she'd felt Nivalis return, terrified. Guarding her.

Guarding her as if she deserved it.

Remiel, gone. Satan had broken in to get Belior, and that was fine. Belior had sworn allegiance to Satan, and that made him Satan's property to dispose of. Who cared what Satan had done to him? But Remiel had run back in to make Belior leave, and Satan had grabbed them both.

But he'd left Zadkiel. Well, why would he want her? She wasn't important.

Mary stopped, and Zadkiel paused at her side. A woman said, "Your house? That was your house? Where will you go?"

Mary said, "I'm not sure."

Mary's arm jerked away from Zadkiel as the woman grabbed her hand. "You must come with me. Stay in my home. You saved my daughter. Now I can do something for you."

Mary said, "Thank you. But there are so many of us."

"Bring all you have," said the woman. "At least stay the night."

It took half an hour in the confusion to find everyone, longer still to get everyone directions to the new house. Someone took Zadkiel by the arm, leading her while reciting one of the psalms. The touch was gentle, and through it all Zadkiel kept feeling her body crying because it was tense and scared and sad, and she felt so, so guilty.

At the woman's house, someone guided Zadkiel to a place to sleep, but she couldn't relax. She didn't even lie down. She just tucked up her knees and huddled around herself. Nivalis she could feel, but she didn't talk to her. She didn't pray. She just concentrated on that burnt-out part of the inside of herself, the place where Mary's house once stood and where now instead stood the very, very deep conviction that she'd caused all this harm and could never make it up to anyone no matter what she did.

TWENTY-THREE

Remiel's head pounded so hard that she couldn't focus while Satan beat Belior. It registered, but it registered more as the pain in her own head from the noise every time Belior screamed or howled or growled, the sparks that flared across her vision with every sudden noise, and the continuous nausea from having been transported heaven-only-knew how far.

Her head hurt again when Satan dropped Belior like a sack of rocks at her side, and he lay there shuddering. He shook for so long that Remiel wondered if she were witnessing a seizure, and if so, what she should do. She didn't want them to kill the host. But "what to do" implied she could do anything at all, and right now she couldn't move.

Eventually Belior stopped shaking, and then he stopped twitching, and eventually his breathing became less shallow and more even.

Satan spat at him, "You can't hide in that body forever. I will get you out of there."

"I keep telling you, you can't. It's involuntary possession." Satrinah sounded urgent, and Remiel picked up her head to try focusing on her. "We tried separating them. He killed one host trying to win free and just got absorbed into another. We tried to make the Christians cast him out, and they couldn't do it."

Flames swirled around Satan. "I don't believe you. After what you were trying to do, he's showing his intelligence and trying to hide. Forever."

He focused his power again on Belior, and the possessed man flexed against Remiel's side, screaming with a hoarse voice.

"Stop." Remiel struggled to get upright. "She's not lying. He can't get out."

Satan pushed her out of the way and blasted Belior with more power. Remiel lay panting, trying to register where she was. A cave. They were in some kind of natural cavern with the echoes of water dropping. Beneath her face she could smell lichen on the moist ground, but there were also the multiple sharp smells of a human body being tortured.

Satan stopped, and Remiel edged toward Belior. "Please, Belior's yours, but don't kill his host."

"I've no authority to kill his host." Satan folded his arms. "I'd have done it by now, trust me. You're very cute," he added, smirking. "Aren't you the lesser Irin, the one that stayed enslaved? A pity that God stuck you in such a weak little body."

Remiel edged further toward Belior, a shape she could decipher only vaguely in the flickering light of the flames around Satan's wings. He was wet, dark, limp. She felt his neck and detected the flutter of a pulse, then rolled him onto his side.

"If I ever let you out," Satan said to her, "you can tell whoever is in charge of you that I don't appreciate having your people coddle my little traitors. If you want to unseat me, go ahead and try. Feel free to invade. I'll feel free to defend. But do not collude with my officers because now you see what I'll gladly do to any and all of them who attempt that kind of subterfuge."

He punctuated that by blasting Belior one more time. Belior seized again, and Remiel held him until the spasms turned into twitches and then eased.

"Talk to me, faux-Camael." Satan paced around the cavern, his wings filling the world and leaving Remiel dizzy with the power he shed. "Which other of my officers are you working with?"

"We weren't working with them." Remiel swallowed hard. "Belior used some kind of new weapon on me. I don't know what it was supposed to do. It didn't work the way he wanted."

Satan crouched down and grabbed her chin, forcing her to look into a brightness that stung. "I thought your kind couldn't lie. Did your Tyrant change His mind about permitting you to deceive? It's about time." Satan glared right into her eyes. "But I'm not deceived. Gabriel's energy is permeating Belior, and Satrinah's is all over you." Remiel recoiled, but he kept his grip. "I know that weapon was designed to trap me and dethrone me. Your assignment may have been to protect *him*," and he looked at Belior with disgust, "but you can count that as yet another failure on your part. The list is getting rather long, but he'll remember it. He always does."

Remiel closed her eyes, but her head kept pounding. The nausea rose again, and she vaguely wondered how Satan would react if she vomited all over him. Probably not at all—he'd just go immaterial and she'd have to deal with the awful taste.

"You getting caught in your own plan is another monument to your own stupidity, but I also don't think your people are smart enough to recognize that, so I'm retaining you for now."

Retaining. That implied he had no authority to torture her, whatever consolation that might be.

"I'm not ignorant of what goes on in my domain." Satan dropped Remiel. "I have informants. And I have my own common sense. Give me that much credit." He turned to Satrinah. "He's disgusting. Clean him up before I deal with him again."

"You might want to move away," Satrinah said, as if bored.

Before Remiel could distance herself, Satan had flashed several gallons of sea water over the top of Belior and doused him thoroughly.

Remiel scurried further away, her clothes soaked through, while Satan did it again.

He vanished. Satrinah went over to Belior and prodded him. "Not too much damage."

Remiel rubbed her hands against her arms. "He was seizing."

"I'm sure he was. You were unconscious through most of that."

The salt water cut down the smells, but Remiel's teeth began chattering. "Why did Satan think you were trying to depose him?"

Satrinah snorted. "I should have known you weren't as smart as you pretended to be."

Remiel huddled around herself while Satrinah tried to get Belior into better shape, longing for warmth she couldn't get from body heat alone. She prayed, and that steadied her. *They were trying to use that weapon on Satan?* Oh, of course, of course, it was so horrible and so like them. In hindsight, it made so much sense: they'd wanted not to get back into Satan's good graces, but to rid themselves of him entirely. They could end the political games with their opponents on the Maskim by deleting the owner of the Maskim from the equation, and then they could use the army to wipe out the other two and establish themselves in power.

Remiel's eyes stung, and she choked back whatever feeling she'd have sputtered out if she'd attempted to speak. Twenty years of working in secret, in ice, with their own little staff of loyal supporters...and had those supporters even realized what they'd been working toward? Or had their idea been all along that they were making weapons to take out God's angels?

Satrinah sighed. "Well, he's about as good as I'm going to get him. I was hoping Satan would be able to yank him out of that body, but even that didn't work."

Remiel said, "You mean you could have stopped him?"

"It hardly matters whether I could or couldn't: I wouldn't have because it made more sense to let him finish what John failed to do." Satrinah inspected one of her outer feathers and flicked off some unseeable piece of lint. "We cooperated, but your nasty Archangel friend went and ratted us out. That's not how blackmail works. We invented it, remember? Blackmail means using your information to manipulate people, not manipulating them and using it anyhow."

Remiel bristled. "Michael didn't tell Satan."

Satrinah folded her arms. "So how'd he find out?"

"How should I know? I've been stuck in this body the whole time." Remiel swallowed hard. "Won't Asmodeus come to get you?"

"Satan took down Asmodeus first. I felt that clear across Creation." Satrinah shuddered. "This whole situation would have been so much easier to resolve if you'd just let me examine Belior in the first place."

"Examine him now," Remiel spat. "Take your time."

"What do you think I've been doing? Or did Camael take all the Irin's intelligence when he left?" Satrinah made enough light to show Remiel the edges of the cavern. Belior lay in a puddle of sea water, and Satrinah tilted him onto his side again so he wouldn't aspirate any of it. "That material is bound up inside him, and I can't figure out how to unlock it. Gabriel looked him over already, and clearly he didn't figure it out, because you're still here."

Remiel rubbed her arms to get warmer. "So since you've got this vast intelligence at your disposal, what's our plan?"

Satrinah tossed her head. "I had a perfectly workable plan. You wrecked it for me, so don't ask me about *our* plan. Any plan I have involves you in no way whatsoever. You can stay here as our master's plaything for the rest of eternity for all I care."

Remiel frowned. "Why haven't you left, then? Take him and go."

Satrinah fired her power at the cave ceiling, and although Remiel flinched, it just shimmered around the outer wall and didn't cause a cave-in. "That, half-a-twin, is a Guard. It keeps angels and their communiques from getting out."

They said nothing further to one another, Remiel more irritated than she should be about Satrinah's attitude and the fact that apparently it was Remiel's fault, entirely, that Satrinah had been caught in the act of treason. She struggled to stay warm, and when that didn't work (thanks to the wet clothing and the lack of sunlight) Remiel went near Belior to check out how he was doing. Or rather, how his host body was doing. Satan could string Belior out at the bottom of the Lake of Fire for all she cared, but the host still had a redeemable soul, and therefore the host needed to survive.

The host had very pale skin, was shivering all over, and was breathing rapidly. "Use that brilliance of yours to shine a bit more on him," Remiel said. "Don't you see his lips are blue? We need to warm him up or he's going to die."

Satrinah said, "If he dies, Belior escapes."

"If he escapes, Satan beats the hell out of you and then finds him again. We need to warm him up."

Satan returned, fire surrounding his wings, bringing with him two other demons. "That one," he said, pointing toward Belior. "This one is for me."

He grabbed Remiel by the arm and flashed her to an even colder part of the cave, leaving her in darkness broken only by the flashes of light that sparked behind her eyes whenever she moved her head. She tried to maintain her footing, but the vertigo brought her to the rocks, and even then the world pivoted like a leaf in a wind storm.

Satan grabbed her by the throat and lifted her off the floor. She closed her eyes and tried to keep still. "Now. What is that weapon supposed to do?"

She coughed, the light flaring behind her eyes again and everything tilting. "It's Death," she choked out. "Sheol material. Weaponized."

He tossed her back onto the rocks so she was facing him. "I already have that information."

Remiel slumped against a boulder, panting, feeling almost distantly the way a human's fear seized control over her body: the longing to run, the urgency, the shaking. She was cold, so cold, and her body hurt, and her heart pounded. She couldn't get enough breath. Satan could kill her if God permitted it, and he'd do so without hesitation and probably the most painful way possible. He was bad enough to deal with when she was in angelic form and he was just a calculating bully. Now he was enraged and she was stuck, and she'd be completely at his mercy if only he had any mercy to be at.

Zadkiel—had he gotten to Zadkiel too? Because for her it would be worse. She'd be blind and at his non-existent mercy. Had she been in that first cavern, beyond the reach of Satrinah's light, still unconscious? Was she already dead?

Remiel reached for God, and even though she didn't feel Him reach back for her, the act of reaching steadied her. She was afraid. Her body was afraid, and that was normal. She wasn't used to the cascade of fear hormones, but at least they made sense.

Satan got closer, and she shivered uncontrollably. "I'm going to treat you worse than Belior if you don't tell me what I want to know."

"Then you're going to have to torture me," Remiel said through chattering teeth, "because I don't have the information you want."

Satan made no move for so long. Remiel huddled around herself, wondering if she'd just freeze to death waiting on him and if they really were right that she'd just stay trapped in this body long after it was dead. Wondering if Michael or Saraquael would be able to find her after the body was dead, and if maybe they'd get someone to resurrect her. Wondered what it felt like to be resurrected. The only thing she knew for sure was it left you ravenous because Jesus had always made sure dead people had plenty to eat once they came back. Maybe Mary would bake her some bread. Maybe being dead for a while wouldn't be so bad.

But then instead of breaking her neck or leaving her to freeze, Satan grabbed her shaking body and yanked her back through space to the main cavern. He dumped her beside Belior and faced Satrinah.

It hurt. It hurt so much. Remiel prayed, *Remember that whole thing about making up what was lacking in the sufferings of Christ? Seriously, how much more could be lacking?*

Satan said to Satrinah, "How do we force him out of that host?"

Remiel could feel what he was projecting behind that: the host was limiting what he could do to Belior, and he still believed Belior was using it as a human shield.

Satrinah sighed. "Again, the Sheol material is pinning him into the host, and none of us has been able to get enough of a grasp on it to release his soul from the human body he's possessing."

Satan said, "Have you tried releasing her?"

"She's not in possession of a human," Satrinah said. "That's a solidified subtle body. To all intents and purposes, at the moment, she herself is human. I assume the mechanism pining her in the form, however, is the same. I also assume Gabriel and his cohorts have attempted to remove the shrapnel from her in order to restore her normal fluidity of form, and because she continues in this fashion, we can assume he failed."

Satan folded his arms. There was heat in his anger, but not enough to warm Remiel. She looked for Belior in case she could huddle up next to him and pool their body heat, but he was conscious again, sitting up and positioned between the pair of demons Satan had brought into the cavern. His eyes were shadowed, and bruises mottled his skin, but he was awake.

Great. Demonic healers. Beat the human body within an inch of death, then restore it and start over.

Satan said, "Give me some theories. What would extract the shrapnel?"

Satrinah said, "We developed several techniques to locate the Sheol material and concentrate it enough to gather it. Once you put it together, though, it has a natural adhesion to itself. It seeks itself out, and it tries to stay together once it's formed up."

Satan looked at Belior. "Aren't you going to contradict her?" He sounded patiently amused even though Remiel suspected he was anything but. "You'll tell her it's not a natural adhesion as much as it's an inherent quality of attraction, and then debate the difference for twenty minutes?"

Belior said, "We've already had that debate. She's using my vocabulary."

He was talking? Oh, but of course, he was no longer under John's authority. He was under a different authority, and that authority demanded he speak.

Satrinah said, "The difficulties here are multiple. First, we have no idea how much of the material destabilized and vanished."

Satan shook his head. "Material doesn't just vanish. It goes somewhere."

Belior said, "When we weaponized the Sheol material, it did become unstable, and it would disappear. We had to keep the setting very carefully Guarded in order to prevent material loss."

Satrinah said, "Secondly, we have no way of measuring how much is in each of them. We could potentially use the Sheol material in Remiel to withdraw the shrapnel from Belior, but if there's a higher concentration in him than in her, then it might have the opposite effect and pull it all into him."

Satan flashed Belior a wicked smile. "I'd come up with a way to get it out of you. Eventually." He returned his gaze to Satrinah. "And there isn't any more in creation? Just what's in these two?"

Satrinah said, "And whatever is in Zadkiel."

Satan's brows raised. "You failed to mention there was a third angel involved."

Remiel straightened. He didn't have her. Zadkiel was safe.

Satrinah said, "It didn't seem important at the time. But she may be holding enough of the material that we could use what's in the pair of them to extract it from Belior."

"Where is Zadkiel now?"

Satrinah shrugged. "I don't know. Given that Remiel was with John, Zadkiel may have been in residence too, but I never made a positive identification."

Remiel checked Belior, but Belior said nothing. Interesting.

Satan drummed his fingers against his thigh. "You," and he pointed to one of the two healer demons. "I want a search party sent. Locate Zadkiel. No interaction. Just reconnaissance."

The demon vanished. Remiel closed her eyes tight and huddled around herself. *God, please protect her. Alert Michael. Please.*

Satan asked Satrinah a few more questions, all of which she answered in that same bloodless Cherubic detachment that Remiel found so incomprehensible right now, while she was shivering in a human body and trying to calm the panic that kept overwhelming her whenever she considered she was trapped underground in an unknown location with enemies who hated every jot of her being. But Satrinah, although she was in just as much trouble as Belior and Asmodeus, answered every question with a thorough attention to detail and as far as Remiel could tell no actual lies. For his own part, whenever Belior got addressed a direct question, he answered the same way.

Satan finally said, "I'm tired of this. You two invented it. You two will un-invent it. Satrinah, I don't care how you do it, but you will extract the shrapnel from both Belior and the weaker Irin, and when I've obtained her, from Zadkiel as well. This is a single-use, weapon, correct? Then once you've done so, you get to pick which of your traitor comrades I use it on."

Belior stiffened.

Satan said, "If you fail to extract the shrapnel, then I'll handle it myself, and when eventually I get that material free, I'll use it on you. I'll give you a few hours. That should be enough. While you're working, you can figure out whether you want to choose your bonded Seraph who goaded you into treason or the Cherub who would just as soon see you on the other end of that weapon." He stretched his wings. "Oh, and in case you need some helpers, I've got a few dozen assistants for you. Be productive."

His light flared, and then it winked out as he vanished. Remiel looked around to find the chamber ringed with demons, all of whom watched the trio at the center.

Belior glared at Satrinah. Satrinah ignored him and focused instead on Remiel. "I'm starting with you."

Of course she was. Remiel rubbed her goose-bumped arms and wished Satan hadn't so transparently set the two Cherubim against one another, or that the Cherubim, for all their wisdom, hadn't failed to recognize what he'd done.

TWENTY-FOUR

Michael had two legions of angels posted in Ephesus, and he kept half of them in or around the houses where John's Christian community had taken shelter for the night. The Romans were still working to extinguish the fires, and several priests and priestesses from the Temple of Artemis were tending to the wounded. John himself was walking the streets with Ignatius, healing whatever of the wounded he could, and Michael made sure he had a strong personal guard.

They'd flushed from the city as many demons as they could, and all of it felt futile because Satan had taken Remiel.

For what might have been the dozenth time tonight, Saraquael appeared before him. "Orders?"

Saraquael wasn't saying, "Give me permission to find her." Michael could feel it all around him, though, how he hungered to mount a search, and instead Michael kept dispatching him to different zones or to check on different crews. Make sure the fire hasn't spread. Encourage the soldiers to create a fire break. Details like that seemed the first order of business: human souls could perish, and Remiel's couldn't. Satan would make her uncomfortable, but not eternally uncomfortable. It was a tradeoff all the angels understood.

And still, he couldn't justify keeping Saraquael here any longer. He was so efficient, so precise, that Michael in some ways owed it to him to let him go.

So Michael said, "Talk to me about mounting a search."

Saraquael folded his arms and flared his wings. "I want to do it."

"Efficacy?" Michael said.

Saraquael's eyes dimmed. "I doubt we'll find any trace of her, given who took her. He won't have gotten authority to take her life, but wherever he brought her in Creation, she'll be under an impenetrable Guard. And that's assuming he kept her on the plane of Creation. If she's being detained in Hell, the degree of difficulty rises exponentially." He shifted his weight. "I want to search, but I have another suggestion."

Michael blinked. "Okay, then. Talk to me."

Saraquael said, "After consideration, I agree with you that Hastle was siphoning the Sheol matter for his own use. The excess material wasn't still on Hastle when Gabriel drew off what he'd taken from you, so we have to assume he's stashed it somewhere."

Michael shook his head. "He's not going to tell us where he hid it. I doubt we could get him to admit he stole it in the first place."

"No, but we've got two reasons we need to track down his stash. Primarily, we can't leave any of it where the demons can make another weapon or figure out how to clone the material from other resources."

Michael nodded.

Saraquael's color had picked up. "Secondly, Gabriel said the Sheol material attracts itself. That means if we gather enough of it, we might be able to draw it out of everyone who's been affected already." His wings had gone a brilliant teal by now, and he was glowing. Giving him free rein had definitely been the right call. "I agree Hastle's never going to tell us how to find it no matter what we do, but it can't be that hard to track it down."

No, of course not. A microscopic amount of a material you couldn't detect, hidden by a demon who was trying to evade the notice of a pair of Cherubim who had spent twenty years working with the material already...that would be child's play to find.

Instead of saying that, Michael chose a milder, "How would you suggest we start?"

Saraquael's hands clenched. "Wherever he was keeping it, it had to be someplace he could get to on a regular basis, somewhere

Asmodeus and Belior wouldn't think it unusual for him to visit, and someplace where he wouldn't be stopped and questioned by other demons. That cuts down our options considerably."

That would eliminate Satan's private work station and the Holy Temple at Jerusalem. That was a start.

Saraquael said, "Gabriel already dismantled the whole lab and set that back up again in Heaven, but it may be hidden in part of that."

Michael said, "I'll instruct his team to search the whole thing all over again."

Beaming, Saraquael nodded. "Meanwhile, you and I have our own places to search."

They couldn't sneak back into Hell to comb the area where Belior's lab had been. Satan had upped security to levels Michael hadn't seen since the Crucifixion, and the very slim chance the two of them could evade the guards only convinced Michael they'd have even less chance getting out again.

Undeterred, Saraquael brought Michael back to the place they'd popped out of Belior's secret tunnel, and it had no especial demonic presence about it. "We can't assume it's safe," Michael said. "By now Satan will have ferreted out and interrogated every demon who collaborated with them."

"And probably several who haven't." Saraquael sat in the field and made himself quiet. "Suppress your signature. I want to get a feel for the place."

It made sense to Michael at least that Hastle would have carried the Sheol material through the tunnel and stashed it on the other end. It would have to be someplace safe, someplace he could secure with a Guard but not someplace where his presence would garner questions. And he'd have to be able to do it quickly.

Michael tamped down his power and prayed. *Please let this work. I don't know if we need this or not to free Remiel, but it seems like the right direction. Please bless our work. Please reveal what is hidden.*

Saraquael finally said, "I can't detect anything."

Michael said, "That doesn't mean it's not here."

Saraquael projected discouragement.

"The tunnel branched," Michael said. "Let's get back into it and check out where it went."

Saraquael moved around until he found the opening, and the "opening" was nothing at all, just an undetectable slit in the fabric of Creation. Undetectable to Michael, that was. "Follow me," Saraquael said, as though everyone found invisible pock marks in reality all the time, and he slipped through.

You couldn't defend in here: that much Michael knew for certain, but he hoped that also meant you couldn't ambush. There was no room to do much except push forward or backward. He tried not to think about how easy it would be for Satrinah to follow them up this slender tube so they couldn't reverse course, then have Asmodeus bottle them up at the far end.

Fully dissociated, they slipped through as pure spirits, moving closer to Hell and further from Earth, and then Saraquael stopped, re-oriented, and branched off to the side. This route felt marginally easier, with less resistance than before, and Saraquael slipped through at a much faster rate. Fine—if it got them out of there faster, Michael wasn't about to object, but he also wondered where it was going to shoot them out, and what would be waiting for them when it did.

Like a bubble bursting on the surface of a pond, they popped back into existence, and Michael solidified into a subtle body to identify where they were.

"Oh, wow." Saraquael sighed, then flexed all six wings and spread his arms. It was cold. It was dark. Reality was thin: they were on the edge of the Void.

Michael said, "This is where Hastle was collecting the Sheol material."

"This makes sense. They needed two tunnels: one to get him here undetected, and then one to get out to Creation." Saraquael turned to Michael, his eyes gleaming like gems in the near-nothingness. "I bet they made this one first, and they formed up the other channel later, once they knew they had enough material to go ahead with their weapon."

In the distance hung the heavy mass of Hell, encased in itself and dull outside but hot within. Sheol would have been attached to Hell between its nearest wall and where they hovered now, assuming directions and distances even made any sense this close to the Void.

Michael spread his wings and glided away from Saraquael. What had Hastle said about his work collecting raw material? *I want that.* This, this emptiness and solitude. The chill, the nearly motionless atoms, the thinning reality that grew harder to move through until it ended and there was nothingness you couldn't reach into because nothing made sense beyond it.

Closing his eyes, Michael listened. Silence. Absolute. Brilliant.

Saraquael said, "Nice as this is, though, it's not what we wanted. He wouldn't have hidden it here."

Michael projected his agreement, then folded his arms. *Oh, God, why Hastiel...?* Because Hastiel had chosen this, of course. There wasn't another answer that worked, but Michael wondered not for the first time if there were something he could have done, could have said, long before the Winnowing that would have redirected Hastiel away from rejecting God. Maybe he could have been out on the verge of the Void with Hastiel instead of Saraquael, picking apart the drifting atoms of the fading universe and joking about whatever prank they'd recently played on Danel. Instead he was with his lieutenant retracing the steps of a demon and trying to think the way a demon might, and the fit was tighter than the inside of that tube they'd traveled.

He glided at the very edge of Creation's fabric, probing through reality as though he were Hastle trying to round up the last lone gem of Sheol's shattered walls amidst the dross. Pretend you found one; call it to you by whatever means Hastle had devised for collecting the things. He'd never been clear about how he did it, but it hardly mattered. Pretend he was using a tiny scoop and pulling it toward him, a tidbit at a time. From there he'd carry his treasure back to Belior and Satrinah, who would turn it into a weapon.

So pretend you're back in the lab now. You're standing guard, calling the weaponized bits back to yourself in undetectable amounts, maybe two or three atoms at a time. You stash them on your person, and then you're sent back out on another mission. On the way out, you pass by your hiding spot and quickly place the stolen material, then continue on.

Michael said, "Are there other tunnel branches?"

Saraquael said, "There were a couple of places where it felt as if there might be, but nothing that opened up."

They had no idea which of the demons had formed this tunnel. It might have been one of the Cherubim, but if they'd set Hastle himself to the task, he might have been able to make an area Guarded off from the others. The whole interior seemed to be sustained by multiple Guards woven around one another. Hastle could have opened a branch in a location only he knew and then Guarded it off.

Michael said, "So in theory, the remaining material could be hidden in the wall of the tunnel.

Saraquael said, "That's extremely dangerous. If Belior and Asmodeus ever decided to collapse that passage, it would have destroyed his stash with the tunnel, and he wasn't taking any chances with whatever he was planning."

True. Michael said, "He's also unlikely to have stashed it in Hell, so we're back to assuming it's somewhere in Creation."

Saraquael said, "And given the very small footprint of the tunnel exit I did find, there's no reasonable way we could search out exits over the whole Earth, let alone if he put it on the moon or in the heart of a star."

Michael tightened his wings around himself. *Hastiel, why did you have to be so thorough?* But of course he had to be: a wolf working among wolves, he needed to protect himself and cover all his tracks at every moment.

Michael lifted his head and studied the Void. No, not at every moment. Out here, on the edge of everything, maybe he hadn't. And maybe for Hastle, that had been a relief.

TWENTY-FIVE

Zadkiel lay in her bed listening to the other women getting up and ready for the day. Remiel didn't come help her. Remiel was gone. Zadkiel didn't know the layout and couldn't navigate. So she lay as if asleep.

She tried to pray, but it didn't come, so she just recited the morning offering and hoped the noises around her meant it was morning. She was so tired that it might still have been midnight, and the taste of smoke lingered in her mouth. She could smell it on her clothes and in her hair, and she assumed it was smudged on her skin.

Remiel had gotten her out of the house, and then she'd gone back in. Because Remiel could see.

It all came down to that: down to one misguided desire twenty years ago. Zadkiel could taste wine right now if she wanted. Perfect wine. Wine as it became when her Lord said, "Wine."

Some consolation. Remiel had been taken, and Zadkiel could have wine.

"Key?" Mary's hand touched her arm. "Are you all right?"

Zadkiel sat up, fighting hunger and the urge to cry. "I'm fine. I don't think I can navigate."

"Here. Count the steps and I'll let you know when you're at the door."

Without protesting, Zadkiel let Mary lead her. It just wasn't worth explaining that she'd caused all these problems and should be left to rot. Instead Mary escorted her to the table, guided her into a seat, then made sure she knew where all the food and drink was before her. The other women helped her, and under their attention she forced down some bites of bread. It tasted like nothing, but somewhere her brain registered that the body needed to eat, and it wouldn't be right to waste food the same way she'd wasted everything else.

The woman of the house came by several times, sounding delighted to be bombarded all at once with so many unexpected guests. What had her husband thought of her spontaneous generosity? But then again, the little girl Mary had prayed over was his daughter too, so maybe the couple were in agreement. Still, it would be a surprise for any family to awaken to dozens of invaders.

And the little girl herself? Her voice came to Zadkiel several times, a high-pitched chatter distinct from the young voices she'd become accustomed to. The girl was thrilled to have so many in her house, especially the other children. After a while they went outside to splash in the fountain before the day became too hot.

Shortly, a group of male voices entered the house: men from the Christian community who had gone back to the site of the fire to salvage what they could. Zadkiel could tell from their voices it was distressingly little, close to nothing at all. That beautiful home, spacious and so perfect a gift for their community, destroyed in a single night.

Sighing, Zadkiel hunched down at the table. Their kindness to her had been repaid with destruction.

Shortly after, the woman of the house came to her. "You're so sad. What can I do for you?"

Zadkiel said, "I'm sorry for bothering you. I'm blind, and I don't know where it would be convenient for me to go."

The woman said, "You can stay right where you are, if you like. Is there anything I can get you?"

Zadkiel shrugged. "I can make fishing nets."

The woman laughed. "I haven't the first clue how to make fishing nets!"

She left, still chuckling as though making things to sell were a great joke, and Zadkiel ran her hands over the table top. It had already been cleaned off.

A minute later, the household's little girl came to Zadkiel and asked her to follow. Taking Zadkiel by the hand, she led her through different rooms until eventually she stopped. "She's here."

Zadkiel wasn't sure if *she* was herself or someone who had sent for her, but then Mary replied, "Thank you, sweetie."

The little girl scampered away, and Zadkiel pivoted toward where Mary's voice had come from. "Here," Mary said, taking her hand. "I'm still trying to track down where everyone went, but at some point our three fishing girls will come for you, and they can take you to the market to buy more rope for a new net."

Zadkiel said, "Selling a net won't repay the damage done to your community."

Mary said, "You didn't do the damage."

"It happened because of me."

"It happened because of the evil one." Mary squeezed her hands. "You're blameless."

And then she heard John's voice. "How could you be anything other than blameless?"

Wait, they weren't alone? Zadkiel swallowed hard. "Sir, the evil one came there for revenge, trying to drive us out. You protected us, and we repaid your charity with evil."

John said, "Beloved, consider." He took her hands from Mary's. "Consider the honor of Christ having asked us to do what he did, to give up everything to protect someone else. Of course we would protect you. Of course we would make any sacrifice God asked of us—what an honor!"

Zadkiel shivered.

John continued, "We're doing no more than Christ who came before us. No, of course you wouldn't have asked this of us. It's always easier to be the giver than the recipient, the protector rather than the protected. But we in no way hold you to blame for the actions of the devil, and in every way we want you to be one among us."

Zadkiel bit her lip. "I should have been able to do more to protect you."

John said, "You are what God made you, no more and no less. Please, release your guilt and stand free in Christ. You are his child, Beloved, as are we all."

Zadkiel only shook her head.

John hugged her. "I'm sorry you are in this situation. I am not sorry we helped you. We lost a building, but rather than destroying us, the fire is giving others the opportunity to be generous. We'll find new places to live and worship. The Spirit will guide us, and even more souls will be added to our number. The devil meant it for evil, but God meant it for good." He kissed her cheek, and then he let her go.

Mary said, "I would take you out into the market with me, but I'm concerned. Satan took Remiel, so if you're spotted with me, you may be in danger too."

Zadkiel had considered that already. "Satrinah recognized Remiel. She hadn't identified me, so they might not know what to look for. Otherwise they'd have snatched me last night as well."

Mary said, "All the same, I'd prefer if you stayed indoors."

Zadkiel shook her head. "That puts this household in jeopardy. There aren't seals on this house yet."

Mary said, "Stay where you are. Remember what Michael said last night, that Belior was Satan's primary target. And if I don't appear to be singling you out for special treatment, he might not pick you out from the crowd."

Doubtful. To all accounts, Belior had recognized who she was, but Zadkiel didn't object further. She let Mary bring her into a room that echoed without people in it, and then shortly Mary filled it with a half-dozen children who needed instruction in the scriptures. "Let's memorize a psalm," Zadkiel said, a little unsteady. "This one was written by David."

The children listened and repeated, and Zadkiel worked with them, translating from the Hebrew David had spoken so beautifully into the Greek in which he'd never imagined his words taking form. She told them the meaning behind some of the images and used every mnemonic device she could think of, and the kids took turns reciting.

And then, in the middle of explaining how one Hebrew word had become a different Greek one, Zadkiel sang it, and then kept going. David had sung this one himself, not just listened to others singing it. He'd sang it before the Ark of the Covenant, saddened that his hands had been too bloodied by war to build the Temple, but rejoicing nevertheless to be so close to the Ark that contained the words of God, the staff of the priesthood and the bread that sustained the people in the desert.

And as she sang, Zadkiel realized Mary was in the room too, and that Mary was herself the Ark of the Covenant, having contained the Word of God, Jesus who embodied the Priesthood, and who then had become the Bread of Life. David had leaped and danced for the Ark, and John the Baptist had leaped for joy when Mary had come to him, but Zadkiel only sang. She thought about the Ark blessing the house of Obed-Edom the Gittite in the hill country and Mary blessing the house of Zachariah in the hill country, and then she thought about the Holy Spirit overshadowing both Mary and the Ark.

Mary was so different from herself. Mary was what God had made her and was acutely aware of God's manufacture: that she had been blessed, that God had done great things for her, and that in all things she was only what she'd been made to be. And Zadkiel must have in some respect denied God's gifts to herself because in so many ways, she should have been more than she was.

It hurt. Zadkiel stopped singing mid-psalm, and the children begged her to continue, but she couldn't go on.

When Michael checked on Zadkiel, his first thought was that she looked despondent, but then he decided some of that was exhaustion. She'd walked across the city last night after the fire, and it seemed as if she'd spent much of the day working with the community's children.

Saraquael alerted her that they were there, then prompted Zadkiel to extricate herself from the children and find a place she could talk to them alone.

Zadkiel made a disbelieving face, and Michael snickered. "You didn't think this through," he said to Saraquael. "There are two dozen people in this house, and the children follow her like ducklings."

Saraquael frowned. "You're right. I'll get Mary."

He vanished. Michael said to Nivalis, "Has everything been stable here?"

"So far. We've had demons crawling through the place, but so far nothing especially different, and none of them seem to have taken any special note of Zadkiel." Nivalis shifted nervously. "Is Satan looking for her too? Mary thinks he might be, and this house isn't sealed against demons."

Michael's shoulders tensed. "I've got a substantial patrol surrounding all the Christians in Ephesus. That should provide some protection for now."

Mary entered the room and sent the children to play in the courtyard, then helped Zadkiel walk to one of the smaller rooms at the back. She seated her on one of the couches, then said, "You'll have at least some privacy here. Do you mind if I don't stay? One of the men is still coughing tonight after the fire, and John is praying over him."

"Go tend him," said Michael. "We'll let you know if we need you."

After Mary left, Michael Guarded the room.

Saraquael moved closer to Zadkiel, warming her with his presence. "We haven't found Remiel yet. We assume Satan's kept her on the plane of Creation, but we have no idea where on Earth she'd be."

Zadkiel nodded. "I wish I could help you find her."

"We think you can," Michael said.

Zadkiel's head picked up. "How?"

Nivalis's eyes gleamed. "That would be great if you could."

Saraquael said, "We're sure one of the demon guards stole and hid a stash of Sheol material, and again, we're relatively sure it's somewhere on Earth."

Zadkiel frowned. "That's a lot of territory to search."

"And it's a substance you can't detect, doubtless under a strong Guard. I know." Saraquael gave a quirky smile that Zadkiel wouldn't be able to see. "But Sheol material draws in on itself whenever it can. It wants to be all of one piece, not in separate little pieces."

Michael added, "We don't think it's a coincidence that all three of you ended up in Ephesus. The material draws itself together in order to remain stable."

Zadkiel's eyes widened. "Oh! And if you combine that pull with the fact that I'm a Seeker, it means I might have a decent chance to figure out the direction it's stored in."

"More than that," Saraquael said, "I'm thinking you could lead us straight to it."

Nivalis raised a finger. "To the stolen stash, or to Remiel and Belior?"

Michael gave a weak smile. "We're not sure which, to be honest. Probably to whichever is closest."

Nivalis shook her head. "I dislike that idea. We could be handing her over to our enemies."

Saraquael said, "We're not going to toss her out into the desert all alone. Michael and I would both be with her."

"And me," said Nivalis, "but Satan's involved now. If he's looking for her, and we bring her to him, I'm worried what might happen."

Saraquael said, "We've got scouts. If Zadkiel wants to try, we can do this in such a way to maximize her safety the whole time."

Nivalis frowned, and a stray emotion slipped: that didn't mean Zadkiel would be *safe*.

Saraquael offered a smile: it was the best they could do.

Zadkiel said, "Of course I want to try. And I'm not worried about my safety."

Michael said, "In the interests of full disclosure, we may have to flash you from one location to another."

Zadkiel grinned in his direction. "In the words of someone we both know, that just means it's going to hurt—it doesn't mean it's not going to work."

TWENTY-SIX

Teeth chattering, Remiel huddled around herself and tried to remember what the Holy Spirit had told her about hypothermia back when she'd weathered that blizzard. She'd spent most of that first long-ago night praying on the rooftop, letting the wind slice through her, facing the gale with her hair blown away from her eyes and her earrings freezing in her ears, and through it all she'd laughed and joked around with God and enjoyed the chaos of nature at its rawest. God, showing off.

Her angelic mind should have been able to remember these things, but her human brain was flooded with all these hormones and neurochemicals, and she couldn't focus past them all. The body kept telling her it wanted to warm up, but she couldn't figure out how. Her body had spent so much of its precious heat drying off her clothes already, and now she just shivered in the thin fabric of her chiton as she curled on the cave floor. She was breathing far too quickly, and she suspected her pulse was racing also, but she didn't have all that much to compare it to.

Belior should have been cold too, nasty thing that he was, but Belior had sent one of the minor demons to fetch warm clothes and warm food and a warm drink. Remiel knew better than to ask for anything herself. The Cherubim were well aware of her discomfort because they'd examined her thoroughly, her soul and spirit and when necessary her body, and there was no reason they would care unless she actually did die—in which case, Satan would probably have at them again.

The only bright spots in this: whatever they'd done in examining her hadn't hurt in the slightest, even when they'd tried to flood her with angelic power; and also, whatever Nivalis had done in infusing her with energy had more than taken the edge off her exhaustion. For all that she'd been transported multiple places and probed and lit up from the inside, her headache wasn't as devastating as the one time Saraquael had transported her to Ephesus.

What was Satan up to? Even though he thought the Cherubim had conspired to use that weapon against him, he had charged them to re-create it and then left them alone, but first turned them against one another. Satrinah wouldn't use it against her bonded Seraph, so if forced, she'd choose Belior. Belior, meanwhile, had been told that if Satrinah failed to extract the material, she'd be the one killed. Therefore Belior had no incentive to cooperate with Satrinah, and Satrinah none to cooperate with Belior, and Satan had then left them under heavy surveillance to do exactly that.

In other words, whatever Satan's primary goal was, it in no way involved input from the Cherubim. He'd parked them in an underground location where they would accomplish nothing and at the same time couldn't team up again to harm him. Either that or he wanted the Cherubim to think the only way out was to use the weapon on him, and therefore be super-incentivized to get it done faster.

Remiel prayed and lay on the ground, watching water drip from the ceiling while the Cherubim argued and experimented in a far corner.

She noted after a while that her teeth had stopped chattering. She felt warmer. She was finally succumbing to hypothermia, maybe, (if only she could remember what the Holy Spirit had said about it,) but then she realized no, the stones beneath her were actually producing heat. That wasn't just a body-temperature thing.

Watching intently, she focused on the cave, but all remained as it was: a ring of demon soldiers and the pair of Cherubim at the center, bickering too quickly for her to follow. And all the while, the stones were just a little warmer than her body, and the goosebumps had receded, and she could uncurl her limbs without wanting to tighten right back up.

Okay. So what's going on?, she prayed. *I wouldn't object to a rescue mission right about now, you know.*

A demon soldier approached Belior with a loaf of bread.

"I don't want this now," Belior snapped, knocking it to the ground.

The soldier approached Remiel with another loaf.

Remiel tensed. Satrinah called out, "What are you doing?"

The demon replied, "Our master says the human isn't to starve. You need her alive."

The demon crouched before her, and she scrambled back into the wall. He handed her the loaf (warm in her hands, which were still chilly) and then passed her a heavy piece of metal encased in a Guard.

As she took it, he removed the Guard from around the piece.

She stifled a cry as it touched her palm. That was her own power, her own signature.

A sigil. Camael's.

The demon guard nodded, then with his wings spread a little further than they had to be, he took back the sigil and set it on the warmed stones. He grasped Remiel by the wrist and flashed her out of the cavern.

It happened so quickly that Remiel had no chance to brace herself. The demon pulled her out through the Guard and into another Guarded cave where she collapsed onto herself, head pounding and vision split by repeated lightning strikes. And all that wasn't as bad as the way her palm ached to have been holding Camael's sigil just a moment ago.

"You got her?" said a familiar voice.

Camael's.

"Like there was any doubt." The demon soldier huffed. "The way the Cherubim were arguing with each other, I could have led a parade band and an army of ten thousand through there. For a pair of insatiable questioners, they didn't even wonder why I was bringing Belior more food when they hadn't ordered me to do it."

Remiel picked up her head, but then someone jerked her to her feet. "They didn't hurt her, did they?"

They could ask her, she thought deep inside herself, still grappling with the vertigo while hearing them as if from a long distance.

"They'd discarded her like broken pottery shards in the corner, freezing." The soldier snorted. "I warmed her up for you."

"They're such idiots." Light flared through the cave, coming from Camael, and Remiel closed her eyes reflexively. "Disgusting. You got stuck in an awful body."

He let go of her, and Remiel stumbled back against the wall, then crept her way down to a seated position with the idea that once she was sitting on the floor, she couldn't fall off it.

The soldier said, "You can eat that. I didn't do anything to it."

Remiel just held the loaf close to her stomach. She managed a weak, "Why?"

"Why what? Why didn't I leave you there to be mistreated by those two buffoons?"

Remiel squinted. "Yeah. That."

"Because they're already so smug." Camael snorted. "Vetzi knew I'd want to know about them taking you, so when they sent him on some pointless errand, he came to me first."

With her hands on the warm loaf, Remiel huddled around it, unable to eat but at the same time craving the heat, the softness of the insides beneath the crusty outside. Her human body was sending dozens of impulses and details, and she couldn't decode them. Her eyes burned. Her mouth was tight. She kept swallowing on nothing.

Camael leaned against the wall. "I kept getting scouted out, and they'd pretend it was nothing. I'm not stupid. That meant they were looking for you, and it also meant they couldn't find you. I'm not without my own authority, so I put out feelers." His eyes glinted. "When I figured out where you were, and what they were doing, I turned them in to Satan." He chuckled. "And I got my reward, but what I wanted was you."

Remiel shivered. "The Cherubim. They'll notice I'm gone."

Camael snorted. "Even if they pick up on it, which is doubtful, they can't do anything about it." He flexed his wings. "They can't call out from that Guard, and they can't leave. And second," he added with a smirk, "they're not going to. My sigil's in there. That's our energy, and they'll just register it as your presence without bothering to double-check if you're actually still around to produce it."

Remiel looked up. "Satan's going to love them for that."

He folded his arms and leaned back. "It's really kind of a shame I won't be there when they realize what's happened."

Remiel whispered, "But you'll get in trouble."

"Do you honestly think they'll tell their master they got tricked by a Virtue?" Camael laughed out loud. "You'll have carved your way out of there with a holy blade long before that happens, trust me."

Vetzi snickered. "They'll slice themselves to pieces rather than admit you escaped with no one noticing. Be prepared to hear tales of your prowess for centuries to come."

Remiel lifted the bread to her face and inhaled the smell, then prayed the meal blessing. She broke it open and started eating.

"They'll say she cracked Satan's Guard too," Camael said.

Vetzi's brow furrowed. "They won't dare spread rumors of that nature."

Remiel swallowed. "What are you going to do with me?"

Camael braced himself. "I'm keeping you here with me."

Remiel's eyes flared. "Forever?"

Camael raised his wings. "At some point those two are going to figure out how to reverse whatever it is they did to you. When they do figure it out, we'll have them set you free of this body as well, and then..."

He stopped. Remiel's hands tightened on the bread loaf. It was still hot.

Camael sounded resolute. "I'm not giving you back to them. That's a matter of pride. I'm disgusted they caught you in the first place. But..."

Again he trailed off. Remiel chuckled. "Satan caught someone who couldn't run away and couldn't fight him. Quite a feather in his cap, don't you think?"

Vetzi said, "You're harder prey than that."

She snickered. "Human. Trapped in a burning building. It didn't take a great hunter to bag me."

Vetzi looked like he wanted to argue, but Remiel waved him off. "I'm just saying Camael doesn't need to be ashamed. Camael wouldn't have been caught so easily because he wouldn't have been in the situation to begin with."

She glanced at her brother, and his whole visage had darkened. Not with anger. It struck her again despite the centuries and despite their alliances, just how alike they were—how identical. Identical in every way except the most important, and how it felt right and wrong at the same time to be looking at his face and interpreting his expressions and knowing what it was he wanted to say before he even said it.

But she couldn't decipher it now, and she hurriedly turned her attention back to the food they'd given her. His attention flickered over her, and the vertigo flared from his proximity.

He crouched before her, and she tensed.

He whispered, "Stay with me."

"I haven't got a choice."

"I'll give you a choice." His voice grew lower still. "This is treason. Satan would pin me down in the Lake of Fire if he heard me say it, but hear me out."

Remiel's head snapped up. Could he? Would he?

"Stay with me." Camael took her hand. "We're one. You renounce your loyalty, and I'll renounce mine. We'll be together, free spirits the way we were intended to be."

She shook her head. "Just come back with me. I'm already free." She pulled his hand closer to her human heart. "You know I want you to come home."

He recoiled before his hand reached her chest. "You're enslaved, and I can't abide by that. But we shouldn't have had to choose sides to begin with." His voice ticked up a notch. "You can stay with me."

Remiel drew back on herself, biting her lip. This human body, clumsy thing, was shaking. Her heart was pounding, and her eyes were watering. It had grown hard to breathe, and she clenched her hands. Camael. Camael.

He edged closer. "I know what I'm asking you to give up. God bribed you in every way possible to stay under His service. He gave you status and power, but he didn't give you *me* because I saw through His ruse."

Remiel tucked her head down on her arm. "Please stop."

"I want you with me." Now he touched her. He flinched as he made contact with the flesh surrounding her spirit, but this time he didn't withdraw. Her head spun from the vertigo of having him so close, his signature an echo of hers, his strength and even the way his soul vibrated so intimately familiar. He was her. She was him. That's the way it was supposed to have been from the start.

"God forced us apart," Camael said. "You can put us back together."

Vetzi said, "I'll help you. After each of you renounces your affiliation, I'll stay with you and keep you protected. Remiel's as good as dead to her folk already, and Camael, you can disappear with ease."

Remiel pulled back even tighter on herself to stop the shaking.

I can't. She pressed her hands against her face and breathed into her palms. *I can't. God, help me. I can't do this.* She wasn't even sure which she couldn't do: couldn't leave God, who she loved and who loved her, couldn't renounce her loyalty and her fealty and the fact that He had created her and sustained her and been with her every moment? Or whether she couldn't say no to her brother, who after all this time apart from her was finally with her again.

One heart. One mind. Irin.

But with God, she also had a oneness. Not the same, but not entirely different either. Camael completed her. God completed her. She loved them both. Had loved Camael. Still loved him, apparently. Never had stopped. And God never had slackened in His love of her throughout. Not even in the moments she least deserved it.

Camael put his wings around her like a shelter while she shook. "She's still cold," he whispered to Vetzi. "Can you make it warmer in here?"

He was warming her up. He wanted her near.

Vetzi said, "Are you really stuck in that form? What did the weapon do?"

Remiel shrugged. "I don't know. No one knows."

"But what was it?"

Camael's wings smelled good, clean. Remiel closed her eyes. "Sheol material. Weaponized."

Vetzi crouched nearer and looked her in the face. "And were you working with Mephistopheles too?"

Remiel's jaw tightened. "Why do you people keep askig me that? We weren't working with them."

Vetzi's brows contracted. "Don't lie to me."

"She's not lying." Camael tightened his grasp on her. "I can feel her signature. And it feels right."

It feels right. It feels so right.

Remiel's voice broke as she pressed into Camael's embrace. "Just come back with me."

"It's not possible. God said it was final." Camael cuddled her to his side. "I can renounce my allegiance, but that won't bring me back to you. You have to renounce yours too." He hesitated. "Why are you keeping us apart? Don't you want to be together?"

Her head reeled. She wanted to tell him to back off and let her think, but she also didn't want him to move away from her. He was right here, after all this time. Breathing together, vibrating in unison. How could she say no?

He sounded as tortured as she felt. "Didn't you ever love me?"

"Don't say that." Her mouth trembled. "You left me."

"So you love Him more than me," Camael snapped.

"Of course I do!" she exclaimed before wondering whether it was true. But it had to be. God came before everybody and everything else. "You're badgering me. You're the one who left. You can't blame me for staying when you're the one who decided to abandon me in the first place."

"We have a chance to be together now," he urged. "I'll hide you."

"You can't hide me from God." She shook her head. "You can't hide me from myself. I can't renounce Him."

"You can," Camael said. "I did."

Her eyes filled with tears. "But you can ask for mercy. I'll ask for you. I'll beg. Please, Camael." She sat toward him, but he recoiled. "I'll offer Him everything I have to bring you home."

"Beg?" He looked disgusted. "And play the servant?"

Her eyes widened. "Then you don't want to be together! You just want me here with you."

Vetzi said, "She's a tough nut to crack, isn't she?"

Camael didn't follow as she backed away.

Remiel said, "That's it, isn't it?" Her voice sharpened. "You're playing me! You have no intention of renouncing anything whatsoever. You just want me to get winnowed alongside you." She glared at him. "We went through that once. Wasn't once enough?"

Camael shot a worried look at Vetzi, but Vetzi only said, "You tried your best. I don't hold you responsible."

Vetzi grabbed Remiel from behind and twisted her arms, then bound her up with his will. She struggled, but his will was far stronger than she'd anticipated...and in the next moment she recognized it for what it was. Satan's power. Vetzi was Satan.

Camael rushed toward her in tears. "Don't do this to me! Please, just stay with me!"

Vetzi pushed Camael aside. He flared like lightning, and when Remiel could see past the glare, he'd dropped the disguise. Twelve white wings, green eyes, cornsilk hair. "You're right, you know. You weren't hard to capture." He chuckled. "But that would have been the same in either form."

Satan dragged her through space again, and this time it hurt. It hurt as her heart got torn away from Camael while he screamed her name one last time, and it hurt as her head howled with pain and her vision whited out, and it hurt when she was dumped unceremoniously on the stone while Satan was saying, "Don't you Cherubim pay attention to anything? Why should I have to bring back your toys like animals that strayed off?"

A circle of warm metal throbbed on the cave floor, directly under her chest. Remiel didn't need to touch it to know what it was. It vibrated with power. Camael's sigil. Camael. Gone.

She collapsed to the floor, landing with the metal against her skin.

TWENTY-SEVEN

Saraquael came for Zadkiel just after dark. She made her way into the courtyard with Nivalis, then asked her child guide to leave her there for the time being. After the child scampered back into the house, Saraquael took form and touched her arm. "Here, you'll need to put this on. It might get cold."

She reached forward and felt heavy fur. "Where'd you get this? Isn't this the clothing Remiel was wearing before?"

Saraquael chuckled. "The same."

Michael sounded amused, and Zadkiel warmed at how relaxed he sounded, and the fact that he was there at all. "How'd you do that?"

"I told Remiel which merchant to go to," Saraquael said as he helped Zadkiel sip the heavy tunic over her chiton, then the coat over that. "I'd scouted him out ahead of time and asked if he had anything warm for a trip up north. That way when these two came to him, he'd be willing to buy it."

Zadkiel worked her feet into the boots with his help. "What did you buy it with?"

"Money. They kind of honor that over in the market."

She could hear the good humor in Saraquael's voice, and she rolled her eyes. "And you got the coins by mining the metal yourself and stamping it with the seal of the emperor?"

"No, silly. I got it from somebody who didn't need it anymore." The boots tightened around her ankles as he fastened the straps. "I searched the bottom of the Mediterranean until I found a shipwreck, and there were coins in the wreckage. I probably overpaid," he added, "but you and Remiel got money when you needed it, and now you've got warm clothing, and the merchant has more money than he started with."

"And the dead ship captain doesn't care," Zadkiel said.

Michael sounded astonished. "When did you set that up?"

"As soon as I realized we might bring them to Ephesus. If we didn't, no harm done. The merchant would have told me no, and then no one would have come to sell him winter gear. Needing the winter clothing again was the only thing I didn't count on."

"Why'd you choose him?" Zadkiel asked. "You realize that merchant was disgusting, right?"

"How so? He was polite to me."

"He made remarks about seeing Remiel naked and buying her from me for his personal gratification."

Saraquael sounded irritated. "Well, then. I guess I need to pray for him specially, don't I?"

Zadkiel grinned. Michael said, "Zadkiel, before we start, have you changed your mind?"

Nivalis's voice sounded unsteady. "You don't have to do this."

Zadkiel shook her head. It was too bad she couldn't project in this form, but body language would help. "I'm good to go."

"Put your arms around my neck," Saraquael said, and she hugged him. He lifted her into his arms and took flight.

She clutched him reflexively, gasping as the air gusted around them. He had his arms around her back and under her knees, and she hoped no demons tried to knock her out of his grasp.

"You're not afraid of heights, are you?" he murmured.

"Only when I can fall." Zadkiel tucked her face down out of the wind and concentrated on the strength of his muscles as his wings beat.

"Like this?" He mock-dropped her, and she yanked closer to his chest.

"Hey!" Nivalis exclaimed. "What are you doing?"

"Making her laugh," Saraquael said.

"I'm going to hurt you," Zadkiel snapped. He was laughing, and she giggled. "Think how much fun you'll have explaining to all the little Greek children how a lady fell from the sky."

"Oh, rats, they'll worship you after Raphael finishes putting you back together, won't they? I'd better not drop you after all."

He leveled out into a glide, and Zadkiel raised her head. The air was notably chillier than it had been on the ground, and it was also harder to breathe. The proximity to Saraquael's angelic power made her ears ring, but it wasn't an altogether unpleasant sensation. Her head ached, and again, it was more like the after-effect of drinking a whole cup of wine. That she could tolerate.

"Okay, fellow Seeker," Saraquael murmured. "We're going to do what God made us to do. I want you to bring that shrapnel home."

Holding close to him, Zadkiel concentrated on Sheol, on Sheol material and death, on what it meant to be weaponized death. She reached inside herself, something she'd been doing since this morning when the archangels had first laid out their plan to her, and she grasped that inner wrongness.

As it had all day, the death inside her felt cold, but with a cold unlike the biting wind against her cheeks and the dry chill tearing at her lungs. This was a solid cold with an immobility to it that dared anyone to budge it from wherever it set its footprint. She couldn't use gloves for this one: with her heart, she grasped the wrongness and didn't try to shield herself.

"I've got it." The wind carried away her voice.

Saraquael pressed his forehead against hers, and she felt him trying to probe through her human heart toward the shrapnel inside. It had dissolved within her; it wasn't in just one place, but rather inhabiting every last bit of her spirit. When he touched it, it parted before him like water around a river rock, and the motion made Zadkiel dizzy.

She tried to draw the shrapnel up to the surface of her heart, but it kept evading her. No wonder it had taken the Cherubim twenty years to work with this: it wanted to escape and hated touch. She let it suffuse her, though, and she tried to draw Saraquael's thoughts into it as well. "Can you feel it?"

He sighed. "Barely. I know it's there, but not more than that."

Nivalis said, "My turn?" and placed her hands on Zadkiel. Gradually Nivalis fed a thread of energy into her the way she'd done into Remiel, giving Zadkiel access to angelic power without overwhelming her. Zadkiel tensed in response, and Saraquael shook his head. She tried to relax, and the energy kept coming. Her head pounded, but she concentrated on the shrapnel.

"Have you got a direction?" Michael asked.

Saraquael said, "It's not responding. We could try moving her so we could detect a change if we happen to get closer."

Michael said, "Is there any response at all? Or just a very weak one?"

"None."

"Then let's go to the next stage." Zadkiel felt Michael draw closer. "Cup your hands."

She unclenched herself from Saraquael's shoulders and left him holding onto her unsupported. It surprised her how scary that felt, how insecure not to have something to cling to. She pivoted away from him, and he corrected for her shifted weight. She stiffened, and then when he felt still again, she cupped her palms.

Nivalis said, "You're okay."

This is terrifying, Zadkiel prayed. *Please bless our efforts.* And then, *Please keep me safe.*

Silly human body, with its human fear of destruction. It occurred to her that it was a good thing she couldn't see how high she was. She could pretend she was on the bottom branch of a tree, swinging her legs while a stream rushed mere inches beneath her toes.

She extended her cupped palms, and Michael placed in them a warm sphere that vibrated out of sympathy with the wind.

Death. She was holding Death.

"The Sheol fragments are under a heavy enough Guard that they're not going to embed themselves in you," Michael said, "but if you need me to, I can lighten the Guard."

Zadkiel cradled the sphere closer to her chest even though it was so immaterial that that wind couldn't knock it free from her fingers.

Nivalis said, "They're all pointing toward you."

"Well that's no good," Zadkiel whispered to the sphere in her hands. "We need you guys to point to the rest of your friends, not have you all point toward each other."

She extended her heart into the sphere, and Saraquael did the same. His touch felt warm around the edges, and the little shards of Sheol material didn't want to be with him. They avoided him, like magnets arranged the wrong end around. For her, on the other hand, they waited, still and poised. They had no motion as much as an air of waiting. Of longing.

Remiel had described them like a school of fish, and Zadkiel concentrated on that image: a dozen or more darting creatures, all lined up together and wanting to stay together. She kept her concentration on the sphere but at the same time thought of the shrapnel in her spirit, and she tried to figure out a way to introduce them to one another, like water poured into water.

"Should I lessen the Guard?" Michael asked.

Deep inside herself, she didn't answer, but she registered that Saraquael was saying not to break her concentration. Nivalis was moving around her too, still passing in energy but with the finesse of someone reeling out the thread of a silkworm cocoon. Zadkiel kept feeling through herself for the splinters of shrapnel that pervaded her spirit.

The energy from Nivalis spiked, and Zadkiel flinched, but then it eased back. In that energy came understanding and tension, and then something more. A question. Nivalis wanted to hold the Sheol material too.

Saraquael's presence backed off. He wasn't able to touch them, but Zadkiel keened inside as he withdrew. Then Nivalis entered into the exchange, and Zadkiel welcomed her presence.

Nivalis reached for the Sheol material, and it responded.

Zadkiel tensed. Nivalis moved through it, and while it didn't follow her, it also didn't run. It vibrated in place, and Zadkiel imagined it like that same school of fish darting for a just-spotted food source.

Next Zadkiel felt Nivalis moving the Sheol material in the Guard, and although she couldn't see it, she could visualize what it felt as if Nivalis were doing: kind of like a German Shepherd taking care of a flock of sheep, she was trying to get the material not to focus on Zadkiel's material but rather to focus outward. And then she sent, *May I?*

Zadkiel shivered. She couldn't speak, but she nodded.

Nivalis dissociated into Zadkiel, merging their spirits together. With an involuntary moan, Zadkiel hunched forward in Saraquael's arms and fought nausea, and he held her tighter, but Nivalis stayed moving in her. It felt worse than the vertigo of being transported. This time her interior was rebelling and her body was trying to reject itself.

Michael said, "Nivalis, stop."

Give me five seconds.

Zadkiel counted, and at two, Saraquael said, "You've got it!"

Zadkiel blew out a hard breath.

Nivalis sent, *I might be able to get the material out of her.*

Michael said, "What?"

Zadkiel didn't have a chance to react. In the next second, a deep dread filled her whole body, coupled with a desire to run and a desire to hide. She made a sound that wasn't a whimper and wasn't a shriek—she didn't know what it was, but her body reflexively curled as if she were hiding, and Michael pulled that sphere from her palms just before she dropped it.

"Nivalis! Out—now!"

The sensation vanished, and Nivalis was saying, "I had it, but it wouldn't come."

Saraquael said, "Michael, they're oriented. They found it."

Shaking, Zadkiel wrapped her arms around Saraquael's neck again as they flew. Beneath the heavy clothes she shivered, her body wet with a dull sweat, and she pressed her face against his neck. That feeling, that emotion—what was that? Limp, she let Saraquael fly wherever the shrapnel was directing him, but her heart kept returning to that dread and the urge to vanish.

Nivalis was saying, "When I linked the stuff inside her to the stuff in the sphere, I was able to handle it. It was slippery, but it didn't resist me. Not the way it resisted Saraquael. I thought I could get it out of her."

Michael said, "It looked like you'd have done that by killing her."

"I'm sorry."

Saraquael said, "You stopped when you needed to. I think you did great work. It's not as if any of us have manipulated this substance before, and here you gave us a compass needle."

Zadkiel fought past the feelings toward the shrapnel inside her, and she found it responsive now. It was all straining in one direction, and she said, "Saraquael, we need to correct course." She leaned in the direction she wanted him to go, and he shifted. All the little bits in her pivoted their direction again, and she listened to them. Seeker: Seekers could listen to the world and find what was hidden, reveal what was concealed. What did that make Nivalis, that she could gather what was scattered?

The shrapnel didn't feel any less pulverized or less diffuse than before. It was just acting as a unit with the material on the outside of her, and now as a whole they were stretching for another bit of themselves they'd been separated from.

"How did you do that?" Zadkiel whispered, but her voice got blasted away by the wind.

Saraquael went lower, and Zadkiel gauged the pressure in her heart. She wanted to be *there*. There was where the rest of this material was, or at least some of it, and it was trying to be all together. Distance didn't matter to it: it reached through Creation and bent space to find itself and draw together. She leaned forward out of Saraquael's arms, and he said, "Whoa, stay put. I thought you didn't want to fall."

"It's out there."

"I know."

No, he didn't know. He couldn't feel that tug, that crazed yearning to be near the other object. *What is this stuff?,* she prayed. *Why does it respond this way?* The original Sheol material hadn't behaved like that. Or had it? Gabriel had developed a way to get it to interlock with itself, but that had been a forced thing. The weaponized stuff wasn't passive. It struggled to be with itself, and she had a hard time staying still against the urgency.

And somewhere, out in Creation, this stuff was yearning to be with her, too, straining back toward her even though it didn't know her or who she was. It just wanted to be all together again.

"Down," she said before she even realized she was speaking, and Saraquael descended, but it wasn't fast enough. Zadkiel fought the momentary urge to jump. He projected a question, and she reached with one hand as if she could grasp the thing she was Seeking. He followed her arm, and she gave minor corrections as they drew closer.

He stopped.

"Keep going!" She leaned forward. "What are you doing?"

"There's a mountain in front of us. Right here."

Her fingertips brushed stone.

"Set me down, then."

He placed her on her feet with a caution not to move too quickly, and Zadkiel embraced the rock. "It's so close," she whispered. She pressed her body against the side of the mountain, then rested her cheek against it too. So, so distressingly close.

Mary finished helping the servant put away the cups and bowls, then turned to find the household's little girl in the kitchen doorway. "A visitor wants you. She's in the courtyard."

Mary wiped off her hands and tucked her hair back out of her eyes before taking an oil lamp from the shelf.

"Do you know who it is?"

The little girl giggled, an amazing sound from someone who'd been so close to dying. "I don't know who any of these people are, Mistress." She took Mary's hand. "But it's fun. Daddy's so confused, but Mommy is happy."

Mary smiled, then turned through the courtyard door and stopped.

It was Remiel, Remiel standing, shaking. "Oh, sweetheart!" Mary rushed to her. "You're back! We were so worried!"

Remiel nodded. "Can I have some water?"

Mary sent the little girl into the house to fetch a cup, and she guided Remiel to one of the benches. "Sit. You're exhausted." More than exhausted: her clothing was damp, and she had bruises shadowing both eyes. She wasn't wearing her sandals, and an air of smoke clung to her from the house fire. "What happened to you?"

"Satan took me last night." Remiel's eyes filled with tears. "I had to fight, but I got free. I came back. Where is Zadkiel?"

The girl brought the cup out to her, and Remiel gulped it down. Mary said, "She's looking for you."

Remiel looked up, eyes wide. "Do you know where she went?"

The oil lamp sputtered a bit, and the little girl went back into the house. Mary said, "I don't know how they planned to find you. I wasn't part of that conversation."

Remiel leaned forward urgently. "Tell me! Who went with her?"

Mary took Remiel's hand. "Don't worry about Zadkiel right now. They'll come back when they can't find you." She gathered herself. "You're so tired. You should lie down and sleep."

"Not until I know what happened to Zadkiel."

The hair stood up on Mary's arms and on the back of her neck. She prayed, *Help me.*

Remiel clenched her fists in her chiton. "Tell me! This isn't a game—she's in danger looking for me, more danger than she knows, but I'm safe! I have to go after her!"

Mary tried to focus on Remiel in the dimming light. "I thought she was your superior officer."

Remiel's nose wrinkled. "Hardly. I'm one of the Archangels of the Presence. She's so much weaker than I am. That's why I need to protect her."

Was this really Remiel? Was it a trap? Mary couldn't be sure. Remiel had been rough around the edges at the best of times, and maybe she felt 'off' because she was scared. Maybe getting beaten up by Satan did that to you. Or maybe it wasn't Remiel after all. She looked like her. She sounded like her. She acted like her, and she felt like her. But how to be sure? Humans weren't meant to make these kind of discernments. *God, help me, please.*

"Please. I have to go after her. I can't just abandon her." Remiel blinked with tears running down her cheeks. "And I'll need you to help me too. When I return, I'm going to be hurt. I'll need you to remind me of what I was because I'll be battered and confused, and if you do that, I'll be able to recover. I'll need you to give it like an order: *Remember who you were. You need to be what God made you to be.*"

Mary took Remiel's shaking hands in her own. They were soft, clammy. "Sweetie, you know I want what's best for you, and you know I'd do anything God wants me to do for you. You came to me for help, and I took you as my guest." She braced herself. "That title you use for me?"

Remiel grimaced. "You aren't going to stand on titles now, are you? This is important!"

Mary waited.

"Fine." Remiel rolled her eyes. "My lady."

Mary stood. "Leave here."

"You're not going to help?" Remiel's eyes widened. "How can you do that to me?"

Mary walked away. "You're not Remiel. Go."

Remiel rushed after her, grabbing her arm. "Anything that happens from here out is your fault! You could have helped!"

Mary said, "You have no authority here. In the name of my Son, leave."

The pressure vanished from her arm. She turned, but there was no one, only the hint of smoke and a pair of damp footprints on the courtyard stone.

TWENTY-EIGHT

Michael made sure Zadkiel wasn't about to slip off the edge of the mountain and plunge a mile to her death. Hastle had chosen a lovely spot to hide his cache of stolen goods: no human was going to randomly stroll into this area, given that it was a thick forest broken only by tons of upthrusted stone. Even to get here required the ability to fly. Either that or skill to stick to walls. Most humans didn't have either.

"Now what?" Nivalis said.

As Michael watched, the color returned to Zadkiel's face. Whatever Nivalis had done to her before, it had left her ash white in a way Michael hadn't seen other than on a soldier bleeding out from a hacked-off limb during a battle. Her blood pressure had dropped, and her brain had output a cornucopia of stress hormones, and when he'd ordered Nivalis to stop, he hadn't even been sure it was soon enough.

Just like stepping off this cliff, in other words. Michael said, "How far inside is it?"

"I'll scout it out." Saraquael pressed up against the rock face the same way Zadkiel was, only he didn't wear the same contented look. "About a wingspan in, there's an opening, like a natural cavern. I bet it's in there."

Eyes closed, Zadkiel nodded.

Nivalis said, "Should we flash her inside?"

"It's this big," Saraquael said, holding his hands apart. "We might get her head in, but not the rest of her."

Nivalis frowned. "So what are we going to do?"

Michael formed up his sword. "Hold onto her," he said, and he sliced through the mountainside.

The rock split beneath the soul-energy of the sword, and he felt Saraquael directing his cuts so they gained access to the area but didn't destroy it. Nivalis steadied Zadkiel, and Michael cut a broader shelf for her to stand on, then made two more slices. Stone slide away down the mountainside, and while smaller pebbles skittered along the rockface, he studied the new opening.

Saraquael said, "This is good. Hang on." He solidified and began removing stone pieces by hand. "Let me know if you feel the material come loose."

Zadkiel said, "It hasn't moved."

Michael and Saraquael shifted stone until Michael found the first opening of the crawl space in the stone. No, not crawl space: Saraquael was right about the size of the thing. Maybe a badger could fit inside, but even that would be snug. Water must have hollowed out this tiny spot over centuries, and then the flow had dried up, leaving just this hollow area.

Yeah, Hastle knew how to hide a thing.

While Michael cleared more of a shelf so Zadkiel would be able to reach the rock cubby, Saraquael shone light inside and sent a warning to any critters that might be living in the area. "No spiders, snakes, or rodents," he called into the hollow. "You aren't wanted right now. We're big scary angels, and we're higher up the food chain than you are."

Zadkiel sounded tart. "I'm not afraid of spiders."

"Humans have this reflex to jump when a bug crawls on them." Saraquael shrugged. "I didn't want your body to take a flying leap while your brain was insisting it wasn't afraid of spiders. At any rate, it's clear now."

"Thanks." Zadkiel pressed her chest against the rock, then her cheek. "It's so close. You have no idea. The pieces want to come together."

Oh, he had the idea. Michael looked at the sphere, all the little shards pressed up against the side nearest the stone, all pointing the same direction, same as Zadkiel was doing. If they could turn her back into an angel, she'd already be in there, curled around the material. Instead she reached a hand deep inside and probed, but Michael could tell she wasn't finding it just by touch.

"Hold the sphere inside," Nivalis said. "I'll go in and get a direction from the shards."

Nivalis vanished, either making herself tiny or else discorporating to enter the cavern. Michael miniaturized himself, leaving Saraquael to keep Zadkiel steady on the rock ledge.

In Zadkiel's hand, the sphere glinted, and Michael sent to Saraquael, *Tell her to move her hand a bit left,* and then, *Have her raise it.* Each time, he streamed a light forward from the points of the shrapnel. And finally, *Have her move it a third place. Anywhere.*

Gabriel had said more than once that with three vectors you could triangulate the location of anything. And right now, Michael had all three.

Where the three beams crossed, Michael found an ordinary stone. He touched it. Ordinary. Solid.

Zadkiel pulled the sphere back from the opening, and she must have passed it back to Saraquael because when she reached back in, she was empty-handed. With Nivalis guiding her movement, she extended her fingers and was just able to brush the stone. Michael heard her gasp. She strained forward, and with her fingertips she rolled the stone out of its niche in the wall.

It dropped, but she found it again, and Michael flashed back outside.

On the ledge, Zadkiel had the pebble in her hands. "It's here. It's Guarded, but it's in here."

Michael said, "Time to unGuard it."

He took back the sphere, and while Saraquael kept Zadkiel secure on the ledge, Michael held both it and the pebble on his palm. He asked Nivalis to create a Guard surrounding both. "I don't want this stuff to scatter, so make it strong."

Within the outer Guard, Michael created a third, tinier Guard encircling the pebble, and he crushed it down, focusing his entire will on the stone. The pebble fragmented, and he let the rock bits pass through the Guard like a shower of powder on his hands. He pushed harder, and at the core he met with resistance, a miniature Guard woven into the rock itself and searing with desperation.

Oh no, you don't. This was Hastle. This felt like Hastle and it vibrated like Hastle, and if he could smell and taste it would have done those like Hastle as well. The Guard buckled but then rallied, and Michael knew that in Heaven, in a sealed cell, Hastle was fighting him, resisting with all his power as the pressure on the Guard intensified every second. Hastle wanted this. Whatever Hastle had been planning, he needed this, and right now he diverted all his strength into it.

Somewhere between Hell and Creation, that tunnel had to be collapsing because Hastle couldn't power both of them. Somewhere in Hell, anything Hastle had tried to stash in secret was now on its own. He was putting every energy into resisting, and Michael kept pressing, crushing it down, determined, relentless, until finally Hastle's Guard caved and Michael's smashed it apart.

"Got it!" Nivalis exclaimed, but she didn't need to. A blizzard of Sheol bits exploded out of the place the pebble used to be, swirled like a cloud, and then rushed around the sphere of other bits. Michael released the inner Guard between them, and they all joined together.

They didn't point at Zadkiel. They were all of them pointing off to the East. Even Zadkiel had turned her face in that direction.

Michael tried to speak, but for a moment nothing emerged. Instead he could only imagine Hastle lying on a cell floor in Heaven, completely bereft.

It should hurt more than it did. Remiel's body should have been bleeding, shivering, convulsing, something, but human bodies didn't show pain the same way an angelic one would. She should have been lying in a pool of blood. Satan had left her, clean and unbroken, in a heap on the floor, but it didn't matter: she didn't move, and she kept her eyes closed because when she opened them, she could see her human body was intact in a way that belied the pain in her chest, the pain in her throat, the pain in her eyes.

She hadn't slept for days in order to avoid this. Satan had done it anyhow in fifteen minutes.

Her heart hurt too much to pray, but she forced herself to recite something. Was it the morning? Well, somewhere it was morning. So she recited the morning offering in her head, then repeated it. She could do words, even if any feelings were beyond her right now. And then she did the evening prayer too, figuring there was an opposite side of the world too and she could make it work either way. *Lay us down, Lord Our God, in peace.* Peace. Peace, she kept repeating to herself. Peace, not being in pieces, two pieces, one of which didn't care what it did to her as long as it could possess her and own her and in the end devour her. It wasn't just missing Camael that hurt so much. He didn't care about her anymore, didn't care about *himself,* and it didn't matter if what brought her to him was a lie as long as he could clamp down on her and drag her into the depths like an alligator with a writhing muskrat in its jaws.

Her body should be hurting, therefore, but it didn't. Just the headache and the nausea, the renewed chill from being on the rocks in nothing but a chiton. She hardly noticed.

Satan hadn't left the cavern. Instead he was working with the Cherubim, and she registered the things he was saying. He'd started off with, "Okay, now that I've settled out Remiel, you two are going to work together, and neither of you will be lucky enough to get destroyed." So either he'd been lying before or he was lying now, and how was that any different from anything else he did? But it made some degree of sense, didn't it? He'd 'parked' the Cherubim until he could try breaking her down. When Camael couldn't swing her to their side, Satan had moved on to the next part of the plan. And so it would go, round and round.

While reciting prayers she knew by heart, she listened to Satan questioning the Cherubim and keeping the resulting discussions on point. She progressed to reciting psalms, and Satan had the Cherubim experimenting on each other. Not on her, for some reason. *It would be helpful to be able to warn Michael about that,*

Remiel said to God. *It's probably significant. He wants that stuff inside me for some reason.*

Satan said, "So tell me how this weapon would have worked." And that was a nice, useless line of conversation for him to explore. Let him become expert in wielding a weapon he'd never have his hands on—what did it matter? He hadn't extracted it from Belior, and so far he hadn't even tried with her.

She closed her eyes. *Well, better in me than in his hands.*

She reached for God, and although He felt faint inside her (human body, broken heart, under Guard) she held to the feeling. She couldn't open up, but she could recite, *Holy, holy, holy* and know His holiness, and she kept it at that.

In the next moments, though, she grew restless. She wanted to be moving, and she pushed up onto her palms to look around the room. Satan noticed her, but although he watched, he didn't move away from the Cherubim. She couldn't leave, and at any rate, there were enough demon soldiers standing watch that she'd be flattened before she could do anything.

But still, the restlessness. She sat up on her heels, then stood in one motion, clutching Camael's sigil in her palm. Once standing, she took a step toward the back wall.

One of the soldiers shoved a lance in her face. "Get down!"

Satan called, "Let her move. Are you afraid of a cute little girl?"

Now that was unexpected. Chagrined, the soldier, stepped back. Remiel glanced at Satan, unsure what was going on, but he'd turned his stare back to whatever Satrinah was diagramming on the table-top in filaments of light.

Remiel took a step toward the wall, and then another. It felt better here. She had no idea why because the rocks weren't warmer, and the stones underfoot were rougher, but she preferred the wall. She moved along it a step, then took another.

With a predatory calm, Satan was studying her again. She hesitated. What was he up to?

Camael's sigil felt heavy in her fingers, but she didn't want to put it down. Now she was actually touching the back wall, and she still felt as if she wanted to move in closer. Restless, she craned her neck to look at the cavern roof where it melted into darkness, then back along the rock.

Smirking, Satan watched her move, and finally she tucked up her knees and sat as close to the stone barrier as she could. She wanted to back into the wall itself, but that had to be a human feeling: naturally she wanted to escape, although why she wanted to escape in this particular direction made no sense. But whatever: her human body had been through a wringer, and those human hormones and neuroreceptors and such had to all be responding to signals she couldn't interpret without a lifetime of experience.

Satrinah followed Satan's gaze over to her, and Remiel shifted. The restlessness was unbearable, except she had no other choice than to bear it. Maybe restlessness was the after-effect of being split from Camael, as if you could run from something you couldn't. *Human bodies make no sense.*

Satrinah's eyes narrowed as she stared at her, and when Satan asked her a question, she didn't respond at all.

That was no good. Satrinah had a Cherub's unbreakable focus, and she was diagnosing something. Remiel huddled tighter. *God, I'd really like to be able to pass through stone right about now.*

Satrinah said to Satan, "What are you really doing?"

Belior's head shot up, and he looked from Satan to Remiel and then back to Satan again. His eyes were wide, white-ringed. *Good call. His master's jerking him around, and by this point even he has to realize he's created a situation that's completely out of his control.*

She allowed herself a wry smile. Satan might have her at his whim, but he had Belior under his power. She wasn't the worst off in this situation.

The restlessness hit again, much stronger, and she rubbed her arms not so much because of the cold but because she wanted to be moving. She pressed into the cavern wall and closed her eyes. Here it felt best. These tons of stone belonged to some unnamed mountain, but for a moment she imagined someone caring about her on the other side. She thought about God, loving her on the other side of the Guard. Camael, walled away from her by his choices but at least pretending to care about her. And through it all, as if just an arm's reach away on the other side, someone who would help her carry this internal heaviness.

Satan folded his arms. "We're up to the next stage in our process. You two keep working on your assignment." He strode toward Remiel. "Everyone, on your guard! We're about to be breached."

Breached? As in—?

Satan's Guard snapped over her and yanked her backward, and Remiel yelped, then crashed to her knees with her hands against her temples.

The wall exploded where Remiel had just been, and she huddled around herself to avoid the rock debris. With a roar, the rubble blasted into the clear force of Satan's Guard, and her head pounded with the noise.

"Quite a dramatic entrance," Satan observed from behind her. "He doesn't realize yet that he can't leave."

Remiel unlaced her fingers from the back of her neck and raised her head. Michael! He'd come for her—and Satan had been prepared for Michael's entrance—an entrance she had somehow presaged by her restlessness.

Satan wrenched her upright, holding her by the shoulders. "You can't leave yet, by the way. You still have my stuff."

The sigil? He could have pried that from her hand. Camael could have called it back to himself. Her head throbbed, and she wasn't thinking clearly, but it had to be the shrapnel. And great, good luck to him getting it out of her after Gabriel, Belior, and Satrinah had failed.

Forcing herself not to struggle, Remiel hunted for shapes through the dust. In full armor, Satan had her in front of him and his sword before them both (*Three guesses what he'll do to me, God!*) with his Guard neatly separating her, the Cherubim, and the demon soldiers from the intruder, of which there was exactly one: Michael.

Michael slashed at the Guard, and Satan sounded bored. "I'd suggest not doing that. My Guard is holding up the cavern ceiling. Your Owner might not permit Remiel to die, but Belior's host would perish, and you've also got Zadkiel to think about."

So Zadkiel was close, truly close. Michael must hidden her, but she'd been on the opposite side of that wall. And Satan had sealed her in too.

Satan looked around. "Did someone send you in here with a message or something? Where's your manager?"

"I have only one message." Michael's eyes glinted. "You can keep Belior. I want Remiel."

"Of course you want Remiel. Unfortunately, I want something Remiel has, and I haven't convinced her yet to be parted from it." Satan tightened his grip, and Remiel kept her body relaxed so he didn't break her shoulder. "You also have no currency with which to bargain. It's annoying when you write me off as stupid, but I have no qualms using your blind spots against you."

For the first time, Michael looked worried, and Remiel reached her heart for God. Those soldiers were going to find Zadkiel, and doubtless Michael had left someone (Saraquael?) with her for protection. Saraquael couldn't hide Zadkiel forever. She was in a human body, and he might be able to keep her screened for a little while, but Satan's forces only had to flush all the oxygen out of the Guarded area, or lower the temperature by fifty degrees and hunt for her body heat.

Satan nodded to his soldiers, and they flooded out of the cavern.

Michael flared with power, and Remiel recoiled against her own will as the stone walls rumbled. He might well bring the whole thing down on them all, Belior's host or not. Stones dropped, and Remiel cringed, but again they crashed off Satan's Guard. Across the cavern, Satrinah had cast a Guard over Belior, and Michael was blasting at demon soldiers in enough fury to keep them from escaping the stones.

Somewhere, Saraquael had to be protecting Zadkiel too. *Please. Please, Father, this is my fault. Don't let her get hurt.*

Satan wasn't defending. He just allowed the chaos to continue, and Remiel closed her eyes because he obviously had a plan, something he'd come up with in only a few hours and yet was undoing them all because Michael hadn't realized his movements were so carefully predicted. Michael had sent in a small force to scout when he could have sent an army, and Satan was ready.

Remiel kept her eyes closed. *You had Israel defeat large forces with small ones. Please, Father. Please help him.*

Satan pried Camael's sigil from her fingers. "Oh, and this?" He held it in front of Remiel's eyes: a flat metal circle with no identifying marks, like a coin struck in the image of an emperor only without an emperor's face to proclaim. "You don't get to keep this. Twin."

His fingers flamed, and the sigil burst apart. The last of Camael's energy vanished.

Her knees weakened, but she tried not to crumple.

There was so much dust and rock by now that Remiel wouldn't be able to breathe if Satan lowered the Guard. Every time Michael flashed with light, or one of the demons, even with her eyes closed, Remiel's head pounded. She might vomit all over Satan after all, small victory. But then the chaos intensified, and in the din, she heard shouting and demons laughing, and then another human body crashed into her, and Satan flung her to the cavern floor.

Remiel grabbed the other person, and it was Zadkiel, shaking violently in that thick northern coat. Remiel pulled her close. "It's me. I'm here."

Her heart sang out inside her as she got her arms around Zadkiel, and in a rush her body tingled from head to toe. She gasped, and she buried her face in Zadkiel's neck with tears streaming down her cheeks. The loss of Camael's sigil burned in her mind, and her heart hemorrhaged with sadness, and behind her, Satan said, "Perfect. Thank you."

He grabbed Remiel by the shoulders and hurled her out through the Guard.

The instant she passed through, debris choked her, and she coughed, doubled over. But her head didn't hurt, and her eyes weren't stinging, and abruptly she registered how much angelic power she could feel. She spread her hands, then reached out with her heart and felt herself extending her wings, shedding her body, stretching out and becoming fully an angel.

She shrieked as power flooded her, and her hands clenched around a pair of swords she formed up out of her own soul material. "Michael, give me some orders!"

She slashed at the nearest demons, and then having won room for herself, she looked back for Zadkiel, crumpled at Satan's feet.

TWENTY-NINE

Michael had barely registered that Remiel was herself again before Satan lifted Zadkiel and transported her across the room to Belior.

Saraquael tried to flash to her, but the Guard bounced him back.

Back to back with Remiel, Michael couldn't concentrate both on the fighting and the conundrum of whatever it was Satan had done that none of them had been able to, and he lashed out at the nearest demon. They'd halved the number of their opponents, but that meant nothing with Zadkiel held by Satan and all of them trapped within his Guard.

"How did he do that?" Saraquael shouted at Remiel.

"How should I know?" Remiel exclaimed. "I didn't even realize it was happening!"

Michael hurled himself at the Guard, but although Belior jumped back, Satan acted as if he didn't notice. Instead he opened Zadkiel's cloak and found, still in her hand, that sphere of Sheol material.

He grinned. He reached for it.

Michael did the only thing he could think of: he took down the Guard on the sphere.

Saraquael yelled, and Satan yanked back, but it didn't matter. Like a flight of arrows loosed, the bits all flew as one into Belior's heart.

"What?" Saraquael exclaimed. "Why?"

Because Satan would have had them if Michael hadn't let them free. It had been the better of two lousy choices, the chance that maybe because the bits were aligned with what was still in Zadkiel's heart, maybe they'd have gone back into her. But instead they'd gone straight toward the only ones of their kind still parted from them.

Satan looked surprised. "Now that's a surprise." He turned to Belior. "Convenient that she'd already expelled the stuff. Since you've got it all in yourself, and you'll be pleased to know you'll make a marvelous weapon."

Bloodless, Belior stared at Satan with inadequately-concealed terror.

Saraquael sent, *Is Nivalis still with her?*

Michael's last orders to Nivalis had been to protect Zadkiel. He hadn't seen or felt her since Satan had seized Zadkiel. Maybe his forces had taken her down.

Remiel sent, *Update me, guys.*

Michael felt Saraquael instill all the information into her, and Remiel received it with no ill effects: she was back. Whatever the Sheol material had done to her, Satan had reversed the effects by pulling it out.

And why would he do that, except if he intended to accomplish something worse?

Satan grabbed Belior by the throat and held him upright. "Remember when you told me all those things you wanted that weapon to do? You're going to get control of all those bits, right now."

Belior nodded. Satan pivoted him so he was facing Michael. "And...now."

Satan's wings burst into flame, and as Belior shuddered in his hands, darkness swirled around them both. Michael had no chance to react: the darkness shot from Belior like a whip and encircled Michael, lashing around his hands, his ankles, and his throat.

Remiel dove at the whip with her sword, but her blade bounced off it without doing more than denting the blade. Saraquael grabbed at Michael, but he couldn't free him.

The glop spread up his arms and legs, down over his trunk, and it began to squeeze Michael down inside itself. He couldn't feel anything out beyond it. Like Sheol itself, it was creating a barrier his senses couldn't penetrate.

Remiel flung herself at the Guard surrounding Satan, but it held.

Satan frowned at her. "You're trouble. Next."

He shifted Belior to face Remiel, his feet knocking into the unconscious Zadkiel. Satan pointed at her, and a second stream of light shot from Belior, grabbing Remiel's hands and wrists.

"You shouldn't be surprised. I'm not stupid, you know." Satan sounded almost stung. "I didn't bond a Cherub because I didn't need to—I figured out what these two wouldn't have done in a hundred years."

Saraquael blasted at the bonds holding Remiel, but the energy ricocheted off uselessly.

"Don't you get it? You can't fight this," Satan said. "They ended up stuck in human bodies because my subordinates weaponized death. *Death.* And our kind weren't made for death."

But neither were they. Michael's world was fading out, and he could no longer speak. *Humans weren't made to die either.*

Michael tried to thrash, but the darkness held him immobile, and as the murk closed over his face like a visor, the last thing he was able to see or feel was Saraquael getting snared in the same ink.

You need to wake up.

Zadkiel's head rang with pain, but she tried to focus on the voice. It had been speaking for a while, and every time it talked, the words smothered her with nausea, so she tried to ask it to stop. But instead it repeated, *You need to wake up.*

The mist felt cool. Zadkiel moved, and she realized she was in angelic form, and next she realized she could see again. The place she found herself, however, was sterile. It wasn't featureless—she was in a mudbrick house, but it was more like a painting of a house than an actual house. Nothing was near her. Nothing seemed three-dimensional. There was a place you'd make meals and a place you'd sit to work, but they didn't feel lived-in.

Where am I?

You're with me, the speaker said, *and I need you to wake up.*

Zadkiel turned. *Wake up?*

You're still in a human body, and I'm making you dream so I can appear in the dream. It's me, Nivalis.

Zadkiel blinked. *Wait—Satan! Satan knocked me out!*

Satan took the Sheol material that was in the Guarded sphere you were holding. I need you awake. You need to save Michael. You need to do it now.

Zadkiel struggled to reach back into the body she'd been trapped in for so long, for the blindness and the helplessness. Slowly the pain of stones swelled up under her body, the ache where she'd landed on a rock, the itchiness of mud on her skin. She reached further and clasped at the memory of wine until the taste flooded her senses and reminded her of everything she'd been and everything she'd become.

She opened her eyes and could see nothing. Okay. Awake.

Don't move!

Zadkiel's human body stayed frozen in fright, even in this painful position. Remiel was screaming, calling to Saraquael, calling for God. Saraquael was shouting suggestions to her, but it sounded as though they were separated. Michael she couldn't hear at all.

Satan's wrapping them up in Sheol material. He took the sphere from you. He's using Belior as a weapon. You need to stop him.

Me? That was the only thing Zadkiel could think, a horrified, *Me?* When Michael couldn't do it, and Saraquael couldn't, and Remiel was trapped?

But she was the only one left. She and Nivalis, but Zadkiel was the only one trained as a soldier. She was stronger than Nivalis. Or at least, she should have been. Should have been.

Should have been.

Zadkiel struggled to breathe evenly. *What can I do?*

Nivalis sent, *There's still Sheol material in you. It's linked to what's in Belior, and that's what Satan is using to trap the others. He's encased Michael in it already. You need to do this now.*

Head pounding from the angelic contact, Zadkiel reached inside to touch the Sheol material. It remained buried, and it was pointing outward. Satan was manipulating it from within Belior, and the stuff within her own heart danced in synchrony to his directions. Relaxing her senses further, she could detect angels on the other end of the feed, but not anything about them, only that they were there and that they were struggling.

Encasing them: Satan was encasing them in Sheol material, and once he was done, would he just cut them loose and leave them trapped? All three of them?

Zadkiel pushed on the Sheol material in her heart, but it didn't yield. It kept gliding like a puppet in time with Satan's manipulation.

I can't do this, Zadkiel sent. *What did you do before, to manipulate it? Do it again!*

Nivalis moved within her, and Zadkiel could feel the other angel's presence against the shrapnel.

You thought you could free it before, Zadkiel sent. *Can you try that again?*

It's anchored to you. It responds, but it's hooked so deep. A warmth enfolded Zadkiel. *Give it to me,* Nivalis said. *Your grief. The thing that's making you so sad you're a kindred spirit of Death. Tell it to me. I need it now.*

Zadkiel went cold all over.

Remiel's scream cut off mid-cry, and Saraquael yelled for her in a panic. On the other end of the chains, Michael had gone still, as if very small and very distant. She needed to do something.

I can't do it! Zadkiel's face tightened, and she tried to stay still rather than run or curl up around herself. *I'm not good enough. I've never been good enough!*

Nivalis projected surprise.

You've always known it! Heat rose within Zadkiel's heart, and her mouth twisted as she struggled to keep the tears at bay.

Nivalis sent, *Hang on. I'm going to work it free.*

You can't. It won't matter anyhow. Nivalis was knee-deep in the emotional blood hemorrhaging from Zadkiel's heart, as if her feelings were all being plunged out of her. *I'm not good enough. I should have had Saraquael's place with the Seven. I'm stronger than he is, only I wasn't good enough, and I disappointed God, and I disappointed everyone. I can't do anything, and everyone knows it. The only thing special about me is the wine, and even that's a liability. And I...*

Zadkiel couldn't go on. Tears traced down her face, and in her soul, it hurt as Nivalis tried to rock that thing loose. It just hurt.

Nivalis had finally seen her as she was: helpless, a failure, and a disappointment to God Almighty who had only ever been good to her.

Behind her, it felt as if Nivalis were warming her by cuddling her. Zadkiel tried to shrink away from her touch, but Nivalis projected reassurance.

Above her, Satan was saying to the Cherubim, "I have to compliment the two of you on your work. You forged an excellent weapon, but this is kind of boring."

Two angels on the other end of the chain were still struggling. The last one ensnared must have been bound up harder because he was fading faster. And Zadkiel only thrummed with how she'd failed everyone again.

In her heart, Nivalis pressed something into her control. *Do you feel this? Try again. Tug on it.*

And as soon as she did it, Satan would know she was awake and would wrap her up in it too.

The fear shot through her whole human body, and for an instant she couldn't move. Then Saraquael called again to Remiel, but Remiel had gone still like a gravestone, so Zadkiel gathered herself. She grabbed hold of that shrapnel in her heart and gave a yank.

It responded, and next a blinding pain shot through her head as Satan kicked her. "Stay down!" he snarled. "You gave me what I wanted!"

Zadkiel pulled the shrapnel again, adding strength from her fear and pain. Nivalis was still with her, still diffused, and as soon as Satan brought her down, he'd do even worse to Nivalis. It was on Zadkiel to protect her even though Zadkiel couldn't even protect herself. But she reached again through the line and groped for whichever angel on the other end was the last one struggling, and she ordered the darkness to let go.

The thrashing on the other end intensified. Maybe that meant whoever it was could win free.

Satan lifted her by the shoulders and shook her so hard her teeth hurt. His power exploded around her, but it couldn't touch her: no authority. The by-blow left her head reeling, and she struggled to contain it.

"She's retained some inside," Belior said.

Satan said, "Linked with yours? Draw it out of her."

Zadkiel tightened her grip. Once Belior pulled it out, the demons would have it all. She couldn't defeat their enemies, but she could at least be an anchor and keep that substance rooted in their side for a while.

And then she thought: what if she could pull everything back into herself? All those pieces Nivalis had united with her own...they were still working in unison. What if they all came back to her?

She could do that. All these years she'd failed God, failed her choir, failed everyone—but at the very least she could entomb all of that renegade material in herself. If death had to claim one of them, why shouldn't it be her?

She reached for the substance and opened wide, pulling it into her heart.

Nivalis blazed inside her. *Don't do that!*

No, no, it worked best this way. Free Michael and Remiel and Saraquael and let them do their work for God's glory. They were marvelous, brilliant. They could defeat Satan. God had elevated them right from the start because they could.

"Stop her!" Satan shouted at Belior.

The shrapnel bits flew into Zadkiel's heart, and then, as more and more came to her, she extended herself further to reach for the ones in Belior.

"No!" Belior's voice pitched up. "You little wench!"

Again her head exploded in pain, and Zadkiel tucked around herself. She was bleeding, and she kept tugging because that was the only thing she could do. And in the distance, as if through a very thick blanket, came awakening motions: the other angels were getting out.

"Belior, I need that power back!" Satan shouted. "Stop her!"

Then came Satrinah's voice, shrill. "Bond him! He needs more energy! Bond him and give him access to yours!"

The stuff anchored in Belior wouldn't come loose, but all the rest was back in Zadkiel now: everything drawn off Michael, everything from Remiel, everything stolen by Hastle. It was hers like a dead weight in her soul, and she let herself sink under its crushing power. *I'm so sorry, Father. I'm sorry because I never did anything worthwhile, but I can do something for you now. I'm so sorry.*

Belior yanked back, and it slipped toward him. Zadkiel shivered, abruptly cold all over, and Belior tugged it again so more went back to him.

She couldn't even anchor it. *I'm sorry. I failed You.*

Nivalis poured energy into her, leaving her dizzy, but Zadkiel couldn't hold fast against Belior. The darkness was slippery, and sometimes when she gripped it, it would slide away, only to stick for a while and then hurt her, and Belior just kept reeling it in. Satan hadn't bonded him—he was just naturally stronger than she was, and he could tear it free from her grasp.

Nivalis tried to anchor it, and Satan said, "Well! Look at this," and ripped her away from Zadkiel with a shriek.

"Let her go!" Zadkiel's head raised. "She's just an Angel! Don't hurt her!"

Blood traced down her neck and shoulders. There would be tears and bruises all over her, and she couldn't do a thing to save anyone. Belior pulled more of the stuff back out, and she was down to just the anchored material. She couldn't feel Nivalis any longer. She couldn't see. And she was losing her grip on what remained.

She reached for God, and wordlessly, she tried to hold that moment.

I'm proud of you.

Her eyes flew open. Surprised, she stared into space, that anchor-tug on her heart still so intense. *How? I've let You down in everything. In everything.*

Proud of you.

Zadkiel pulled, and it came back to her a bit. Proud of her? She pulled again, and more of it came. But how? How could God be proud of her when in every way she'd been outshone by lower angels, lesser in power or strength and yet promoted to so much more than herself?

"Belior!" Satan hollered, and Zadkiel pulled more, then reached along the line toward where she thought she'd felt Saraquael struggling last of the three. He was more than she was. Created with less, but promoted over her into the Seven, and yet God was proud of her? She extended toward him where Death surrounded him and sealed him in place like a sarcophagus. But her heart could slip along it, probing for an opening.

"Stop her!" Satan shouted, and she felt him grasping over Belior's hold and yanking the material. Zadkiel called it back into shape around herself, imagining the shrapnel the way Remiel had described it, a school of tiny fish all pointed in the same direction. She pointed them at her, and then she pointed them back to Saraquael and sent them toward him, gathering all their fellows and calling them to her.

Proud of her. Not just tolerant of her, but God was proud of her. By now the shrapnel kept responding, and she imagined holding it in one hand and her own feeling of inadequacy in the other, and they worked together. She didn't need to pull everything out of Belior. She just extended as far as she could into the attachment and probed for Saraquael, and in one moment of brilliance, he grasped back at her as if through a hole in a very thick wall. *I'm here,* she sent, almost jubilant. *I'm here, and you're coming back with me.*

She pulled, and he slipped toward her through the connection. Satrinah was screaming at Satan to bond Belior now, do it now and break it later if they could figure out how, but bond him now—but Satan struck Zadkiel instead.

Zadkiel hit the ground, the world gyrating so crazily that couldn't figure out which way she'd even go to get upright again. *Help me,* she prayed.

He was proud of her. It kept coming back to her: God had said He was proud of her, and He loved her, and she was His own.

Saraquael was still reaching for her, and she grasped back for him, and they clasped. It was strength she needed now, but trapped as he was, he had nothing to offer.

Satan kicked her again, and Zadkiel curled around herself.

She reached again for God, and instead she tasted wine.

Wine, as wine existed when her Lord said, *Wine.* Wine as it was, as it should be. And herself, as she was, as she should be.

Before Satan hit her a third time, Zadkiel felt it coming, and she rolled to the side so his blow glanced off the heavy coat. She stumbled to her feet, then ducked as he struck at her again.

Wine. It flooded her, and she called it to the forefront of her mind. Again she darted to the side, this time crashing into Belior and then rolling away from him just as Satan blasted the spot with power.

She had no time to think. She extended again for Saraquael to pull him out of Death, and instead she found him pushing his sword at her through the opening.

She unsheathed that weapon from Death and unreality, bringing it up just in time to crash against Satan's own weapon.

"You're not clever," Satan snarled. "You can't use that toy."

Saraquael had flooded all his power into his sword, and Zadkiel let Saraquael's sword itself guide her defense. Every time Satan struck, wine coursed through her like blood through her veins, and every painful breath intensified the memory. She was the only one who could do this. The only one. And God was proud of her.

She parried twice against a blade she couldn't see, then pivoted in time to defend against a blow from Satrinah.

Satan got a blow in at her side, and as she crashed into the rocks, she raised her sword to deflect an incoming surge of power.

She couldn't keep doing this: even with her sight, she'd have been overmatched. She reached again into the shrapnel, hoping to find Remiel, but one of them hit her, and she went down, her head reeling.

Come to me, she thought, pulling on the shrapnel bound to her heart. And as she pulled, it came to her, came into her heart, and then surged up through her arm and out into her sword.

Belior shouted, "Watch her!"

Zadkiel raised a weapon that suddenly thrummed as if alive, but it was the opposite of life. It was hunger; it was loneliness; it was isolation. All that in her palm. She pivoted toward Belior's voice and pointed. "Come to me! Now!"

Belior screamed as she opened wide to pull with a strength she'd never felt before in all existence. Flamed engulfed her, but she gathered the shrapnel up like a shield around herself so the heat didn't turn into pain. *All of it. Now. All of it, to me!*

Her heart thrummed, and as the shrapnel came to her, it thinned out over Saraquael and Remiel and Michael. Satan was shouting something at Satrinah or Belior, but she couldn't make out the words over the roar. Instead she was alone inside a sphere of Sheol, bearing a sword imbued with Death, and Saraquael was tearing free of the sickly membrane that had overwhelmed him.

And then light came to her, light she hadn't been able to see since Belior first set off the weapon in the ice caverns. Her human form was yielding to her angelic power. The last bit of shrapnel to be released was the material embedded in her heart, and God was proud of her, and it was coming out.

Zadkiel aimed toward Satan, and she blasted the Death energy at him.

All around her, the cavern rumbled. "Don't!" Belior shouted. "He'll drop the ceiling on us!"

Sounding groggy, Saraquael projected, *You did it. You finished their weapon.*

Sides heaving, bones aching, Zadkiel took a ready stance.

Satan flew at her with only one objective: get that weapon. She raised it and met his strike, parried, met him again, defended with every bit of energy she had. She wasn't strong enough. She knew it, but she didn't have to be stronger than him: she had only to hold onto the sword and direct it. The power felt comfortable now: a familiar ache that fueled her defense. Saraquael was getting to his feet and reaching for Remiel, who had just clawed free from her own cocoon. Michael lay in a heap on the stone, but it was Zadkiel the demons attacked. Satrinah and Satan struck with a choreography just short of perfect, but she was able to keep them distant.

Belior tackled her against the wall, and as her spine slammed into the rock, the sword fell from her hand.

She twisted and lunged for it, but Belior knocked her backward again, and her head cracked against the stone. She struggled up, but Belior dove for the sword.

Before Zadkiel even had a chance to cry out, Satan flashed the sword to his hands.

He raised the sword and leveled it at her—and then Remiel crashed into him, once again wearing a human body and wrestling the weapon away .

"Let go, wench!" He ignited, and Remiel's clothes caught fire. "I'll hurt you beyond anything you ever dreamed!"

"Hurt me," Remiel gasped, holding the sword in both hands. "That doesn't mean I can't do it."

Zadkiel flung herself onto Belior to keep him from jumping Remiel. And then, as Satan snatched at the sword, light flared through the cavern.

Michael stood over Satan, holding the sword high and engulfing it in his light.

"Enough!" He flared his wings, and a strong wind swept the cavern, extinguishing the fire around Remiel. Michael pivoted to face Satan, his eyes like twin stars, and he pointed the tip of the weapon at him.

Satan vanished, taking his Guard with him.

The cavern shook. Chunks of stone plummeted from the cavern ceiling in a waterfall of rock and dirt. Zadkiel pushed Belior down and threw herself over him to protect his host, and then Remiel was over her, and the ceiling caved in.

Everything hurt already. Zadkiel couldn't figure out if it hurt more or hurt less, or if she were dying or if she were pinned or just too scared to move. She reached for God, but with a mute shock;

she could only pray without words. It was dark again, as if she were once more blind, and the air tasted of dust.

Beneath her, Belior struggled. She couldn't find the strength to tell him to stay down.

THIRTY

When the cavern caved in, Michael flashed toward Zadkiel, but there was no way to anchor a Guard for protection. He tried to stream the collapsing rubble around them, but then a blow from behind sent him down.

Satan: back for that sword.

Michael flooded his power into the weapon. It wasn't his own, so he couldn't just call it back into his soul to keep it safe. The energy making it up was Saraquael's, but with the Sheol material bonded to it, Saraquael couldn't call it back into himself either. No matter what Michael did, it wouldn't go less solid than it was, and it had a slipperiness that made it difficult to grasp.

So for now, Michael had to protect a thing he neither wanted nor would use.

Satan still maintained the larger Guards around the cavern. Michael couldn't flash away and couldn't call the reinforcements he knew were trying to blast through from the outside. Saraquael was still groggy. Remiel and Zadkiel were buried, although Remiel at least should have been able to reattain her angelic form. The fact that she hadn't was more than a little scary.

Satan spread his wings as he grappled for that sword, forcing Michael backward. Michael fought the urge to go desolid—as soon as he did, he'd lose his grasp and Satan would have it. Even in a subtle body he could barely keep a hold on the thing.

Zadkiel!, he sent. Was she still alive under all that rock?

Satan forced Michael down with a knee in his chest and grasped him by the wrist. Satan smashed his hand back against the stone, then did it again, eyes blazing, wings cupped over them both.

239

Satrinah joined them, wrapping her hands around Michael's throat. "Take it!"

Satan's teeth clenched as he fought the weapon free of Michael's hand bit by bit.

Then up through Michael's chest shot Saraquael, discharging all his power in Satan's face. Satan let go in surprise, then slashed at him with one of his wings, but Michael pivoted and curled around the sword as much as he could with Satrinah tightening her grasp.

Satan grabbed Saraquael by one wing and hurled him aside.

On Michael's other side, a hand reached up through the ground and took the sword from his hand.

Nivalis. She dragged it beneath the ground.

She'd made it desolid, something he hadn't been able to do—and with his hand now empty, Michael manifested his soul's own sword.

Satan turned toward him, shedding light like a super nova, and reached for the weapon.

Michael brought up his blade and slashed it right into Satan's neck.

Light and heat erupted from Satan as Michael hit. Nivalis stabbed upward through the rock at Satrinah, who released Michael and rushed toward Satan, hemorrhaging power.

Michael got to his feet, wings spread and soul vibrating with anger. Nivalis appeared beside him, armored and wielding Belior's weapon.

"You take Satrinah," he said, and sprang at Satan.

Nivalis didn't hesitate even though Satrinah had nearly a hundred times as much power as she did. A moment after, Saraquael pulled himself up and joined her.

Michael squared off against Satan with two objectives: keep that sword from him and bring down the Guard. Satan's objectives numbered precisely one: get the weapon. With no interest in engaging Michael, he went straight for Nivalis.

Michael got between them and deflected, slashed, parried—because Nivalis was the weakest of them, and yet the bearer of that sword. Saraquael had engaged Satrinah, but there still was no way out of the cavern, and until they got Nivalis out, the weapon wasn't safe.

Satan never let up for a second, attacking Michael on every front while simultaneously trying to get around him. With Saraquael, Satrinah was attempting to do the same. As for herself, Nivalis had gone for the pile of rubble pinning Zadkiel and Remiel. Semi-solid, she slipped through the stones like a pearl diver seeking treasure.

Saraquael blew back Satrinah, and he projected at Nivalis, *Transform it!*

Hidden, she projected back a question.

Gabriel said it's very plastic. Change it!

He didn't get out anything else because Satrinah blasted him with soul energy, and he threw out a Guard to shield himself.

Michael had no breather with Satan, each keeping the other fully engaged. Satan couldn't advance toward Nivalis, but neither could Michael break through the Guard to get her away.

And then he realized his senses were contracting. Behind him, Saraquael exclaimed in surprise. Satan was tightening the Guard around the cavern.

He was going to squeeze them closer and closer to one another until there was no room. He would slip himself outside the barrier. He might even let Satrinah go. But he'd keep everything else sealed and crushed together until he was able to extract that weapon.

Nivalis! Do it now! Michael sent.

He couldn't sense her other than her terror. Beneath the rock, she'd worked her way down to Zadkiel and Remiel, but Satan's barrage kept him unable to feel anything else. *Nivalis!*

What do I change it to?

Under a renewed attack by Satan, Michael couldn't answer.

He felt her running through the possibilities. The shattered walls of Death itself, Sheol, had been transformed into the bricks of the New Jerusalem. But this wasn't Death. This was weaponized Death.

And what was weaponized Death? It was grief.

Her shock rocketed through Michael, and he used the energy of it to push Satan back momentarily. But the Guard kept shrinking around them, and Satan wore a dazzling smile. All he had to do was keep Michael occupied, and Michael wouldn't be able to push back on the Guard.

Nivalis was still putting it together: that the weapon had not affected Michael because Michael had no unresolved grief; but Remiel had a very large, very complicated grief that she'd held onto until Satan forced it to the surface; and Zadkiel had a grief she'd never resolved because until now she'd never admitted to it. By its nature, grief wasn't stable. It had to become something.

But it didn't have to be a weapon.

The Guard had closed in so much now that Michael and Saraquael fought shoulder-to-shoulder right through the rubble entombing Zadkiel and Remiel. "Nivalis!" Saraquael exclaimed. "For pity's sake, *now!*"

Satan's wings were in flames, giving off a stifling heat. It wasn't hurting the angels, but what about the humans? Behind him, Saraquael disarmed Satrinah, but she only laughed when he pinned her against the Guard. With her in one place, though, he started applying counterpressure to Satan's ever-decreasing Guard. At least they wouldn't be crushed.

Satan aimed his power at the rock behind Michael, but then Nivalis emerged from the rubble.

"You're hurting the humans." She stepped forward, her wings pale and her hair bedraggled. "Stop. There's no need."

She extended her hands, and in them was a fist-sized lump. The muscles stood out on her arms from the weight of the thing, and with her wings slack she trembled, but she held it at arm's length toward Satan.

Satrinah screamed. "What have you done?"

Michael couldn't feel the thing in her hand at all. It must have been Sheol material. Changed. She'd done it.

Satan's eyes flared. "You little worthless wench!"

He blasted her with white-hot energy before Michael had a chance to move, but the blast parted before her outstretched arms, streaming to either side of that blackened stone.

She didn't flinch. She just looked at him, eyes liquid and soft.

"That was worth more than fifty of you!" Satan bellowed. "You worthless, weak, stupid Angel!"

He shot at her again, but this time Michael watched only the stone in Nivalis's hands. She stood tall in the fire, eyes glistening, and the stone took it all.

Satan glared at Satrinah, then flashed her out through his Guard.

Behind him, Saraquael dove for the pile of rubble and dirt, hauling rock out of the way and shoving it against the sides of the Guard. The dust was so thick the humans wouldn't be able to breathe, so Michael said, "Back away," and he tried to filter out the air within the confines of the cavern.

It wasn't working. He turned to the Guard to smash it apart.

The Guard vibrated hot against Michael's touch, but he pushed his thoughts outward against it. His soldiers would be outside, pushing inward too, and he extended his heart toward the ones he knew must be there. He prayed, and he reached for God because that was the one reach that couldn't be denied. Not by Satan, not by his angels, not by distance or even death.

Nivalis came up beside him, and she pressed the stone in her hands against the wall of the Guard. It flamed up at its touch.

Michael gave a wry smile. "We beat you. Jerk."

He gave one more blast with his sword, and Satan's Guard shattered.

A squadron of Archangels flooded into the cavern, and Michael brought up a wind, calling, "Raphael! To me, now!"

He turned to find Saraquael grasping a pale, dust-coated hand jutting out from the rubble. "Clear them!" Michael shouted to the newcomers. "Get them out of there."

Within seconds, the rocks had been desolidified and moved away. Saraquael hauled out a limp Zadkiel, and then out climbed a pale Remiel. At the bottom was Belior, still stuck in the body of the magician.

Saraquael knelt beside Zadkiel. "Come on," he whispered, rubbing her arms. "Be okay. I really don't want to find out what happens if you die in human form."

Remiel was rubbing her face and coughing up blood, but Nivalis sat at her side, wings around her. Belior, or the magician, just stayed waist-deep in rock dust, stunned.

And Zadkiel still lay there without moving.

"I tried to protect her," Remiel was saying, her voice urgent.

Beside Michael, Raphael appeared. He rushed to Zadkiel and pressed his hands into her flank, then her head, then crouched beside her in the dust with his forehead against hers.

Michael lowered his sword, shoulders slumped, then called the blade back into his soul. He approached Zadkiel where her human body lay, ashy pale wherever it wasn't covered in dirt.

Wrapped in prayer, Raphael glowed with a creamy light, and he crouched over her, focusing the light here and there but mostly keeping it trained on her chest and her left arm. Michael couldn't feel a signature from her.

"Don't quit on me," Raphael whispered, straddling her waist in order to get a better reach on her. He arched all six wings over her and breathed into her face, then repeated, "Please, don't quit on me."

Michael felt warmth at his side: Danel. Also praying. So Michael reached for his hand and closed his eyes, and they prayed together.

"There!" Raphael sounded urgent. "Come on! You've got it— just a bit more."

Zadkiel coughed, and Michael's eyes flew open at the best sound in the world.

Saraquael scooped Zadkiel into his arms, and she groaned, then flinched. "Hey, she's got to stay still," Raphael said. "I'm not done yet. She's still stuck in that body, and she battered it up pretty good."

Remiel dropped to the rocks at Zadkiel's side. "Battered makes her sound like a piece of fish."

"Beaten?" Raphael was still staring right through Zadkiel's ribs to where he must have been mending internal injuries. "No, that's more like an egg. Ask Saraquael. He's the poet."

Saraquael didn't respond, just kept his face pressed into Zadkiel's hair.

Zadkiel extended a hand, and Remiel caught it, saying. "He's fixing you. You're going to be okay."

She breathed, almost inaudible, "The weapon?"

"It's done," Saraquael said. "We're safe."

Zadkiel closed her eyes, then lay against him to let Raphael finish working.

"So you might not have known this," Raphael said, "but if your rib cage gets crushed, you can't actually breathe. It's known as a blunt force chest injury, and I'd prefer if you avoid those in the future."

Zadkiel squinted at Remiel. "Why...?"

"Why'd I get back in a body and then jump in overtop of you trying to keep you from getting killed by tons of stone?" Remiel chuckled. "It's a mystery."

Zadkiel forced a smile. "You could have gotten hurt."

"Doesn't mean it didn't work." Remiel stretched, and then she returned to her angelic form. "Raphael, I distinctly recall saying I needed to take you to task for saying I was cute."

"Well you're not cute anymore, so it's all good." Raphael stood. "Zadkiel, I think you're all patched up now."

"You knocked out the headache, too, thanks." She started to rise, but Saraquael helped her up to her feet.

Danel went to Zadkiel and took her hands. "I apologize for interrupting, but Zadkiel, you need to come with me. You've been summoned."

Zadkiel went paler than before, and she swallowed hard. "Before the Throne?"

"Into the Temple," Danel said. "I'll bring you to the Sanctuary, but you'll go in alone."

Saraquael closed his wings around her. "Can I go with her? She still can't transcend."

Raphael said, "That's not right. You should be able to," and put his hands back on her head.

Michael turned to find Nivalis at his side, staring at the ground. He said, "Go to her."

Nivalis stepped up to Zadkiel, then closer. Zadkiel's cheeks went pink, and Nivalis whispered, "I'm sorry." She moved closer, then said, "But thank you. Thank you for trusting me."

Zadkiel reached out from Saraquael's wings and touched the stone in Nivalis's hands. Nivalis reached for her and embraced her, surrounding her in pearly wings.

An instant later, Zadkiel's coat dropped to the ground, sending up a shower of dust. She laughed, spreading her wings. "I'm free! Thank you!"

"Hey, be careful with that coat." Remiel's eyes flashed. "Oh, and I've waited a while to do this"

She hauled the magician to a stand. "You. Out of him. Now."

The magician groaned, snarled, then shouted, and a moment after, the air felt lighter: Belior had gone.

The man collapsed, and the soldier behind him caught him under the shoulders. "Take this guy back to Ephesus." Remiel flexed her wings. "They said he has a house just outside the city walls, near the temple of Artemis."

The soldier flashed him away.

Finally, Michael turned to Nivalis. She had wrapped her wings around herself, the stone cuddled against her chest, and she looked stunned.

"I didn't realize what it was," she whispered. "Not right until the end."

He held out a hand, and she laid the stone in his palm. The weight of the thing was unbelievable, but as Michael traced it, he recognized the shape. Four chambers. Muscle tissue. She'd turned the weapon into a human heart.

"I was scared. I couldn't think of a shape for compassion." She swallowed hard. "This was the best I could do, but it's useless now."

Michael shook his head. "It's not useless at all. This was what it should have become all along."

THIRTY-ONE

"**H**e doesn't want to leave."

Michael folded his arms and frowned at Hastle's interrogation team where they stood arrayed before him in his office. "He doesn't have a choice. We're not running an inn for demons. Kick him out."

The Principality said, "He keeps insisting you owe him a favor. I agreed to ask you if that was true before ejecting him out into Hell."

Michael glared out the window. "I never promised him anything."

Across the room, Saraquael said, "What kind of favor is he asking for?"

Michael stared in shock at Saraquael, who shrugged. "I'm not saying we're going to give it to him. I just want to know what he wants."

The Principality opened his hands. "It's going to be a fight to get him to leave. The other demon blazed out of here the instant we opened the Guard, but Hastle only Guarded the place again on his own and demanded that you repay him a favor."

Saraquael squared his shoulders. "I'll go with you."

Startled, Michael said "Really?"

Saraquael nodded. "Normally I'd tell you not to talk to him. But at this point, let's just do whatever gets him out of here soonest. Hear him out, tell him no, and then we throw him out."

"Well, then." Michael huffed. "You realize I'd rather do anything else, right?"

Saraquael grinned. "That's why you're in a good state of mind to talk to him."

They flashed to the cell. Michael suspected he'd have been able to get through on his own if he'd transported directly inside, but the Guard would have stripped off Saraquael. So instead he called through. "Take this thing down and I'll come in."

Hastle replied, "You can come inside."

Michael said, "I have no reason to come alone. Take down the Guard within ten seconds or on the eleventh I'll have a legion of Archangels take it down and hand you over to Satan like a trussed boar."

Five seconds later, after Hastle must have run through all his options, the Guard flickered and then vanished. Michael and Saraquael entered.

Hastle huddled in the corner, disgusted. "You can't send me back. You have no idea what they're going to do to me. Asmodeus is going to beat me mercilessly, and then Belior and Satrinah are going to come up with something even worse. You stole my safety net. You owe me now."

Michael said, "Your bad decisions are hardly my debt to repay."

Saraquael sent, *Impressive line.*

I rehearsed it.

Behind him, Saraquael snickered.

Hastle snapped, "You think it's funny? They're going to torture me."

"You tried to double-cross your employers." Michael opened his hands. "None of them are particularly charitable with regards to failure or treachery. You knew what you were doing. That's a dangerous game, and sometimes you lose it."

Hastle jumped to his feet, wings spread. "I had a plan! You screwed up everything for me, but it would have worked! Don't you understand?"

Michael tilted his head. "You were going to build a weapon of your own, and then what? Become the most powerful sub-sub-sub-demon under one of the most powerful sub-demons on the Maskim?"

"And then use it on myself!" Hastle shouted. "I didn't need much! Just a little more and I'd have had enough to build my own permanent sphere and seal myself inside! They'd never have found me. That thing would have been undetectable, and I'd have disappeared. No one would even have noticed, and the only ones who did notice wouldn't have been able to report it because saying anything would have tipped Satan off."

Michael's feathers stood on end. Behind him, Saraquael projected horror. "But…you'd never have been able to get out."

"I'm in Hell!" Hastle's eyes glistened with angry tears. "Do you think it matters where I am? Hell is inside me, but I never want to deal with those others ever again! The noise, the back-stabbing, the maneuvering, the hatred! When I went out there to pick off the last of the Sheol material, it was so quiet, and I realized that's what I wanted. I don't care if I can't ever get out again. I'm already trapped!"

Michael couldn't relax his wings. He turned aside. "It didn't matter. You couldn't have kept that material anyhow. They'd have found it again and broken it open."

"Not if they didn't think it was missing. They thought it had fizzled away into nothing, so why look for it?" Hastle's voice broke. "Please, Michael. Give me back the rest of my stuff. Seal me inside it. After that, I don't care what you do to it. Drop it into the Lake of Fire. Entomb it in the ice fields. I don't care." Hastle was crying now. "They're going to torture me. It's never going to end. Isn't Hell enough? Please, Michael."

And Hastle didn't even know Asmodeus was planning *a long, long reckoning*. Michael fought to look unaffected. Hastle was manipulating him. That didn't mean he wasn't being honest, though. It just meant he wanted something and had no idea how else to get it.

Michael shook his head. "After the stunt they pulled, Belior and Asmodeus aren't going to be on the Maskim anymore. How could Satan trust them again?"

"Satan never trusted them in the first place!" Hastle's fists clenched. "He'll use their uncertainty to tie him closer to him, and they'll sacrifice me in a second. Michael, I need that Sheol material."

Behind him, Saraquael spoke with an uncharacteristic hesitancy. "There isn't any more. It's all been changed."

Hastle crumpled back to his knees, then wrapped his arms and wings around himself. He projected despair.

And then: *Just let me stay here.*

It wouldn't work. Michael knew that: at the Second Coming, Hell was going to be sealed off, and even if he stayed for now, Hastle would be ejected back into Hell then. Eternity was a long time. It almost didn't matter how long he hid if he was going to be spending eternity beaten and tortured by his humiliated superiors.

Folding his arms, Michael stared at the floor.

Saraquael's voice was quiet. "I have a suggestion."

Hastle didn't even raise his head. Michael's shoulders sagged. "Let's hear it."

For Saraquael's plan to work, Hastle had to cooperate, and he must have been telling at least some of the truth about wanting to disappear, because he answered their questions and even demonstrated some of the technique he'd used in Belior's employ. Saraquael sat in the far corner, spinning light filaments into coils while Hastle criticized his technique and Michael sat, praying. *Please, please, Father, if this isn't your will, if this offends you, please let me know. But Hastle...Hastiel...this doesn't interfere with your justice.*

And then, after miles of coil and three different types of weaving, Michael snuck back into Hell, Danel at his side in a black uniform. They slipped in and lost themselves in the upper caverns, worked their way through the lower ones, bypassed the Lake of Fire and entirely skipped the areas of impenetrable darkness.

In the ice, Michael drilled for what felt like miles, a fist-sized hole directly downward through the ice layers. They were nowhere near the lab Belior had used, but the wind blasted them with the same ferocity, and bits of ice pelted any parts of them they'd left exposed. Danel stood with his wings clasped around his body.

Michael got to his feet, brushing the ice off his gloves. He looked at Danel, who met his eyes.

The wind was too violent to speak. Danel opened his hands and revealed a palm-sized cocoon. Melded into the fabric of the cocoon was a Guard woven by Saraquael, braided with a Guard from Michael and an emotional repulsion from Hastle. It was the same technique their enemies had used to create the tunnel between Hell and Creation. With Hastle's input only on the inside, none of the demons would be able to detect it when they searched. If someone came close by accident, they'd want to leave it alone. And at the very center was the soul of Hastle himself.

Only one step remained.

Danel handed the cocoon to Michael, who crouched over the shaft he'd cored through the ice. When after a few minutes he still hadn't let it go, Danel squatted at his side and held his hand on Michael's. He pressed his forehead to Michael's temple, and Michael felt him praying. He joined in the prayer, and then, when the cocoon slipped from their hands into the long icy shaft, they together followed it with a gentle heat to seal the ice tube behind it.

Michael wrapped his wings around himself, and Danel wrapped his wings around Michael, and although the wind howled, the pair of them stood silent in the lashing sleet.

Mary looked up from kneading bread to see a girl: short, blonde, and bedecked with earrings.

"Remiel! You're safe!" Mary rushed to her and embraced her, and Remiel snuggled against her: so warm, so soft. She squeezed Remiel, then held her at arm's length to investigate. She was wearing the same clothing she had been when Satan had taken her, but no smoky smell clung to her.

Remiel beamed at her. "It's all right, *Kecharitomene*! We're all fixed up." She grabbed her by the hand and tugged her to the courtyard. "Come see!"

Remiel was playing up the little kid routine, and Mary chuckled as she let Remiel take her out to the courtyard. Blinking in the daylight her eyes fell first on Zadkiel, and then on—

Her son! She rushed to him, and he took her into his arms. Him. So warm, so present, so alive. She reveled in the feel of him, his realness and his love. "I've missed you so much," she whispered.

"You're always here with us, but I've missed hearing you, talking to you."

"I know." Jesus kissed her on the top of her head, and he held her tighter. "Just a little longer."

Mary ought to ask Zadkiel if she was all right, ought to invite them in and offer them hospitality, ought to do so many things, and she put them all out of her head because right now she just wanted to stay where she was forever.

Finally Jesus relaxed his hold, and with reluctance she stepped back. She looked into his face, and it felt so good to see him again. That last look had been so many years ago, and whatever she saw today would have to hold her for more long years. She swallowed hard. "How long will you stay?"

Jesus said, "A couple of my angels wanted to thank you for your help. I decided to accompany them."

Zadkiel reached for her, and it surprised Mary that she was still blind. But she'd said as much—it wasn't a side effect of the weapon that had blinded her, but the deal she'd struck with God. Of course that would still be in force. Mary took Zadkiel's hand, and Zadkiel suddenly smiled. She looked more relaxed than she'd been the entire time of her stay. "Thank you for all you've done for us." Zadkiel bowed her head. "We appreciate your sacrifice and the protection you gave."

Remiel bowed and gave her own thanks, but Mary could barely concentrate on them. She reached again for Jesus's hand, noticing as she did how he still bore the nail marks through his wrists. Would those ever go away, or were they the jewels of his Kingdom, a permanent brand showing his right to the Kingship?

Jesus said, "You were baking bread."

Mary's head picked up. "Would you like some? No one bakes bread like your mother."

Remiel laughed out loud, and Mary rushed to the kitchen, took one of the warm loaves, and brought it out to Jesus along with a cup of wine mixed with water. After praying over the food, Jesus sat with her in the courtyard to eat, and while she sat at his side, Remiel and Zadkiel told her how they'd finally been freed of the shrapnel.

Mary rested her hand on Zadkiel's. "You were grieving too?"

"Apparently." Zadkiel gave a self-conscious laugh. "God summoned me before the throne afterward, and I'm going to be on furlough with Him in adoration while we get all this worked out."

Jesus said, "And Mom, as my own special thanks, I want to offer you a gift." She waited, and he said, "Whatever you want. Ask for a reward, and I'll give it to you."

Reeling, Mary realized what that meant. God saying He would give you anything meant...anything. *Make me Queen of the Universe* would be perfectly reasonable, as would, *Give me eternal youth.* She could ask for the wisdom of Solomon or for the restoration of Jerusalem from the Romans.

What had Belior said? That God wouldn't refuse her anything? And here she was actually in that position. It was insane.

But that was how temptation worked, after all. God's enemies had to tempt you with good things because nothing else would have appealed. Good things you shouldn't have, or maybe shouldn't have yet. What had Belior offered her? The ability to heal. Brilliance in preaching. Knowledge of everything. All good things, but not things she should have had from his hand.

She'd refused, but now she could have them anyway.

At last she broke the silence. "So many people come to me, asking for help. It's not just Remiel and Zadkiel. Your Church needs so much right now, and so many people have asked for prayers, asked for advice, asked for assistance." Mary wrung her apron in her hands. "I do for them whatever I can, but I can't do the most important." She reached for Jesus's fingers, avoiding the wound on his wrist. "So the favor I'd ask is this: when people come to me for help, please, lead them to you. Don't let them stop with me. I'm your mother, and I guess that counts for something, but I want you to give them the grace that leads to you because you're my Savior also. "

"Let it be done." Jesus leaned forward to kiss her, and she tried to savor his nearness and not cry, not now, not until he left again. "Be steadfast," he whispered. "It's only for a little longer, and then there's our Eternity."

"I want to be with you." Her voice broke. "Don't let me leave you. Not even in the smallest ways."

"You will be with me in Heaven. You have my promise." He squeezed her hand once more, and when she looked up, he was gone.

Remiel and Zadkiel remained, and Remiel snuggled close to her. No doubt about it: she had definitely made herself younger than before. Zadkiel put her arm around both of them, and Mary tried to keep the warmth of Jesus's presence in her heart for as long as she could after he'd gone.

"Key!" A young girl's voice penetrated the courtyard stillness, and all three of them looked up. Shortly they were swamped with girls: the fisherman's daughters as well as the daughter of the household. Zadkiel was laughing, and it turned out she had a bag with her that Mary hadn't noticed, and it contained a completed net for their father. The girls climbed over Zadkiel, asking her for a story, and Zadkiel agreed.

Remiel pressed a heavy container into Mary's hands. "It's the wine made from honey. I promised you a jar, and here it is."

Mary wrapped her fingers around the ceramic, and she looked down at it in her lap. "How long are you planning to stay?"

Remiel folded her arms and leaned against the wall. "Long enough to intercept and debate with a former magician who's en route to this house right now."

Before Mary could react, the youngest cried out, "Daddy! Daddy, Key finished the net for you!" and she brought her father over to them, half pushing and half tugging.

The widowed fisherman inclined his head, then kissed Mary on both cheeks. He said, "I wanted to thank you for helping with the girls. They've been telling me the stories you've shared with them about your god." His cheeks were flushed, and then he added, "I was wondering if you could tell me some of those stories too."

Mary's heart thumped, and she prayed. *Thank you.* She closed her eyes and let the sunlight warm her face, and she felt God's presence warm her heart. *Thank you, and thank you again.*

Keep reading!

I've got an excerpt of another novel, *The Wrong Enemy,* following the credits. Think of this as a Marvel movie. You wouldn't want to miss out on the Easter eggs.

I would love to hear from you. Please consider joining my mailing list at http://eepurl.com/bcnCNX. I don't send out much on the list, but I'll use it to notify readers of any new books, potential discounts, and ask for people who want free books in exchange for honest reviews. Everyone who signs up gets a free copy of the *Seven Angels Short Story Bundle*, too!

Speaking of honest reviews, good books can always use them. Forget what Mrs. Miller told you in third grade: a book review can be a couple of lines and doesn't have to be anything more than "I laughed so hard I fell off the subway bench" or "Boring. Don't bother." You can post a review on the book's page at Amazon.com or Goodreads, and I hope you will.

Thank you for the gift of your time and the privilege of having my angels into your home.

THE WRONG ENEMY

One

Raguel waited at the back of the Judgment Hall to hear the verdict passed on the boy's soul: Heaven. He nodded as he registered the word, but without rejoicing as he should have. Based on the expressions of the other witnesses, neither was anyone else. Half the angels in the room watched the boy as he leaped in delight and hugged the angel at his side, but the larger number studied the angel who stood at the back of the hall, Tabris.

Tabris had not reacted to the echoing verdict. Staring only at the chains binding his wrists and securing him to the floor, he stood like a horse at a hitching post. Only once did Raguel see him look up, struggling to get a glimpse of the boy before the other angels crowded into his line of sight, but then they'd taken him away, and Tabris said not a word.

Two Archangel guards flanked Tabris, one wearing a thousand-mile stare and the other struggling against grief. Everything about their posture read *duty* to Raguel, broadcast without words in their alert stance, the readiness of their weapons, their raised chins. Between them, Tabris seemed smaller, slumped, his two-toned wings touching the floor. With a shudder, Raguel realized at least one of the guards had probably been his friend.

They had no idea how to act. And rightly so. Angels didn't usually take one of their own into custody.

In the wake of the boy's removal, motion animated the hall. Some celestials left, but many more took seats on the benches in front of and to the right of the judgment throne. The intensity of the Father's light heightened to a brilliance that made Raguel gasp, but Tabris brought up his wings as a shield.

God, have mercy. He looked again at Tabris, and the words cycled in his mind, a prayer tinged with dread when he considered what would happen next.

One of the Archangels glanced at the other, and Raguel felt them exchange an unspoken question.

He flashed to the trio, reappearing there the same instant he vanished from the previous spot. He had the highest rank of any present—one of the Seven Elite as well as the officer in charge of all guardian angels—and at his appearance, both Archangels saluted. Tabris recoiled and wouldn't meet his eyes.

With a gesture, Raguel made the chains disappear. The Archangel with the thousand-mile-stare snapped to and looked at Raguel with relief, but the other guard protested.

Raguel said, "He can't run anywhere. And unless God damns him, he's still one of us. Don't forget that."

Tabris shivered. Even with the chains gone, he didn't move.

Raguel reached out with his emotions to reassure Tabris, a communication process angels use more efficiently than words, but Tabris retreated from his soul's projection.

Uneasy, Raguel advanced to the long table at the front of the room and leaned his muscular form on the edge to await the next phase of the trial. With raised wings, he inspected the broken angel. Then, sighing, Raguel turned toward God's throne.

One of the angels sounded a Shofar, and the room came to attention. The pair of guards escorted Tabris to the fore.

For the last millennia, only humans had stood this kind of trial, the sorting of those who should enter Heaven from those who belonged in Hell. This time, the subject was Tabris, an angel, and until an hour ago, a guardian angel. Until an hour ago, just as sinless as the rest of them.

Without any presentation of evidence or arguments from either side, God presented to all the witnesses what Tabris had done, and what he deserved for the crime.

Raguel could feel the guards recoil, but Tabris remained still. His hands: he kept staring at his hands.

Swallowing against nausea, Raguel stepped toward Tabris. "Do you have a statement in your own defense?"

Tabris didn't look up. "No."

"Then I do." Raguel turned to the throne of the Lord, his face bathed in the radiance that had dispelled chaos in the first moments of creation and acted as his beacon ever since. His heart trilled as he glimpsed infinity, but he focused himself. "I would beg you for mercy." He ignored the tendrils of hope and outrage that swirled from the other angels. "Tabris panicked. I don't think his crime was premeditated. If he'd thought about it at all, I'm sure he would have stopped."

"The boy's dead!" shouted a voice from across the room.

Raguel forced himself to look only at God rather than toward the voice. "Tabris's intentions—"

"I said—" the voice continued, closer, "the boy is dead. Regardless of Tabris's intentions, Sebastian died. Tabris short-circuited God's plan in the worst way possible, a plan that—if you recall—one-third of the angels were thrown into Hell for failing to fulfill. And now you want—"

Raguel said to God, "One more angel in Hell won't resurrect the child."

The accuser took form immediately beside Raguel. "That would be justice."

Raguel still wouldn't turn. "Tabris is sorry. It was a rash action, not a rejection of You."

The accuser said, "The boy is dead. That's all the rejection possible."

At that moment, the light of God took form at the head of the room as Jesus Christ. The angels bowed, but Tabris prostrated himself.

Jesus advanced to the accuser, who looked him dead in the eye.

Jesus said, "Your point is understandable."

Raguel turned for the first time to look at the accuser, who wore an icy glare and had every feather on every wing standing out, typical for a demon.

"*Understandable*?" said the demon. "Everything here is perfectly understandable. Angels have only one written law, am I correct? And that law is shown to every single guardian angel before beginning his assignment, am I still correct? Including Tabris? No one forgot to show it to him because they were too busy polishing their harps and reciting your cute scripted praises?”

Jesus waited him out. Raguel had less patience; his sword had manifested at his side, and his palms itched.

Jesus glanced at Raguel, acknowledgment in his eyes.

The demon cocked his head and folded his arms. “And would I still be correct if I were to recall that the law says, explicitly, *Do not kill your charge*?”

Jesus said, “You have a thorough grasp of the facts.”

The demon said, “Shocking that you even need such a written law. But your playthings want so badly to brainwash their toy monkeys and get them here, so it makes sense. Polish them to a high shine and then kill them. Ta-dah, instant sainthood.”

Jesus said, “Again, you have a good grasp on the guardians’ desire to get their charges into Heaven.”

“The only thing I can’t grasp is this,” the accuser said, his voice flat. “If I’m in Hell for far less a crime than he committed, I fail to see why he should receive the mercy you denied the rest of us.”

Jesus said, “Tabris still loves me.”

“You have to admit,” the demon said, stepping closer and lowering his voice, “that his demonstration of that love falls short of ideal.”

Jesus turned to Raguel, who forced himself to look away from the demon. “Why are you pleading for Tabris? He hasn’t pleaded for himself.”

Raguel folded his arms over his chest, but Jesus touched his shoulder, and Raguel looked up. “My Lord, he’s in shock. I’m convinced he had no intention of doing what he did, and given the chance, he’d change it. He’s condemning himself. I think you want better than that for one of your own.”

Looking at Tabris, Jesus said, “How much do you believe in him?”

“I wouldn’t challenge your judgment,” Raguel said.

“But you want that judgment to be favorable?”

Oh, God, Raguel thought, *thank you for an opening here.* He ignored the demon’s outraged huff. “Please have mercy on him.”

He looked again at Tabris, still prostrated, still not projecting any of his emotions. Raguel wondered if maybe he’d stopped himself from reacting to his own Creator debating whether to discard him.

"He does still love you." Raguel's voice turned urgent. "For that alone, you might be able to show him mercy."

Jesus stepped toward Tabris, who pulled his wings tighter over his head, a brown and green shield of feathers. Raguel noted both the brightness and softness in his Lord's eyes as he studied the prostrated angel, the contemplation that stretched into a question-mark, and for a moment Raguel feared it was God lingering over a last look. Tabris himself had gone motionless, and Raguel fought panic as Tabris's fear filled the room.

As if voicing Tabris's own thoughts, the demon said, "There isn't a choice. He deserves to burn."

Jesus kept his gaze on Tabris. "Raguel, answer me, how much do you believe in him?"

"Completely."

"Then I release him into your custody. Do with him as you wish."

The demon let off a flare of rage. The rest of the angels in the room reacted with simultaneous surprise and relief, tainted by confusion and anger.

Raguel bowed. "My Lord."

"Tabris?" Jesus's voice sharpened, but Tabris still didn't raise his head. "You're on probation. One more act of disobedience means damnation. You are clear on that."

Tabris projected his emotions so all could hear him: understanding, and thanks.

Jesus looked Raguel in the eyes. "Accompany him to his next assignment."

Jesus vanished even as Raguel felt himself filled with that assignment's details.

The demon pushed past Raguel to Tabris. "They've only delayed it. You're still mine."

Raguel put his hand on his sword, and the demon vanished.

Tabris raised his head, then got to his feet, his eyes wide but otherwise expressionless. The other angels watched as he looked at the spot the demon had stood, then to the last place he'd seen the boy.

Raguel touched his hand. "Come with me." And they departed.

Tabris still trembled with fear, with hopelessness, with desperation. He followed Raguel by doing automatically what would confuse any creature with a body, *going* somewhere without a destination. Angels traveled by thinking about where they wanted to be, and they arrived without passing through the intermediate space, whether the thought was "corner of 83rd and Park" or "wherever he's taking me" or even "wherever Gabriel is right now." This time Tabris's intention had been the second, so he felt surprised when he found himself surrounded by the paperish scent of Raguel's study, a familiar room in one of Heaven's "many mansions." Familiar because he'd gotten his previous assignment here. Being brought back at the end felt like a mockery of closure, the breaking of that long-ago promise.

Raguel had Tabris sit. "Take a few minutes to get yourself together. I'm going to leave you here, and I think it would help if you prayed."

"Please—" Tabris's voice sounded uncertain even to himself. "I'd rather you didn't."

Raguel hesitated, and Tabris waited for the inevitable recoil, but instead Raguel settled on the couch beside him. Tabris inclined his body away but found himself searching out Raguel's eyes. What he wanted wasn't there, of course. He couldn't find what wouldn't be found.

Raguel said, "I wasn't going to lock you up here. I wanted to go ahead of you to your next assignment."

"To warn everyone? That way they can resign before they have to work with a—"

Tabris's voice refused to complete the sentence, but the final word rang in his head like an echo in an underground cave.

Sebastian had gotten into Heaven. Hold onto that thought. Because that was good, the only good to come from this whole disaster. It wasn't Sebastian's fault that Tabris had taken his life. Tabris, however, was guilty of murder, and murder cried out for nothing less than damnation, sharp and swift. If only to keep the other guardians faithful, Tabris had seen no other way things could unfold.

He'd felt the other angels' agitation about God sparing him, and really, Tabris himself wasn't sure how he felt. Even here, sitting on

Raguel's couch and feeling like a homesteader after the tornado has blown past, he knew he was by no means out of danger.

"I—" He quelled the instinctual projection and forced himself to translate into words. "I wanted to say thank you. For pleading for me. I..."

He couldn't continue. He wanted to push the words, but they wouldn't come. *I didn't deserve that.* Deserve. Didn't deserve anything.

Raguel reached for Tabris's hand, and the reassurance flowed from him, unrestrained emotions from an unsullied heart: Raguel would have done it for anyone.

"You did it for me." Tabris's voice deserted him again. He strangled down his feelings until he could figure out how to keep speaking.

Raguel said, "I won't be gone long. But I want to go ahead of you."

"I know what's going to happen." The inner darkness surged, and Tabris stared again at his hands. "Wherever you stick me for this next assignment—if it's a small city, a corporation, an apple tree out in the middle of the Great Plains—no one's going to want me there."

Raguel said, "I'm going to intercept their objections," and beneath the words, Tabris sensed a tease: he hadn't guessed it.

Tabris looked up. "A star? I could handle that. Make it about a thousand light years from anything else." His voice dropped. "And make sure there aren't any black holes near by. Just in case."

Raguel squeezed his hand. "You're being hard on yourself, and it's not all about you. Stay here and get your equilibrium. I'll be a few minutes."

"The reality couldn't possibly exceed imagination." Tabris's eyes narrowed. "What am I assigned to?"

"Not what," Raguel said. "Who."

"What?" Tabris leaped from the couch, his wings flaring as he backed across the room, eyes round as full moons. "I hope you mean an animal!"

Raguel shook his head.

"No!" Tabris exclaimed. "Absolutely not! I—you can't! The one-person rule!"

Raguel stood. "It's been suspended so you can guard a second human being. And you won't be the primary caregiver. It's a secondary guardianship."

"But—"

"You can't refuse." Raguel's voice turned insistent. "You *cannot* refuse. You're under obedience to take it."

Tabris covered his face with his hands. His thoughts ricocheted like atoms in a nuclear reactor, and every attempt to get them under control only sped them up. Another person? A human being? Someone else whose life he could screw up—could *end*? Why would God do that—unless God wanted him in Hell all along and wanted to prove it wouldn't have helped to be merciful. No one would plead for Tabris again. No one.

Eventually he whispered, "What about the other guardian?"

"He'll have no choice. He's under the same directive you are."

Directive. Oh, God, please, no. He'd *had* a directive! The word *Sebastian* was strong enough to break through every barrier Tabris had thrown up against it, and he knew when it hit Raguel like an arrow in the heart. *Sebastian.* Little one. Brown-eyed, clever, assertive, curious, responsible, generous, impulsive—and *his*. His charge. Not his charge anymore.

Tabris groped for a chair, and then, huddled with his arms wrapped around his waist, he did everything in his power to push it down. Stop thinking. Just stop thinking. Everything had changed. He couldn't go back.

Raguel neared him, and Tabris shook his head. "If you're going to do it, we should do it now."

Raguel hesitated.

"Waiting won't make it easier."

Tabris took a few deep breaths to steady himself, his color darkening, his wings enriching to a deep jade and an even deeper mahogany. He regarded himself momentarily, then looked back at Raguel, and in the next moment, Raguel took him away.

Thank you again for reading! If you want to read the rest of The Wrong Enemy, you can pick up a copy in paperback or ebook format at Amazon.com at http://amzn.to/1sCjOfY.

www.ingramcontent.com/pod-product-compliance
Lightning Source LLC
Chambersburg PA
CBHW071748190726
48292CB00003B/911